"Tell me. Tell me about it." Amelia's palm smoothed over the raised skin, imagining the knife, the blood, the curious pleasure in the pride Dorothea must have felt at enduring this sacred ritual. "I should like to know what happened."

"Well," began Dorothea, "it was about three years ago, as I recall. I had been commissioned by the Royal Archaeological Society to travel to West Africa and study the sexual and initiation rites of the tribes. Whilst there, I heard rumours of the existence of a tribe of women; women who never met with men, and who perpetuated their tribe's existence by taking young women from neighboring villages and initiating them into their ways, as though they were their daughters. I determined at once to find these women, and I set out for the heart of the forest.

Also by VALENTINA CILESCU:

The Haven
Mistress Mine

the Rosebud Sutra

VALENTINA CILESCU

ROSEBUD

The Rosebud Sutra

First Rosebud Edition 1994

First Printing December 1994

ISBN 1-56333-242-6

Cover Photograph © 1994 by Trevor Watson

Cover Design by Julie Miller

Manufactured in the United States of America
Published by Masquerade Books, Inc.
801 Second Avenue
New York, N.Y. 10017

Chapter 1

Women are hardly ever known in their true light, though they may love others or become indifferent toward them, may give them delight or abandon them, or may extract from them all the wealth that they possess. —The Rosebud Sutra

From the journal of Dorothea Strong,
London, January 1885

Hearing of my knowledge of India, Her Imperial Majesty Queen Victoria has lately commanded me to travel there and conduct a study into the wealth of exotic archaeological and anthropological curiosities present in the subcontinent.

On hearing the news, my maidservant Floss professed herself distraught that she would not be accompanying me on my journey. I remain unconvinced by her tears, for I know full well that she has been giving her favors to more than one other woman during the time that she has been sharing my bed. Some few months' separation may perhaps teach the shameless girl that she would do well to show a little more constancy toward the mistress who puts the clothes upon her pretty back.

I had intended to delay my departure for India for a few months, until after my annual summer lecture to the Royal Archaeological Society. However, today I obtained some startling new information which prompts me to set out as soon as I can make the necessary arrangements.

At breakfast, I received an unexpected invitation from the Ranee of Patnador, who is at present residing in London, staying at one of the townhouses owned by the renowned poetess and society belle, Lady Erlingham. The ranee and her enchanting daughter, Soraya, invited me to partake of afternoon tea with them. No doubt they had heard of my studies of their country and its culture, but I suspected a second motive behind their invitation. The ranee and her royal circle are noted practitioners of the sensual arts of Sapphic love, and I wondered—nay, hoped—that they might have a less scholarly interest in my company. As it turned out, this indeed proved to be the case....

In due course, I arrived by hansom cab at 31 Euston Square, where a heavily veiled woman in eastern dress duly conducted me into a ground-floor drawing room to await my hostess. The room's decor gave ample evidence of Lady Erlingham's long and fruitful association with India—and of her appreciation of the beauty and love of women.

The walls were lined with the most exquisite Indian watercolor paintings depicting scenes of unrestrained revelry, and the whole of the wall opposite the window had been decorated with a huge painted frieze. Dancing girls, naked save for their brightly colored jewelry, were performing the most extraordinarily gymnastic display for a richly dressed princess and her consorts, two high-born courtesans with painted lips and almond eyes thickly lined with black kohl.

As the dancers tumbled and sprang, their taut, naked flesh as appetizing as *café crème*, the secrets of their bodies were opened up to the viewer in the most stimulating detail. One girl was caught in the middle of turning a cartwheel, her gold anklets sparkling about her slender limbs as she supported herself on her hands, her thighs parted like the juicy branches of a young sapling, revealing a deep pink furrow that simply yearned to be kissed.

The girl by her side was bending backwards, crablike; her arms and legs were arched and outspread so that her shaven sex-lips pouted and gaped, and the deeper pink of her inner folds was exposed in all its glossy perfection. What sweet honeydew dripped from those parted lips, anointing the dusty ground where it fell and making it bloom anew?

The mere thought of taking my refreshment at that eternal spring made my own juices begin to flow in abundance. Tight-laced in whalebone and linen, I could feel the hardening buds of my nipples chafing against the inner surface of my chemise, causing me no little confusion. Surreptitiously, I let my hand roam over the front of my dress, pressing lightly on the pleasure-buds and producing the most deliciously tormenting excitement.

To the right of the frieze was an ornate fireplace, clearly Indian in origin and carved from rosewood. The carving had been executed by a skilled hand, and the natural grain and patterns of the wood had been used to spectacular advantage. The mantelpiece— engraved with Indian characters grown a little worn and indistinct with age—was supported by several brackets in the form of naked girls, their firm young bodies stretched into sinuous curves as they hung like figureheads beneath the wooden shelf, thrusting out breasts as round and glossy as polished apples.

At either side of the grate stood rosewood pillars in the form of veiled women, a filmy fabric clinging to the contours of their faces and breasts as they held up the veil to cover their modesty. But oh! Their pretended modesty was all to no purpose, for their nipples pushed through the fabric as hard and appetizing as betel nuts, and beneath the waist-deep fringe of material, their bodies were utterly bare, utterly exposed.

They were standing with their legs slightly apart, and between their parted thighs I made out the intricately carved forms of their quims, the outer lips agape and the inner slightly protuberant, like a mischievous tongue. Both women were pierced with rings that passed through the outer lobes of their sex, and their navels were set with two enormous, perfect, glittering rubies.

Curiosity getting the better of me, I stepped a little closer to the fireplace and made an attempt at deciphering the writing carved into the mantelshelf. But the characters belonged to some obscure dialect that I could not easily comprehend, and they were too indistinct to copy down easily. Besides, my eyes kept straying from the object of my academic interest to the objects of my lust—the intricately and most lewdly carved figurines that adorned the fireplace. They were so exquisite, so real, that I could almost imagine them coming to life, touching me, kissing me, drawing me down into their own private world of lascivious fantasy.

"Memsahib Strong? Her Royal Highness is so gratified that you could accept her invitation. My name is Pushput. I trust you have not been waiting too long?"

Startled out of my reverie, I wheeled around and saw a veiled young woman standing behind me. How long she had been there, I could not begin to guess, for I had truly been lost in my sensual daydreaming; I could only hope that she had not obtained any inkling of my sexual excitement.

But it was difficult to suppress that excitement, for despite her veil the girl was undoubtedly beautiful. At eighteen, her breasts were no more than tiny buds beneath her filmy garment. My heart quickened as I looked at the way the nipples pushed against her sari, their flesh seemingly pierced and distended by heavy metal rings. Her waist and hips were slender, her frame graceful, her eyes bright, and I longed to see her face, kiss those long, pierced nipples.

Reminding myself that I had come to meet one of India's most powerful women—a woman that it would be foolish indeed to displease—I forced myself into some semblance of composure.

"Not long at all, thank you. And this room…it is most diverting for a scholar like myself."

The young servant inclined her head in a respectful nod. Her voice was quite high-pitched, but musical and soft; the voice of deeply sensual submission.

"Her Royal Highness has heard of your studies and discoveries, memsahib. She is most eager to make your acquaintance. You will come with me now, please?"

I followed her out of the room, almost regretting that I must leave this place of sensual enchantment. What need had I of some formal tea party when I could simply close the door and remain in here with this bewitching girl?

Pushput led me down the dark panelled hallway past a line of incense burners. Their thin, upward-winding smoke filled the corridor with a heavy, spicy scent of sandalwood and patchouli, reminding me of the happy days I had spent in my youth, at the house of a royal courtesan in Calcutta.

The corridor led through the house to a very fine conservatory, and this is where I found the ranee and her daughter. Both were rather handsomer than I had envisaged they would be: fine-featured women with long ropes of glossy black hair ornamented with gold and jewelled chains. They were so alike that they might have been sisters, rather than mother and daughter. Soraya, in particular, captured my interest, with her mischievous sloe black eyes and the crimson oxbow of her painted lips.

"Your Royal Highnesses." I curtseyed, not for one moment taking my eyes off the adorable Soraya, with her firm apple breasts and tall, slender frame.

"My dear Dorothea. We are so delighted that you could come to lighten our wearisome hours."

"Your Highness, I assure you the honour is all mine."

The formalities over, the ranee indicated a heap of soft brocade cushions and I sank down gratefully onto them, somewhat overawed by the splendour all around me. The conservatory was opulently furnished in the

Indian style, with brightly patterned fabrics and heavy cloths woven with silver and gold. In the middle of it all sat the ranee and her daughter, their delicate frames perched regally on carved thrones of gilded wood inlaid with ivory.

The vast expanses of glass between the iron pillars let in the full force of the afternoon sun, and even in winter this was sufficient to create a sultry warmth. Indeed the sun's rays—combined with assistance from the glowing coals in a cast-iron stove beside the outer door—created a steamy, rather overpowering heat. Subtropical plants wove in and around the pillars, ripe mangoes and papayas hung just above my head. It was like being in some deeply exotic, deeply sensual jungle rather than the centre of modern London. In my heavy winter dress of grey woolen serge, my many petticoats and constricting stays, I felt both excited and slightly faint.

"You may leave us, Pushput." The ranee clapped her hands and, to my slight regret, the slender girl left us, pressing her hands together and bowing low as she retreated silently from the room and closed the double doors behind her.

"She is very graceful," I remarked by way of conversation. To my surprise, Soraya laughed, her sweet laughter like the tinkling sound of a mountain stream.

"Pushput is to your liking?"

"Indeed, your Highness. Even without seeing her unveiled, I discern that she is both beautiful and accomplished."

Soraya burst into another peal of laugher, which I confess quite baffled me.

"Indeed!" she said, with an air of mischief and mystery. "Most accomplished."

I glanced questioningly at the ranee, who lifted her hand to silence her daughter.

"Our guest is perhaps not well acquainted with the particular customs of our house, Soraya."

She sipped a little iced lemon sherbet from an engraved silver goblet; it left her delicate lips covered with a thin sheen of moisture which I longed to kiss and lick away. But I was no more than a humble guest here, and it would be a terrible insult if I were to presume...

"Your customs, your Highness?"

"As you know, Dorothea, in our country it is usual for women of high rank to be cloistered, secluded from public life..."

"The life of purdah, yes. The harem..."

"Such seclusion would be intolerably burdensome to ladies of our refinement and...disposition." She exchanged glances with her daughter, who smiled most modestly and colored as she lowered her eyes. I yearned for her to look up again and gaze into my eyes, reading there the hunger that burned for her. But the ranee continued, apparently unaware of my interest.

"Fortunately, the rajah is agreeably liberal in this important matter, having spent a good many years in Europe as a young man. Consequently he places as few restrictions as possible upon us, and indeed encourages us to pursue such innocent pleasures as will divert us from the idle luxury of our existence. As you probably realize, Dorothea, he and I lead entirely separate lives. His sexual interest is entirely in other men and as for myself..." She laughed, her expression turning to a slightly teasing smile. "I have always infinitely preferred the company of women. Attractive, educated women such as yourself, Dorothea."

I felt a thrill of pleasure run through me at her words. Could it be that my first instincts had been right? Had I been brought here not to discuss my scholarly life, but to provide the ranee and her beautiful daughter with a new form of diversion?

"I am most honored by your interest, your Highness," I replied, sipping from my cup of sherbet. My mouth had grown abominably dry, and in the heat I longed to shed my outer skin of constricting clothing. "But what did you find so strange in my appreciation of Pushput's charms? Is she not a most attractive young girl?"

Soraya smiled.

"Pushput is not quite what she seems, Dorothea. She—or rather, *he*—is a boy. Or at least, he was once..." She placed her silver goblet on the table before her, running her fingertips lightly over the inlay of ivory and mother-of-pearl.

The color must have been washed instantly from my cheeks, because when Soraya looked up at me she giggled.

"Let me explain," the ranee intervened. "The rajah is happy for us to lead our own lives and—to a limited extent—to go about in society. He is not a barbarous man. But it would simply not be permissible for a rajah to allow his wife and daughter to travel abroad without guards to...ensure their fitting behavior. Pushput—and the others like him—are our guards. They are eunuchs, Dorothea—pretty boys dedicated to our service as tiny children and brought up as women. They are entirely happy in their lives—they know no other."

I gasped, scarcely believing that I could so easily have been deceived.

"A eunuch! But..."

"But you were right, Dorothea," interrupted Soraya, looking me straight in the eye for the first time. "Pushput and his kind are indeed very accomplished. They are taught from infancy how to give us pleasure. Indeed, their only way to achieve any sense of pleasure themselves is to give us delight. They are particularly skilled in the use of the mouth and tongue, the pleasing little pastime we call *Auparishtaka.*"

"You are welcome to sample Pushput's charms," added the ranee, with completely ingenuous charm. "As a rule, Soraya and I much prefer to indulge in congress with our female courtesans, but Pushput is capable of giving great pleasure. Even if we were freed from the necessity of being guarded, we would doubtless keep our eunuchs for their beauty and skill—as curiosities, you might say."

Naturally I declined the offer to enjoy Auparishtaka with the eunuch; my interest was now entirely directed toward my charming hostess and her daughter. Swiftly I directed the conversation toward a subject dear to my own heart.

"I understand that your Royal Highnesses are yourselves very expert in the ways of Sapphic love," I hazarded, by now reasonably confident that I would cause my hostesses no offense.

"In the northern countries of India, it is a sacred duty of all high-caste women to learn the arts of pleasure," replied Soraya simply. "Is it not also the case in your country?"

"Would that it were," I replied, thinking of my own repressive upbringing. "Alas, Englishwomen are encouraged to know as little as possible about the arts of love."

Soraya held up her hands in horror.

"But that is terrible! How then do they please their mistresses?"

"They have no mistresses," I replied. "They are taught that such desires—indeed, any desires—are unclean."

"And what of your sacred books of sexual lore? What do they have to say on the matter?"

"We have none. Your Highness, I have spent my whole life searching the world for ancient teachings of sisterly love—teachings that would liberate Englishwomen from the tyranny of their own guilt." I did not, of course, add that such a find would also advance my archaeological career, as I felt that evidence of altruism, rather than ambition, would advance my station in Soraya's eyes. But the quest is my great dream, my one true obsession. I paused, then spoke again. "My life's great quest is to find the legendary Indian book of love lore, the *Rosebud Sutra.*"

There was a brief silence, and I saw the ranee and her daughter looking at each other. There was something in their eyes... Could it be that they knew more than they dared say? Or perhaps I had been mistaken.

"Ah yes. *The Rosebud Sutra*. The greatest book of Sapphic love lore that the world has ever seen." The ranee crossed her elegant thighs, so that the gossamer sheer fabric of her many-layered robes seemed to cascade over her skin like a glittering waterfall. "But of course, it is only a legend. Such a pity."

"You do not believe it exists?"

"It never existed," replied Soraya firmly.

"And if it ever had existed," added the ranee enigmatically, "it would be a foolish woman indeed who tried to find it."

I did not reply. What could I say? It was plain that

this aspect of our discussion had been brought decisively to a close. But thoughts were still whirling around in my head—suspicions admittedly, just the merest suspicions, but could it really be true that the ranee and her daughter knew something of the *Rosebud Sutra*? I burned to know more, longed for the courage to take the questioning further.

I would do anything to find the *Sutra*. Anything. It is like a madness in my soul. For hundreds of years, scholars have disputed its very existence, but I have always believed that it is there to be found—if only I knew where to look.

To my surprise, the ranee got to her feet, smoothing down her robes.

"I must leave you now," she said, with the faintest hint of a knowing smile. "I believe my daughter wishes to have a private discussion with you."

"Your Highness?"

She took my hand and pressed it to her lips. The touch was cool and moist, yet it burned me with the flame of a sudden, unquenchable desire. The ranee's eyes were dark, deep pools in which I read an answer to that desire.

"Later, Dorothea, when you and Soraya have finished your discussion, you may come to my private apartments."

And then she was gone, her robes swirling with a shimmering fluidity about the fullness of her tall, elegant figure. Once again I was filled with the yearning that had begun within me the moment I stepped through the door of the drawing room and set eyes upon the watercolor prints, the carved fireplace with its nut brown forms of naked, willing women. Would Soraya also be willing...?

We were alone together now, and all was silence save for the rhythmic tick, tick, tick of the long-case clock hanging beside the door.

"It is very lonely here sometimes, Dorothea. I am so glad that you came to see me."

Soraya's voice recalled me to the present, and I turned to see her stand up and begin unwinding the long, broad band of her sari, turning slowly as the fabric floated around her, like a bright star within the heart of some great-petalled flower. Her jewelry caught the light as she turned; the golden headdress and the nose-chain glittering with emeralds and rubies and the long, silky rope of her jet black hair twisting between her shoulder blades like a sinuous snake.

The end of the fabric floated free, and Soraya appeared before me, naked except for her jewels and the tight sari-blouse stretched across the ripe apples of her breasts. Their stalks pressed hard against the inner surface of the gold-embroidered silk and all at once I longed to suck and bite them, releasing their infinitely sweet juice.

In the intensity of my lust, I hardly dared let my eyes roam downward to the flat, coffee-colored flesh of her belly and beyond—to the succulent, dipping V of her pubis; a wiry tangle of black hairs cresting the mound of her womanhood. And down still further, to those slender yet strong thighs, tapering to graceful calves that were half-hidden in the bright, floaty mass of unwound silk that lay in a loose spiral about her feet. The gossamer nest rested like a pile of crumpled tissue paper lying around an unwrapped present.

She turned her back to me and I saw the long line of tiny buttons running down the back of the sari-blouse. It was clear what she was asking me to do, and I was only too ready to oblige her, though my fingers were trembling as they fumbled awkwardly with the tiny mother-of-pearl discs.

The flesh beneath was a light honey color, satin-smooth and covered with the tiniest, finest hairs which stood instantly erect as I ran the tip of my tongue slowly and hungrily down the shallow valley between her shoulder blades. She did not speak, but I could feel her whole body tense at my touch and then relax with a great, soul-deep sigh as I slipped the sari-blouse from her shoulders and let it fall to the floor.

For a few long moments we stood there together, not moving; my hands resting lightly on Soraya's waist, her body naked and deliciously vulnerable in my embrace. My mind was reeling. I could hardly believe that this was happening; that a princess of the highest rank was presenting herself to me, offering me her sweet flesh as though it were some toothsome sweetmeat.

My eyes travelled down over her body, loving her with my gaze, coveting her with my every thought. Her long, glossy rope of black hair swung forward over her shoulder, baring both of her lovely golden shoulders and the long, satiny sweep of her back. Her waist was tiny, her hips flaring out into soft yet firm buttocks that I longed to kiss and bite.

At last she turned to face me, so smoothly spinning her body round in my clasp that when she had turned and was looking into my eyes, my hands were still about her waist.

"Will you join your nakedness to mine?" she asked me, and she pressed her lips lightly against mine. Her breath was scented with jasmine, her lips juicy-soft. The very tip of her tongue flicked over my mouth for a fleeting second, and then the kiss was ended.

"Gladly," I replied.

I reached up to unfasten the buttons of my sober grey dress—which now seemed even more curiously out of place in this exotic world of fantasy—but Soraya laid her elegant hand on mine.

"Permit me," she breathed.

How could I refuse? Her touch was so beguiling, her caresses so persuasive. Light as a butterfly, her fingers fluttered over the front of my dress, opening it up, peeling away the stiff, unyielding fabric to reveal the bare flesh beneath.

"You are a very beautiful woman," she murmured, kissing my throat again and again as she eased the bodice down over my arms and felt for the buttons at the side which fastened the skirt. They yielded easily, almost gratefully, and in moments I was standing before the ranee's daughter in my petticoats and chemise.

"And you, your Highness, have the devil in those fingers," I replied, throwing caution to the winds as I seized her hand and covered it with kisses, taking each of the tiny fingers into my mouth in turn and winding my tongue about them.

My breasts ached with need, and I felt a familiar warm wetness spreading from my belly, moistening the secret triangle between my tightly pressed thighs. I squeezed my legs more tightly together as she rubbed her hands over the front of my chemise, savouring the agreeable sensation as my pussy-lips were pressed against each other and the hood of my clitoris slipped slowly back and forth over its swollen head.

"Your nipples betray you as a very sensual woman," observed Soraya, unbuttoning my chemise so that the thin cotton fell away, baring the hard pink nubs of my breasts. My stays were laced very tightly, pushing my breasts up into two hard white globes with a deep crease between, and I shuddered with pleasure as Soraya pushed her tongue tip into the crease, letting it dart in and out and giving me the most thrilling sensations.

All the time her fingers were working away at my clothes, undressing me with the skill and gentleness of a nurse, the knowing sensuality of a practised lover. Never before had I enjoyed such pleasure from the simple action of being freed from my constricting clothing. The heat in the conservatory seemed even more intense than before—or was it simply that the burning in my belly was growing hotter, more intolerable? I could feel little beads of sweat bursting from my skin, forming little salty trickles which Soraya lapped up with apparent enjoyment.

Sliding her hands under my breasts, she lifted them out of the corset and pressed her face between them. Her skin felt so smooth, so cool against my overheated flesh, and I trembled as she stroked and kissed and caressed my breasts, taking first one nipple and then the other into her mouth.

At last she bade me turn around and began unlacing my stays. The glorious release, when it came, made me half-faint with delight. Suddenly I felt free and sensual, all my desire liberated from the cruel prison in which it had so long been hidden. I heard myself sigh and moan with pleasure as Soraya slid off my camisole and petticoats, then unfasten the knotted tape which held up my knee-length drawers.

"Why do Englishwomen cage themselves in so many clothes?" asked Soraya, wonderingly.

"We do not cage ourselves," I replied. "We are caged." But I had no appetite for further philosophical discussion. I had well-nigh forgotten that Soraya was a princess of the blood royal and that I was nothing but an impoverished English archaeologist in search of fame and fortune.

My drawers slid down in a whisper of crisp, starched cotton, and I stepped out of them gladly, happy to be naked with my delectable Indian princess, whose fingers were so skillful, whose kisses and caresses so knowing.

Soraya fell to her knees and set to kissing me with a passion that inflamed me. Her mouth pressed again and again against my belly, my haunches, the flesh of my thighs.

"Open for me. Let me kiss you properly," she pleaded, and her slender hands stroked me, persuading me to move my feet a little farther apart so that my thighs would part for her kisses.

Never had I even dreamed of the pleasure of those kisses. Soraya's tongue was long and expertly tutored, for it sought out swiftly the heart of my desire. Beginning at the flesh of my inner thigh, she worked her way quickly upwards to the margin of my cunny-lips, the thicket of dark curls fragrant and moist with the juices of my need. These she sucked and licked, whilst her fingers toyed with me, stroking and soothing my bare flesh, lulling me into the acceptance of other, lewder caresses.

How I longed for her to be bolder; how I moaned with delight as the very tip of her tongue parted my cunt-lips, the fleshy, pointed blade slicing neatly through all my resistance and instantly finding the hot, hard bud of my clitoris. It throbbed with a terrible hunger, and such was the brutality of her kiss that I could scarcely bear the painful torment of the pleasure it gave me.

"Please, please," I gasped, but Soraya paid me no heed. She was lapping at the honey-sweet ooze from my parted cunt-lips as greedily as a kitten laps cream. Never before had I been so skillfully, so sensually stimulated, and I could hear myself making a low groaning sound as the pleasure became almost too much to bear.

As she licked at me, Soraya's fingers moved slowly across my backside, the flats of her hands making smooth circles on the willing flesh. Sweat was trickling down from the small of my back; Soraya smoothed it over my buttocks as though it were some costly essential oil.

I responded instantly and instinctively to her touch as she grew bolder and her fingers crept into the deep furrow between my arsecheeks. Hardly able to bear the intensity of this new stimulation, I tried to wriggle free but she was inexorable. Already her fingertips were probing the secret garden of my arse, her long, sharp nails teasing the hypersensitive membrane of my perineum. And all the time my cunt was oozing its hot tribute, thick and sweet as mango juice, all over Soraya's ecstatic, upturned face.

Her fingertip entered me, brutal and sudden. I gasped, but there was no evading the pleasure. Soraya's entire finger disappeared through my forbidden gate, burying itself up to the knuckle in my flesh. And then she began twisting and turning it as she sucked and licked me, as though the sole purpose of her entire life was to bring me to the brink of despair. A dozen times she brought me to the very edge of orgasm, and then, at that last crucial second, refused me the release that would turn my torment to delight.

I pressed my cunt down hard against Soraya's face, and instead of pulling away she opened her lips wider, as though she wanted to take the whole of my cunt inside her mouth. Still she was sucking and licking, and then she seemed to home in on the engorged stalk of my clitty, and as I sobbed for the pity I knew she would not give me, her lips closed very tight around my love-button.

My poor tortured rosebud was aflame with pleasure as her teeth skillfully pushed back its outer petals and fixed on the juicy, blossoming heart. I could feel my whole body screaming as she flicked her tongue over the clitty head, all the time biting gently at the root of the stalk.

The pleasure was agonizing, never-ending. Never in my life had any woman brought me to such an immense, crashing orgasm. It seemed to go on forever, the pleasure and the pain mingling, the fear of still greater and more unbearable pain only serving to enhance the wealth of sensations I was feeling.

Floods of honeydew seemed to cascade out of me, like some hidden underground spring suddenly bursting to the surface in a glory of crystal-clear waters, warm and sweet. Soraya drank it all down, each fat sugary drop, and through the red mist of my pleasure and pain, I could hear her sighing and groaning.

How she had succeeded in prolonging my crisis so beautifully, I could not begin to imagine. What subtle skill hid in those gentle fingertips, those fiendishly cruel lips and teeth, and the hard, muscular shaft of her tongue?

I looked down at her. Her face was still pressed against my pubis, her nostrils slightly flared as she breathed in the scent of my spending. Her lips and cheeks were wet with my dew, and I thought how good it would be to lick my own taste off her skin, then let my tongue joust with hers, sharing the taste and texture of our coupling.

She opened her eyes and returned my gaze. She seemed to be tempting me, daring me, urging me to better her sweet excesses. It was a challenge to which I was more than eager to rise, though I suspected I held not one ounce of her skill in my own fingertips.

I laid Soraya down on the ground. She made no attempt to resist, and I marvelled at the sinuous beauty of her long, smooth limbs, the little tuft of black hair that gleamed so invitingly on the summit of her love-mound.

I burned not only with carnal desire, but with a lust to know where she had learned her sensual skills, and as I began stroking and pulling at her pubic curls I murmured to her of this other desire.

"Tell me, Princess. I beg of you...tell me who taught you to give such pleasure."

She giggled, almost overcome with pleasure yet not so unguarded that she would willingly reveal all her secrets.

"How can I tell you that? Mother would be so angry with me. And with you..."

"Princess..." I knew I was dicing with danger, but I no longer particularly cared. I had faced danger before—and in any case, I would have paid any penalty to know what she was refusing, so prettily, to tell me.

"No, no," she moaned, twisting and turning as I pinned her down and slipped my finger a little lower, letting its tip part the plump, hairy margin of her cunt-lips.

I bent lower over her, and took her right nipple into my mouth. It was sweet and brown as a nut, puckered to a rubbery consistency that simply begged to be sucked and bitten, rolled on the tongue whilst the little points of my teeth teased the oh-so-willing flesh into ever greater hardness.

And all this time, my hand was between her pussy-lips, my fingers rubbing back and forth along her thin, wet crack with a gentle insistence which drove her, little by little, to a frenzy of need. As I sucked and bit her nipple, I could see her hands clenching and unclenching into fists. She was fighting the feelings inside her, but her sensual nature was proving to be her downfall. I wondered if that was what she had wanted all along.

Her honeydew was oozing freely out of her now, inundating my fingers with the abundant evidence of her desire. And her clitty had swollen to an iron-hard bud of longing beneath the pad of my thumb. I rubbed it greedily, imagining that I could taste its slick wetness as I sucked at Soraya's breast.

I could hear her moaning, whimpering, sighing as her body twisted and writhed in the torment of her need; her ascent toward pleasure served also to excite me to new heights of desire. I longed with all my heart to have her tongue on my clitoris again. But I fought down the need and continued with the sensual torture of my willing victim. I felt her whole body tense, and a second rush of sex-liquor poured out of her onto my fingers. Her pleasure was near. I had only to rub her a little harder, nip her breast a little more unforgivingly, and she would give up her soul to me in a great climactic flood. But would she also give up her secrets?

"I shall have what I want, Soraya. You know I shall."

Judging the moment right, I took my fingers from Soraya's cunt, leaving her utterly bereft. I felt a great sob of longing shake her, and a gasp of desolation escaped from her pretty, painted lips.

"No. Please. Don't stop..."

I stroked her, very lightly, with the ball of my thumb, and she shuddered convulsively as flesh met flesh and the love-bud of her clitoris throbbed into painful, yearning life.

"Please!" she squealed, unable to control herself.

She was trembling all over, her eyes tightly shut as though she was concentrating all her ebbing strength on the helpless, hopeless quest for orgasm. Ignoring her pleas, I took my thumb away. Her nipple fell from my lips, standing dusky pink and hard on the tense globe of her breast. So beautiful. So irresistibly kissable.

I saw her hand stray from her side, and move stealthily toward her love-mound, but I stopped her. She gave a little moan of loss.

"No, Soraya. I shan't let you."

"Please. I must..."

"The only way you are going to come is if *I* make you. And if you want me to make you come, my sweet princess, you must tell me what I want to know. Tell me where you learned the secret sensual arts that you have at those pretty little fingertips."

"There is nothing to tell. Nothing."

I whispered my retort: "Don't lie to me, Soraya." And my finger pressed down once, quite hard, on her succulent rosebud. She shrieked her protest, and for a moment I feared that her mother would come back into the conservatory and discover my ingenious little game.

"No, please. I cannot tell you that."

"Tell me, Soraya. Or I won't let you come. And you want so badly to come, don't you, Princess?" I know not what black, malevolent hunger overwhelmed me, but I had resolved to deny her all release until I had extracted the truth from her, the truth that I had already so nearly glimpsed. I let my fingernail run in a wide circle around Soraya's clitty, each movement making tiny adjustments to the position of her clitty-hood and making her sob with anguish. Tears were rolling down her cheeks, and her mouth was open as though in agony. "Tell me."

"I…I can't. Mother would be so angry with me."

Again I stroked her—tantalizingly, fleetingly, with a short-lived brutality that so very nearly took her to the edge of orgasm.

"Tell me. You have seen the *Rosebud Sutra.*"

"No! No one has seen it. It doesn't exist…"

"It does. And you have seen it, learned from it."

I took the hard, blush pink stalk of her clitoris between my finger and thumb and pinched it hard. Soraya gave a thin, high wail of protest but she had no strength to resist me.

"Yes, yes. *The Sutra.*"

A warm glow of triumph washed over me. At last; at last I had some small evidence to back up what I had known all my life—that the *Rosebud Sutra* truly did exist. I slid down Soraya's body until I was kneeling between her outspread thighs.

"I could suck your clitoris, Soraya."

"Yes. Oh, yes."

I bent and ran my tongue, very lightly and playfully, along the grooves on either side of Soraya's swollen clitoris.

"I could lick you out and make you come. Would that not feel agreeable, Soraya? Wouldn't you like to feel my fingers up your cunt and my tongue lapping at your clitty?"

"Yes! Oh, Dorothea, please."

"Then tell me." I pressed my face to her pussy-lips and kissed the glossy black tangle of her pubic curls. "Tell me where the *Rosebud Sutra* is hidden."

"Anything, Dorothea. Ask anything of me, but not that. The penalty for giving away the secret..."

"I don't care, Soraya. Tell me now. Or I shall keep you in this agony of need until you do."

My cruelty surprised even me; I had perhaps not fully understood quite how desperately resolved I was to track down this object of my obsession. But, whilst I had never seen the sacred pages of the *Rosebud Sutra*, I had made a lifelong study of the Sapphic arts and prided myself that I knew some of the more esoteric paths of persuasion. There was a demonic ferocity in my caress as I ran the sharp point of my fingernail over the hypersensitive flesh surrounding Soraya's clitoris.

"I...will tell you all I know," she panted, half fainting from the pain of her frustrated pleasure.

"Hurry—tell me. Tell me now." I pressed my nail a little harder into her flesh.

"I do not know where the *Sutra* is kept, I swear I do not," sobbed Soraya. "But if you seek it, you must go..."

"Where, Soraya? Where must I go, my sweet Princess?"

"To Jainapur," she whispered, and as she nearly fainted away I at last rubbed hard on the head of her clitoris, releasing her from her torment with the gift of an orgasm that shook her frail body as though it were no more substantial than a leaf. "To Jainapur, in the foothills of the Himalayas."

She lay before me, not moving, for many moments, and I thought she had swooned away. The scent of her arousal was so strong that I could taste it, and I put my wet fingers to my lips, savoring the heady aroma of her intimate perfume. She had not entirely satisfied my longing for knowledge, but she had filled me with an exultation that aroused my whole body to a new peak of sensual need.

A voice from the doorway made me look up. The ranee was standing there, a curious smile on her face.

"Now you have conquered my daughter, you must also conquer me," she whispered, and I watched, mesmerized with longing, as she slowly unwound the long, shimmering folds of her robe.

Chapter 2

When a maid arrives at the age of puberty, her mistress should keep her secluded, and when others ardently desire her on account of her seclusion, and on account of the difficulty of approaching her, her mistress should then bestow her hand on such a person as may endow her with wealth and happiness.

—The Rosebud Sutra

Jainapur, northern India, Spring 1885

Amelia Courtnay was dreaming. Such a silky soft, sensual dream. She could not quite understand what it meant, but in the drowsy moments between deep sleep and waking, when she was almost but not quite conscious, the sweetly seductive world of the dream seemed infinitely preferable to the imperfections of reality.

In her dream, she was naked. Her eighteen-year-old body, white and smooth as marble, was moving slowly through a forest where curtains of many-colored foliage brushed her bare skin, curled and wrapped around her with the utmost gentleness. She looked down at the orange and purple and crimson leaves, and saw them transformed into thousands of caressing fingers and tongues, smoothing over her body again and again as though their only desire was to bring her pleasure.

She sighed and snuggled down in the bed, sinking into the dream of this faraway, jewel-bright world where all was softness and delight. As she walked across a carpet of crimson lilies, springy yet yielding beneath her feet, the long waving tendrils of their flowerstalks and leaves sought to wind themselves about her legs. Their soft, probing tips pressed between her parted thighs, teasing and stroking their way towards the gently-burning heart of her desire.

Amelia found her way barred by a hanging curtain of brightly coloured vines, their fruit and flowers pendulous and tempting. Reaching up to touch them, she found them as warm and soft as living flesh. At her touch, the curtain parted to let her pass, but as she walked between the hanging vines, their tendrils curled about her face and arms, extending down to touch and caress the hard white buds of her breasts. As the vines wound about her breasts, the warmth seemed to spread into them, making the white, waxy flesh blush pink. A fine tracing of blue veins throbbed and tingled just beneath the skin, and Amelia felt her whole body coming to life.

Where was she? What was this magical world into which she had strayed? The heat about her was tropical, the air steamy and heavy with moisture. She could feel little beads of sweat prickling the skin of her neck and back, the beads bursting to form little trickles that ran down into the small of her back, into the deep crease that began at the very top of her smooth, rounded buttocks.

The whole world seemed to be caressing her; even the hot breeze that shook the vines was like a lover's hand, smoothing and stroking her timorous, virgin flesh. Amelia had never known the touch of a lover, but as her body awakened to the first glimmerings of womanhood, she could feel the need growing within her. The need to be touched, caressed, made love to in ways that she could not yet understand…

"Five-thirty, girls! Are you so lazy that you must lie abed all day long?"

The sound of a handbell jolted Amelia from sleep. Miss Catherstone's voice barked out discordant commands that provoked a chorus of groans and sighs from the sleeping girls. Half past five! Why did they have to get up so early?

In the bed beside her, Amelia's friend Katherine stirred, groaned, and turned over. Amelia snuggled up to her, put an arm about her waist. "Time to get up, sleepyhead."

Katherine gave a grunt of protest. "Tormentor! Anyone would think you like getting up at this unholy hour."

Amelia and Katherine had been sharing a bed in the dormitory for two years now—ever since Amelia had come to the academy from her parents' home near Lahore. Colonel and Mrs. Courtnay had been killed in a sepoy uprising, leaving Amelia and her brother Alfred to fend for themselves. Alfred—a strapping eighteen-year-old—had gone directly into the army, but that had not solved the problem of what to do with a fifteen-year-old girl whose only accomplishments to date had been playing the piano and doing fancy embroidery. For a time, it had seemed that she would have to be sent directly back to England, to earn her keep as a governess. And then her Aunt Jocasta had heard about the academy.

The Jainapur Academy for the Daughters of Gentlewomen had been in existence for over fifty years, its sole purpose being to educate the orphaned daughters of gentlewomen and army families. Its stated aim was to provide a "respectable" upbringing for girls who no longer had any means of supporting themselves; keeping them safe from the temptations of the outside world and—when the time came—finding them suitable occupations or attachments, as befitted their class and accomplishments.

Miss Catherstone, a thin-lipped woman of forty-five, was headmistress of the academy, and had her own views on the upbringing of young gentlewomen. She was fond of telling people that luxury and idleness must, at all costs, be avoided, since these might lead to lewd thoughts and temptation. But sometimes, Amelia thought to herself when she looked at Miss Catherstone, it seemed almost as if the detection of such lewdness in her pupils provoked similar feelings in the headmistress. But, of course, it was wicked to think such things about Miss Catherstone.

What Miss Catherstone seemed not to realise was that the environment she had created was perfect for the development of attachments between the girls, who slept two or even three to a bed. What could be more natural than that, during the long, cold nights, they would cling together for comfort? At eighteen, Amelia was just beginning to discover the innocent pleasure which could be had from her own body, finding out, through chance and play, what caresses were most pleasing on her soft, white skin.

Amelia wrapped her arm more tightly around Katherine's waist. The starched white cotton of her nightdress felt crisp and clean over the softness of her young body. Katherine was remarkably well developed for her years—so much so that Miss Catherstone tried to force her to bind her breasts with tight linen straps, to inhibit their growth. "Such oversized breasts are the work of the Devil," she would snap. "The unfailing sign of a sluttish and unclean mentality and an enticement to the lascivious gazes of men." It was no use Katherine protesting her innocence; the punishment was always the same: to sit naked to the waist in the school quadrangle, whilst buckets of ice-cold water were thrown over her breasts—"to shrink them," Miss Catherstone said.

But Amelia could not help noticing how Katherine's nipples stiffened into hard pink nubs at the touch of the cold water and the way that trickles of freezing-cold water dripped off their tips. The sight invariably made Amelia feel curiously warm and excited; whenever she turned to look at the headmistress, she noticed that Miss Catherstone seemed excited, too. She seemed unable to draw her eyes away from the spectacle of Katherine's huge, naked breasts.

The handbell rang out again, and Amelia heard Miss Catherstone's voice booming out from the junior girls' dormitory on the other side of the landing.

"Ten to six, girls! Inspection in ten minutes."

With a groan of protest, Amelia nuzzled her face into the back of Katherine's neck. Katherine had long chestnut hair that took endless washing, and it smelt comfortingly of spring flowers, the mingled scents of the wild geranium and hibiscus that grew in colourful profusion on the slopes above Jainapur.

"Time to get up. It really is."

Katherine thrust out her backside a little, and Amelia did not edge away. She liked the feel of her belly hollowing to mould itself to Katherine's soft, round backside, and wondered what it would feel like to do it without their nightdresses on—bare flesh to bare flesh. The very thought made her feel hot all over, and her nipples went all tingly and hard, as Katherine's did when the icy water was poured over them.

"Do we have to get up?" murmured Katherine, clutching at her hard, feather-filled bolster.

"You know how we'll catch it if we're not up when Miss Catherstone gets here," sighed Amelia. Her hands moved slightly upwards and she felt a little thrill as she touched the underside of Katherine's heavy breasts. They felt big and soft, like two pillows. She wanted so much to unfasten the front of Katherine's nightdress and take them out so that she could try to cup them in her hands—not that she would be able to, because they were so big that the soft flesh would spill over her fingers like warm bread dough.

She wondered if they would smell yeasty and appetising if she were to lie with her head between them, pillowing her wavy blonde hair on the yielding pink flesh of Katherine's lovely breasts. She had seen them when her friend was dressing and undressing—beautiful pink-white clouds of flesh with bright pink nipples, and areolae that seemed as big as saucers.

Regretfully, she slipped out of bed and her feet met the cold linoleum of the dormitory floor. All around, the other girls were getting up, pulling off their nightdresses and washing before putting on their camisoles and long cotton drawers. This done, they must stand in a neat row beside their beds to await Miss Catherstone and her daily inspection.

Katherine slid reluctantly out of bed, yawning and stretching. Her chestnut hair was held in a long, loose plait which fell down her back like a rope. As Amelia watched, she took off the ribbon and it floated free—a glorious, fragrant mass of color. Amelia longed to kiss it. And then, perhaps, to pull away the hair that covered Katherine's neck and plant kisses all along the hairline.

She watched, spellbound, as Katherine unbuttoned the high-necked white nightdress she was wearing and lifted it over her head. As her arms raised the nightdress above her head like a white tent, Amelia saw Katherine's whole beautiful body stretch on tiptoe, her flesh growing firmer and tauter and her heavy breasts thrusting out, curiously buoyant, as she arched slightly backwards.

A little sigh of longing escaped from Amelia's lips. Then she glanced at the clock and realised that she must hurry if she was not to incur Miss Catherstone's wrath—as it was all too easy to do.

Fumbling with the tight buttons that held her high-necked nightdress modestly closed at the throat, she succeeded at last in unbuttoning them and peeling down the sides of the dress. Swiftly she wriggled out of it, pushing it down over her hips and thighs until at last it formed a little white cloud about her feet. She picked it up, quickly folded it and thrust it under the bolster, straightening the bedsheets and smoothing down the thin counterpane.

The water for washing was carried up from a well in the central courtyard by the school servants. Most of these were Indian, but one—a brown-haired, bright-eyed girl called Mary Bates—was the orphaned daughter of an English corporal in the Indian Army. The headmistress had considered the girl's lowly station in life wholly unsuitable for a place at the academy, but had condescended to take her on as a school servant, allowing her to attend a few classes in writing and arithmetic in return for her long hours of labour.

Amelia approached the washstand and saw Mary standing at the top of the stairs leading down into the servants' quarters. She was smiling broadly, and at once Amelia felt her spirits lighten perceptibly. Colour came to her cheeks and she turned away, afraid of betraying her pleasure at seeing the girl standing there. Whatever would Miss Catherstone say if she knew that one of her pupils had been striking up a loving friendship with one of the school servants? She would surely be expelled, and Mary dismissed instantly from the school's employ!

Looking sideways, she saw Mary smile and mouth the question, "This afternoon?" Before she could demur, Mary was gone and there was no time left to do anything other than have a very cursory wash in icy water before putting on her camisole and drawers.

Miss Catherstone insisted on all her senior girls wearing split-crotch drawers and a camisole in coarse, unbleached linen. This was a design which she herself had perfected, and she considered the drawers both hygienic and "minimally conducive to unclean thoughts." As Amelia stepped into her drawers, she thought that they were merely scratchy and uncomfortable. But as she watched Katherine dressing, she could not help thinking how comely she looked, with one foot on a chair and the vent from belly to arse gaping so wide that the chestnut tufts of her pubic curls were clearly visible to any casual observer.

How pleasant it would surely be to kneel in front of Katherine, to press her face into the blissfully warm, damp, fragrant valley between her thighs and breathe in the sweet, spicy scent of her. The thought made Amelia feel hot between her own thighs, and she thought with sudden panic of the inspection. What on earth would Miss Catherstone say?

Seconds later, Miss Catherstone strode into the dormitory with her usual retinue of school prefects. Tall and thin, she was habitually dressed in a gown of plain grey serge, even on the hottest days, with a stiff, high collar of starched linen that pushed up against her chin and a belt from which jangled a large bunch of keys. One of those keys was to the punishment room, mused Amelia with a frisson of discomfiture. That was the room where Miss Catherstone kept her store of whips and canes to punish the recalcitrant or the impure. Amelia recalled her last visit there—the caning she had received as she bent over the rough wooden bench, surrounded by harnesses, straps, and buckles—all the paraphernalia of the very strictest discipline.

"Girls! To your stations."

The girls scuttled to their beds, waiting in obedient silence as Miss Catherstone walked the length of the dormitory, keys swinging and jangling at her waist.

"At once, now! Idleness and sloth are sinful and will be punished most severely." She paused at the bed next to Amelia's, opened the small wooden cupboard beside it, and took out a folded pair of linen drawers which she spread out on the counterpane.

"These are yesterday's drawers, Jane?"

"Yes, ma'am."

Miss Catherstone picked them up and examined them closely. They were spotless and, when she had finished, she handed them back to the girl—almost regretfully, thought Amelia.

"These are satisfactory. You may go to your prayers now."

The girl curtseyed and hurried out of the dormitory, bound for the early-morning chapel service, after which there would be a meager breakfast of bread and gruel. Amelia paid the girl no heed. Her head was reeling, her palms damp with sweat as Miss Catherstone turned toward her.

"Ah, Amelia. Amelia Courtnay."

"Yes, ma'am."

The headmistress's thin lips curled into a condescending smile.

"Now that you have passed your eighteenth birthday, we really must consider your future." The smile grew glacial, and Amelia felt her mouth grow dry. "You are sometimes guilty of immodesty, but you do have certain…physical assets. Already I have had a number of interesting approaches."

Approaches? Amelia knew only too well what this meant. She had seen it happen all too often before, to her friends. As they approached their eighteenth birthdays, Miss Catherstone kept her girls even more strictly confined than ever, so that they could know as little as possible of the world beyond Jainapur and the academy. It was rumoured that, through her network of contacts, Miss Catherstone would invite wealthy women to make "offers" for her pupils—offers of employment, homes, companionship...and perhaps other things, too. Things that Amelia was not yet quite ready to understand.

The prospect both excited and terrified Amelia. What would become of her if she agreed to go and live with a complete stranger who—for some unaccountable reason—desired her company? She wasn't at all sure that she wanted to be sold off like some commodity. Not that she would have very much choice in the matter.

Seeing that she did not reply, Miss Catherstone repeated herself, this time with a note of menace in her voice.

"Several very promising approaches, Amelia. I must remind you that you should be grateful—grateful for anything. After all, my dear, I plucked you out of the dirt." She reached out and ran skeletal fingers down Amelia's cheek and throat. "You had nothing then—and without me, you would have nothing again."

"Y-yes, ma'am. Thank you, ma'am." Amelia knew what she must do. She lowered her eyes modestly, not daring to return Miss Catherstone's steely gaze.

"Show me your undergarments, Amelia." Miss Catherstone held out her hands, waiting impatiently for her pupil to comply.

Amelia fumbled in the wooden cupboard beside the bed and took out the previous day's camisole and drawers, handing them over with trembling hands.

"Now, let me see."

Miss Catherstone unfolded the camisole and held it up to the light, inspecting it minutely for any stains or marks. To Amelia's great relief, there were none.

"Some small degree of creasing, but this is satisfactory." The headmistress refolded the camisole and laid it on the bed, spreading out the drawers on the counterpane so that the long central split gaped wide. Miss Catherstone took a long, indrawn breath, and instantly Amelia felt all eyes upon her.

"Is there something wrong, ma'am?"

"Something wrong?" Miss Catherstone's eyes burned into her with a ferocious intensity. "Child, have you no shame?" She held up the drawers and ran the tip of her finger along the central vent. The faint shadow of a stain quite clearly darkened the material as she held them up against the early morning sunlight. "See? See that stain? It is the stain of your filth-ridden soul, Amelia Courtnay!"

"But ma'am..."

"Silence!" Miss Catherstone crumpled the rough linen drawers in her bony, yet strong hands. "That stain is the stain of impure thoughts—sluttish, unclean thoughts which must be banished from your head." She turned to Cordelia Johnson, one of the house prefects. "Fetch me a gym shoe. Hurry now."

Amelia exchanged worried glances with Katherine, but there was nothing she could do.

"Bend over the end of the bed," Miss Catherstone instructed her. Face burning with fear and embarrassment, Amelia obeyed. Dressed only in her camisole and drawers, she felt terribly exposed. Everyone in the room was staring at her, sharing or delighting in her humiliation. "Legs wider apart. I want to see you properly."

She complied, and the long, unforgiving vent in her drawers parted wide as her legs slid apart on the cold, smooth linoleum, baring the guilty secret of her sex.

Miss Catherstone's finger slid dispassionately into the valley between her thighs. She shivered, suddenly unsure if this was a torment or a pleasure. No one had ever touched her there before. There was something at once repellent and delicious about the touch of that bony finger, running over flesh already grown damp and slippery with some half-understood longing.

"You are indeed a slut," whispered Miss Catherstone, her voice no longer strident but low and husky. "Your private parts are wet with the filthiness of your desires!"

Amelia clutched on to the brass rail of the bedstead, her head hanging down, her eyes tightly shut and her mind filled with sudden, inexplicable images. All at once the image of the forest came back to her—the sensual wonderland of her dream, where everything had been warm and soft and moist, where her body had not been something to be ashamed of but the instrument of her pleasure.

She felt so confused, so mixed up. Was she really an evil slut, as Miss Catherstone said she was, or were these feelings natural and good, as Mary Bates kept telling her they were? She thought how she had almost given in to Mary's blandishments the previous day when she had sneaked out of detention to go walking with her in the hills. Mary's kisses had seemed so sincere, so passionate. How could that be wrong?

Miss Catherstone's voice silenced her thoughts, made her cringe in fear.

"Whilst you are here, you will keep yourself pure from all taint," she snapped. "And if you have not the moral strength to do it for yourself, I am quite prepared to do it for you. Those who are generous enough to become your mistresses when you leave here insist upon complete purity in the girls they take into their homes. Must I beat purity into you, you willful child?"

Amelia did not answer. How could she? Her whole

body was tensing for the inevitable, the pain that would surely follow.

Fingers unfastened the drawstring at her waist, wrenching her drawers down to her knees and exposing the white swell of her twin white globes.

"Wicked, disobedient girl," growled Miss Catherstone, and Amelia thought that she caught a hint of excitement in her headmistress's voice. A second later, she heard the hiss and whistle of the gym shoe cutting through the air as Miss Catherstone brought it down hard on her bare backside.

The first slap of rubber sole on bare skin sounded deafening in the silence—the only other sound the hoarse, rasping breathing of her tormentor. Amelia bit her lower lip, trying desperately not to make a sound. She had never had a slippering before. In the past, it had generally been just the flat of the hand—or the supple birch cane, which caused such acute discomfort that Amelia had almost swooned from the pain.

The gym shoe felt different, though. The second stroke hit her backside, making the flesh quiver and redden, and Amelia let out a little gasp as she was thrown against the brass bed rail and all the air was knocked out of her. There was pain, yes, a stinging, burning sensation—but it was more heat than pain; a tingling, searing feeling that was on the borderline between pain and pleasure.

Could pain be pleasurable? The thought had never occurred to Amelia before. But here, bending over the bed with her backside marbling pink and white at each new slap from the gym shoe, she felt that it could perhaps just be possible. What other cause could there be for the spreading warmth in her belly, the oozing, dripping wetness she could feel between her parted thighs?

Ashamed of her weakness, and confused by the conflicting sensations spreading through her, she tried to shuffle her feet together, hiding the evidence of her shame. But Miss Catherstone prevented her with an even harder swipe of the gym shoe.

"I forbid you to move, slut!" she hissed between clenched teeth, and Amelia was forced to remain stock-still, awaiting the next blow whilst the juices of her forbidden joy began to ooze and trickle out of her cunt, moistening her inner thigh.

The blows fell again and again, and she began to lose track of time and place. Where was she? What was happening to her? All that seemed to matter was the rhythm of the gym shoe, falling with a regular smack, smack, smack on her bare bottom.

"This. Will. Teach. You. To. Defy. Me." Miss Catherstone's hand came thundering down again, each word punctuating the blows from the shoe. Amelia had long since lost count of the number, but her backside was throbbing now—no longer stinging with the same vicious intensity, but dulling to a pulsing heat that was not quite pleasure, not quite pain.

Lost in the delicious torment of her punishment, Amelia scarcely noticed when it ended. Miss Catherstone threw the gym shoe to the floor and wiped her hands on a white cotton towel handed to her by the senior prefect, as though trying to wipe away the taint of her unruly pupil's impurity.

"The rest of the inspection will take place after morning service," she announced. Her voice was completely devoid of emotion, as though discussing the weather. "Hurry now—to the chapel."

Katherine stepped forward to put her arms around Amelia, but Miss Catherstone shook her head sternly.

"Leave her. She must have time on her own, to repent her sinful weakness."

Still bending over the brass rail of the bedstead, too afraid and too confused to move, Amelia heard footsteps moving away across the linoleum, fading into the distance and down the stairs toward the chapel. A door slammed. Moments later, all was silence.

She was so dazed that she did not notice another pair of light footsteps travelling across the linoleum toward her. It was not until she felt cool hands on her burning flesh that she awoke to the reality around her and tried to lift her head.

"Don't...Miss Amelia, let me. You'll hurt yourself." Mary's arms were strong and steady as she helped Amelia straighten up, then led her toward the bed. "Oh, Miss Amelia, what have they done to you this time?"

Amelia winced as Mary eased off her drawers, lifting first one foot and then the other to pull off the stiff white linen. The throbbing of her backside intensified once again to a burning as Mary helped her onto the bed, face-down on the counterpane, for her skin was so sore that she could not possibly bear to lie on her back.

"Mary...oh, Mary, how it stings!" murmured Amelia, her face turned to the side and her ruffled blonde hair forming a fluffy cloud about her head.

"There, there." Mary's voice soothed like a sister's, but her fingers were those of a lover, gentle yet experienced. She stroked them down Amelia's bare flank, skirting the large area of reddened skin that glowed with an inner heat.

"I must have been very wicked," sobbed Amelia, her body tensing as Mary's cool pink tongue touched her skin, leaving a filmy trail of saliva as its tip skated over the hard pink dome of her arsecheek.

"Don't be daft!" chaffed Mary, raising her face from Amelia's throbbing backside. "That's just old Catherstone's way of making you feel guilty. She don't beat you just to punish you, you know."

"No?" Amelia's eyes widened.

"'Course not. She just wants an excuse to touch your bare bum, that's all. Gets her all excited, it does."

"No, surely that can't be true!"

Mary ran her tongue in a long, winding trail from the top of Amelia's thigh, up over the swell of her left buttock and into the deep depression at the base of her spine. Amelia let out a long, low sigh of satisfaction. She hadn't ever thought it could be so pleasurable to have a dear friend licking her backside, but Mary's saliva felt just like a cooling, soothing salve on her injured flesh.

"It's true as I'm here," retorted Mary, climbing up onto the bed and kicking off her shoes. "That Catherstone bitch only runs this place so as she can have her pick of all the prettiest girls. That Betty Tinniswoode, remember her?"

"Mmm...yes, I think so. Tall girl, very slim, with dark hair. What about her?"

Amelia winced slightly as Mary's hand skimmed the burning surface of her arsecheeks. Even the lightest touch was painful, and the flesh seemed to radiate heat. She longed for the renewed touch of Mary's tongue as she wriggled her body on the counterpane.

The rough material offered its own clumsy caresses, but Amelia couldn't help imagining how much nicer it would feel to have Mary's tongue on her backside, her belly, her breasts. Other places too, perhaps.

"Used to spend the nights in Catherstone's bed,

that's what," replied Mary, a note of triumph in her voice. "Catherstone told her it was important 'training.' Anyhow, once Betty got near nineteen and Catherstone was tired of her, she sold her off to some slave merchant in Kalka. You know—some native woman who finds pretty young playthings for bored princesses."

"A slave merchant!" Wide-eyed with horror and disbelief, Amelia tried to roll around onto her back, but the pain prevented her and she gave a sob of discomfort. "No, no, I can't believe that."

Mary shrugged.

"Please yourself. But that's what I was told, and I can well believe it. At any rate, Betty disappeared all of a sudden, and we've never seen her again, have we?"

Amelia lay in silence for a few moments, then whispered: "What's to become of me, Mary? Do you think she intends to sell me too?"

"Don't you worry—I'll look after you. Mary Bates knows all there is to know about this bloody awful place. I won't let her do anything to you, you'll see I won't."

Mary silenced Amelia's fears with an embrace so agreeably sensual that Amelia felt all her tension melting away. Mary was kneeling between her parted thighs now, the cheap material of her maid's dress rubbing roughly against Amelia's bare skin. She bent and planted lingering kisses on Amelia's rump and Amelia raised herself a little on elbows and knees, so that her backside lifted and her arsecheeks separated slightly, revealing the long pink cleft of her cunny and the dark amber rosebud of her arse.

Mary shivered with pleasure at the sight of such sweet, virgin delights. Although Mary was not much older than Amelia, it was a while since she had lost her virginity to a rather beautiful Indian dancing girl, who had visited the hill-station of Jainapur with a travelling troupe to entertain the garrison. Mary had learnt a great deal from the veiled girl with the sloe black eyes and the pierced navel set with a huge dark emerald—a gift from her wealthy mistress.

Even now, as she began licking Amelia's upraised arsecheeks, Mary thought back to the moment when she and her first lover had been caught together by the girl's mistress, remembering the terrible threats and fury, and the sharp dagger that had been held at her throat. Only quick thinking and sensual initiative had saved her that day—it had been fortunate that the mistress enjoyed making love to two girls at once—but Mary was confident that if necessary her quick wits would save her again. Yes, and save Amelia Courtnay, too. For Mary had taken to the girl and felt a deep sense of injustice that she should become the latest victim of the hated Miss Catherstone.

But her thoughts turned quickly to the delicious taste of Amelia's bare flesh, still fragrant with the carbolic soap she had washed with and now lightly sprinkled with the sweat of the kindling Indian sun. The first chill of the early morning had passed away, and the heat of noon was only a few hours distant. Already a low-burning warmth was spreading through the dormitory, molten rays of sunlight falling on Amelia's bare back, making her martyred arse glow like a second sun.

Mary slid her hands under Amelia's belly and bent lower so that her face was between Amelia's nethercheeks. As her fingers worked gradually down toward Amelia's pubis, her tongue made little darting movements into the deep amber crease, teasing and tormenting with the very lightest of touches.

"Oh! Oh, Mary, please. Please don't..."

Mary paid little attention to Amelia's protests or to the frantic wiggling of her hips as she danced to this new and seductive tune. Amelia was an innocent, naive little virgin, and quite naturally all virgins were afraid of giving up their secret treasure. *Most* virgins, that is, thought Mary; she herself had been desperate to lose her virginity to the first woman who desired it. Mary had been brought up never to be ashamed or afraid of her essential sensuality.

"Please, Mary!" cried Amelia, as Mary's fingers met the crisp blonde tangle of Amelia's maidenhair, and she amused herself by winding a few curls about her fingertips. The slight pulling sensation seemed both to frighten and excite Amelia, for Mary could smell her juices flowing, and seconds later felt them running out of her, warm and sticky, forming great glutinous dew drops at the margin of her fringed cunt-lips.

"Don't be afraid, Miss Amelia. Just let me—let me do it to you."

Without waiting for Amelia's reply, Mary pressed her face hard against Amelia's arse cleft, her lips kissing the secret rosebud that seemed alternately to pucker and open itself to her kiss.

"No, no, no! Not that, I can't!"

Sensing that Amelia's resistance was too great—and fearing that her cries might alert Miss Catherstone—Mary let her tongue slip down, regretfully, from Amelia's arse to the deep, succulent furrow of her virgin cunt.

It tasted so good; honey-sweet, running with juices as clear and pure as the waters of a mountain stream. Mary let her tongue tip run up and down the deep pink folds, curling to scoop and drink the sex fluid as her fingers moved stealthily between the fringed margin of Amelia's plump sex-lips.

Mary wanted so much to give Amelia pleasure; wanted, even more, to relieve her of that troublesome virginity which Miss Catherstone had guarded so jealously and so long. Her clitty throbbed with the anticipation of such glorious pleasure, the pleasure of feeling her fist inside Amelia's tight, wet cunt, hearing her little cries of pain and ecstasy as she broke through the last barrier of her resistance.

Her tongue tip pushed against the entrance to Amelia's womanhood at precisely the moment when her fingertip brushed the fleshy hood of Amelia's clitoris. The touch was butterfly-soft, and the violence of Amelia's reaction surprised even Mary.

"Oh, oh, *oh!*" gasped Amelia, her last cry a screech of astonished ecstasy as the combination of finger and tongue tip brought her to her first-ever orgasm.

Mary felt the full force of her climax, her open mouth flooded with the sudden deluge of Amelia's clear, sweet juices as her virgin cunt tensed in the first spasms of overwhelming pleasure. Mary's own feelings were mixed: the taint of disappointment mingled with a triumphant lust as she felt the power of her skill coursing through Amelia.

As the last spasms of ecstasy ebbed away, Amelia's body fell limp on the bed, her bare back and buttocks glistening with the sweat of her pleasure. Her backside was still reddened from the slippering she had received from Miss Catherstone, but she rolled onto her back, scarcely aware now of the pain in the afterglow of her delicious climax. Her face was filled with questioning wonder.

"What…? What happened to me, Mary?"

Mary laughed and wiped her mouth with the back of her hand. Amelia's juices smelt strong and spicy-sweet, and she thirsted to taste them again.

"Have you never felt that before?"

"No, never!"

"That was your crisis, Amelia, your spending. Surely you have heard of such things?"

"Yes, but…I have never felt anything like that before."

"Don't you play with yourself?"

"I…don't know how. I touch myself sometimes, but it doesn't feel like that. Not like that at all."

Mary edged a little closer. Her breathing sounded loud and harsh in the silence, punctuated only by the ticking of the wall clock and the distant cries of flower and spice sellers in the bazaar below.

"I could show you how."

Her fingers crept down over Amelia's shoulder and cupped the firm globe of her breast, still thinly veiled by the linen camisole but a treacherous betrayer of her lust, for the nipple was hard as a nut, pressing insistently against the inner surface of the fabric as though begging to be released from its torment.

Amelia felt her head spinning. It was all so new, so delicious, so…forbidden. Mary's hand on her breast felt like heaven, and it was giving her the strangest of notions. She wanted her to squeeze it hard, so hard that it almost hurt. And she wanted her to release her from the constricting camisole and bite and pinch her breasts. Something told her that it would feel so, so good.

"Let me show you. I'll be gentle."

Amelia turned her head to look at Mary and saw

something disturbing, something scary and almost animal in her eyes. It was like looking into the eyes of a hungry tiger. Amelia felt the juices spilling out of her cunt-lips, cooling on her inner thigh, and thought that she would like Mary to show her how to make herself feel like that again. The memory of the feeling was so strong and so sweet. And yet…

"No. Not here."

Gently, she lifted Mary's hand from her breast and slid off the bed. Mary watched in an agony of frustrated lust as Amelia walked toward the window, still naked from the waist down, her firm round buttocks quivering slightly as she walked barefoot across the linoleum.

"But Amelia…"

Amelia half-turned and smiled.

"Someone might come in. Chapel will be over soon, and they might see us. Somewhere else, perhaps."

Mary got off the bed and joined her at the window, wondering what all the people in the square below would think if they knew that the prim young English rose looking down at them had a naked belly and thighs, a naked cunt and the most succulently naked arse…

"When and where?" Mary reached out and ran her fingers lightly down Amelia's bare arm.

Amelia gave a little sigh of luxurious pleasure. She might be an innocent virgin, but she had an instinctive understanding of the game she was unconsciously playing—the teasing, tormenting game of mutual lust.

"Tomorrow…or perhaps the next day. You know that I cannot always get away from my lessons. Miss Catherstone is most strict in her supervision."

She turned back to the window, revelling in the feeling of Mary's longing eyes boring into the side of her face, the delicate touch of her fingers on her bare flank, the scent of her own spending, wafting like incense around her in the hot, empty room.

It was market day in the hill station of Jainapur, and a variety of figures were already milling about in the town square below. Brightly coloured Indian robes and starched white dhotis mingled with the red jackets of the local garrison and the impossibly thick brown tweed and serge of the English community, who believed in "dressing warm" even at the height of summer. Brown monkeys and hoopoes chattered in wooden cages, and a man with a tray of amber trinkets cried his wares in a thin, quavering voice.

As Amelia watched, a swaying jampan—a sort of curtained sedan chair—entered the square, and its four turbanned bearers set it down. Immediately the curtain swished back and the passenger alighted: It was a tall European woman in her early thirties, her glossy dark brown hair cropped almost as short as a man's. She was dressed in dramatic black and white, her dress businesslike and unfussy in its cut, yet clinging alluringly to her body like a second skin.

The woman paid the jampanees, then set off across the market square, bag in hand. As she stepped over a patch of mire, she lifted up her skirts with one hand, and Amelia glimpsed the shiniest, most ladylike ankle-boots she had ever seen. Made from black patent leather, narrow-cut with high spikey heels, they were decorated with a long line of buttons and straps, and seemed quite at odds with the rather sober dress, plain white gloves, and simple jet jewelry.

Amelia leaned forward a little to get a better view, and, as though sensing her presence there, the woman paused briefly and looked up at the barred window.

Their eyes met. Amelia felt a sudden thrill pass through her as she looked into the woman's face, sensing an electricity that made her tremble and feel almost faint. The woman seemed to feel something, too, because her lips curled into a smile that turned Amelia's legs to jelly and filled her belly with an unfathomable, inexplicable hunger. She seized Mary's arm and pulled her closer.

"Who is that?"

"Who?"

"That woman down there—the one who just looked up at me. The one with her hair cut short like a man's."

Mary followed Amelia's gaze to the woman, now walking away toward the stone gateway which led away from the ancient part of the town to the English quarter and the barracks.

Mary giggled.

"Oh, her. That's some Englishwoman who's been sent over here by Queen Victoria—at least, that's what they say in the town."

"Why would the queen send her here?"

"She's an archaeologist. Now what was her name? Strong, was it? Yes, that's right. Dorothea Strong."

Chapter 3

If the maid desired be living with some other woman, then her suitor shall cause her to be stolen away, and—having made her a slave—shall place the maid in her harem.

—The Rosebud Sutra

From the journal of Dorothea Strong, May 1885

Upon my arrival in Jainapur, I went directly to the villa inhabited by the British consul, where I met with Lady Fortescue and her three delightful unmarried sisters.

The villa is situated in the most charming hilltop position above the town, stone-built in the Tudor style and surrounded with such verdant greenery that one might think one had been transported back to the lush

English countryside. Only the turbanned servants and the little troupes of brown monkeys who scamper across the tennis lawns remain to distract the eye from the contemplation of a perfect English villa. These and, of course, the mountains, whose snowy heads tower high above the little town of Jainapur, reminding me of the mysteries that lie deep in those Himalayan fastnesses.

During dinner that night, Lady Fortescue told me a little about the history and geography of this mountainous and beautiful area of northern India. It would appear that the garrison is yet an ever-present necessity, since wealthy Jainapur is from time to time troubled by the incursions of lawless bands of thieves and brigands who live in the mountains which lie in a broad arc behind the town. Some of these men are rebels against British authority; the larger number are simply fugitives from honest British justice, violent criminals who prey upon the vulnerable and the innocent.

Although Lady Fortescue tells her stories with great sincerity, I have little doubt that she exaggerates the dangers of this region. She is merely relaying the lurid tittle-tattle which finds such fertile soil among the idle rich of the ruling elite. I, most certainly, have no intention of curtailing my movements through fear of attack. In any case, in my youth I was trained in all the arts of self-defence and can handle both sword and pistol with greater skill than most men I have met.

To delay here in idle luxury, however pleasant, is a distraction from my main purpose—to win Her Majesty's favour by presenting her with a trophy worthy of her imperial greatness. I must, with all despatch, seek a way of finding the ancient book of love lore, the *Rosebud Sutra*. Now that I know for certain of its existence, I burn with the need to have it in my hands, to possess it.

Within its ancient covers lies the key to certain fame and fortune, and wondrous sensual secrets that will unlock the hidden and suppressed sexuality of Western women, too long condemned to a life of celibacy and forbidden the pleasures of self- and sisterly love. Best of all, it will ensure my fame and fortune forever.

Last night I took myself once more to a house of pleasure, much frequented by the Indian women of the town, yet shunned by the English, who condemn it in their ignorance as a place of sin and ill-repute. There I met Shushila and Panjeet, two young girls raised in the arts of pleasure since early childhood. It is the custom in some mountain villages to dedicate young girls at birth to Kali or some other goddess of the sensual mysteries, training them in the traditional ways of the Tantra so that they may more perfectly pleasure their mistresses and sisters. This strikes me as an entirely civilized custom.

Upon attaining puberty, these girls are taken to the pleasure-house where they will live for the whole of their lives. There, they are put under the direction of what we Europeans might call a "Madame"—the mistress of the house, who regulates their lives by a strict timetable of service and devotion, and continues their training as they begin their commerce of love.

I first encountered these Indian pleasure-houses when, as a young girl, I was sent to live with my aunt and uncle in Delhi. Already somewhat of a rebel, I rejected all their pleas to "make a good marriage," and at the age of eighteen I ran away to live with a young courtesan, who sheltered me and taught me some of the arts by which she lived. In later years, when living back in dreary, foggy London, I have often thought back to those blissful nights I spent in her young and tender arms.

As soon as I arrived at their house, Shushila and Panjeet greeted me with the greatest courtesy, embracing me warmly and assisting me to undress. In these pleasure-houses, it is customary for the guest to be naked whilst she is entertained by veiled and jewelled dancers who gradually reveal themselves to her. This gradual unveiling is a great awakener of lust, and the herbal drinks which are furnished by the house are concocted according to ancient and closely guarded recipes designed to arouse and excite.

I settled myself down on a pile of soft embroidered cushions. All about me, clusters of joss sticks burned in engraved brass holders, their incense wafting in fragrant clouds about me, making me half-dizzy with desire. I had abstained from all congress for three days prior to visiting the house, for I knew that I would need all my sensual power to match the skills of these two Indian beauties.

Panjeet sat cross-legged on the floor and began to play for me upon a wooden pipe, her robe open from waist to ankle so that the dark fluff of her pubis was clearly visible between her outspread thighs. The light from the small oil lamps was smoky and inconstant, casting ever-changing shadows as the incense smoke swirled about us, at first veiling then revealing the most succulent inches of caramel-coloured flesh, the half-hidden, glistening crack between Panjeet's black-furred muff.

The music was liquid and light, bubbling like a stream, leaping and swooping like my own light heart. The beaded curtain swished and parted, and in danced

Shushila, graceful and mysterious in her many veils of gossamer-fine tulle. I glimpsed her lithe and slender body beneath the thin fabric as she twisted and turned, and although I could not see the lower part of her face her kohl-rimmed eyes glittered and glistened like jet.

I reached out to touch her but as soon as she was almost within reach she danced away, beyond the grasp of my eager hands. I knew that she was toying with me, using her body with coquettish skill to tempt and inflame me. Joyfully I drank more of the sweet cordial from its simple wooden cup and felt the desire grow bright as a flame within me. As I watched the dance, I grew still more lascivious, running my own hands over my body, feeling how good it was to have the touch of gentle, knowing hands on my skin.

Panjeet swayed from side to side as she played, her long dark rope of hair swinging between her shoulder blades and the light, diaphanous fabric of her robe floating free—now almost covering the sweet valley of her sex, now shamelessly baring it, so that my hungry eyes could feast on the dark pelt of her sex, the coral pink oyster within. I thought of the pink pearl that lay cloistered within this pink satin casket, so prettily trimmed with glossy black fur, and the anticipation of its touch, its taste on my tongue, made me half-mad with need for her.

Her eyes never leaving mine, Shushila unfastened a long veil that wound round and about her graceful frame. As it fell away, it revealed the swell of one creamy breast, across which swung a host of clinking silver chains that reflected the light.

The second veil bared her right leg from thigh to foot, a circlet of silver bells adorning her slender ankle. As she danced and bent her supple body, the bells and chains jingled a rhythm, the rhythm of my heartbeat, fast and urgent. I wanted her with all my being, longed to have her nakedness next to mine, her pussy-lips rubbing against my own as we ground our bodies together in a harmony of lust.

The music and the incense, the sweet herbs and Shushila's swaying form, all began to mesmerise me and I could feel myself gradually losing control. The lust within me was my only guide now, and I could think of nothing but the delight of Shushila's nakedness. Veil by veil she revealed herself to me, with such painstaking slowness that I thought I would die of longing before I would ever see her naked before me.

The last veil—a scrap of silver-spangled scarlet cloth—wound over her shoulder, covering her right breast, the taut plateau of her belly, and the dark pussy mound I so longed to kiss. With agonising slowness, she unfastened it and let it fall away, revealing the last perfect piece of her erotic jigsaw puzzle. Bending over me, she ran the scrap of scarlet fabric between her thighs, moistening it with her juices, then let it float gently into my face. I caught it and breathed in the irresistibly erotic scent of her sex, heightened by the musky perfumed oil she had rubbed into her pubic curls in preparation for the night's pleasure.

"Come to me," I beseeched her, reaching out my arms to her. She caught my hands and pressed them with the greatest ceremony to her breasts, then to her pussy-lips, and finally to her mouth. Her crimson-painted lips felt hot and moist on my skin as she opened her mouth and took my two index fingers inside, working her tongue about them as though it were some lewd serpent, coiling and uncoiling about my flesh.

I scarcely noticed Panjeet putting down her wooden pipe and slipping out of her robe. But as Shushila sucked and licked at my fingers, I felt the other woman begin stroking and biting the long sweep of my bare back.

Before I could seek to regain the upper hand, the two women of pleasure had me totally under their spell. I was enchanted by them, willingly bewitched by the sweet insistence with which they made love to my aching, yearning body. Whilst Shushila's tongue played with the sensitive tips of my fingers, Panjeet took a small pot of oil warmed on a bed of hot coals, and put into it three drops from a small flagon of scented liquid. As soon as the perfume met the oil and mingled, its scent spread through the room, more powerful and more sensual by far than the scents of incense that wafted around me.

Bergamot and patchouli, jasmine and sandalwood; all these scents seemed contained within those few drops of precious liquid. These perfumes and others, more subtle and musky, more infinitely sensual, met and mingled in the air and created a sexual magic that found its way into the deepest recesses of my soul.

I gasped with pleasure as Panjeet lifted the pot of sweet-smelling oil and tipped a little of it between my shoulder blades, so that it ran down my spine like the long, slow kiss of an amorous lover. Her fingers caught it as it reached my waist and scooped it up, then began working it into my skin with sweeping circular movements. Over my flanks, up toward the nape of my neck, into the hollow between my shoulder blades, loosening away all the tension and letting the sweet, sultry warmth soak into me, right down to the bones.

Shushila left off sucking and licking my fingers, and got onto her knees in front of me. I sank a little deeper into the soft pile of cushions, welcoming the boldness of her embraces. Through my half-closed eyelids I saw her smile, and then those red lips came closer and fastened on the bud of my right breast—with such demonic precision that I gave a loud cry, half of astonishment at her boldness, half of ecstasy at her sweet, matchless skill.

Whilst her lips were working away at my nipple, her left hand cupping the breast and gently squeezing it, the fingers of her right hand were journeying ever downward, toward the secret garden between my thighs. Instinctively I, too, got onto my knees, sliding them a little apart so that Shushila's fingers met with no resistance as they reached the tangled brown of my pubic hair.

"Such skill," I sighed, happy in the torment of my pleasure. I had not known such delight since my adolescence, since those balmy days when I had made my first excursions into the sensual secrets of the Indian subcontinent.

"Our whole life is the giving of pleasure," replied Panjeet serenely, working more of the warm oil into my skin. Her hands were working their way down over my buttocks, massaging them hard so that the flesh quivered and imparted a most delicious sensation to my arse and quim. "The giving...and the receiving. For in pleasuring you, we receive our own reward."

Her voice was soft and sweet, apparently so submissive, yet I heard the steel within the velvet and knew that it was she, not I, who was in control. She held all my desire in the palms of those small and perfect hands. And, for once in my life, I cared not one jot that I was not the pleasure mistress in this pretty tableau.

Panjeet's fingers moved inward from the fleshy pads of my arsecheeks, working their way into the deep and secret furrow that longed for her touch. I could feel the puckered sphincter of my anus pulsing, dilating and contracting like the mouth of a sea anemone as her finger slipped between my arsecheeks, brushing a thin, warm slick of oil from the base of my spine to the gaping lips of my cunt.

My breath was quickening, my heart racing with the excitement of the caresses lavished on my greedy body. Shushila's fingers were sliding up the inside of my thighs, pressing lightly into the crease between thigh and cunt-lip, moving firmly apart so that my cunt opened still wider, dropping sweet, fat dew drops onto the beaten earth floor. As her fingertips fluttered into the hypersensitive folds of my quim, I felt Panjeet's touch on my arse—bold, insistent, indiscreet, she was pressing her thumbnails against the fragile membrane, demanding entrance to the inner sanctum of my pleasure.

I began shuddering, trembling with the glorious need for release as my lovers wrought their inexorable will upon my helpless body. Shushila's fingers flicked back and forth over the head of my clitty, exciting it to paroxysms of need which made me twist and turn, unable—and unwilling—to escape from this terrible, unforgiving pleasure. Panjeet's sharp-nailed thumbs forced their way into my arse in a single thrust that left me gasping and sobbing, impaled upon the spike of her flesh.

Relentlessly, Panjeet began working her thumbs in and out of my arse, pulling them apart little by little so that she stretched my poor arse almost to the point of tearing. I had lost all control; I no longer knew or cared if I could halt the headlong rush toward orgasm, and as Shushila's fingertip penetrated my vagina, I knew that I must surely spend...or die.

My orgasm seized me with such suddenness that I was quite unprepared for it. In an instant, my whole body was transformed into a raging inferno of lust; my quim clenched in a shattering series of spasms and I felt my arse tighten about Panjeet's fingers, as though cunt and arse longed to draw both of my lovers in, absorbing them into the pleasure of the moment.

As the spasms died away, I found myself thinking of the pretty blonde girl I had seen standing at an upstairs window of the Jainapur Academy for the Daughters of Gentlewomen. Such a face she had—so open, so pure; a face like hers could only be the face of a virgin. The thought of the girl's sweet, unsullied flesh almost made me spend again, and I wondered idly if I might contrive some innocent stratagem by which we might meet. How much pleasure I might bestow upon her pretty body—perhaps more pleasure even than Shushila and Panjeet had bestowed upon me, with their knowledge of the secrets of the East. And how much delight my possession of her would give me.

As I sit here, writing my journal, I cannot help thinking how much more pleasure I shall enjoy when once I have won the prize which glitters grail-like in my mind's eye—the matchless prize of the ancient *Rosebud Sutra*...

"Amelia Courtnay."

"Yes, ma'am?"

Miss Catherstone took off her steel-rimmed spectacles and laid them on the desk before her. Amelia shifted uneasily from one foot to the other, certain that she was about to be punished—but not knowing for what. Could it be that someone had seen what she had done with Mary Bates, a few days before, in the dormitory? Had she committed some other transgression, without even realising it? She slid back her chair and stood up in front of the class, very conscious that all eyes were on her, that there were whispers behind hands, stifled girlish giggles.

"Come here."

Amelia walked nervously to the front of the class, where Miss Catherstone was waiting, as tight-lipped and enigmatic as ever.

"You have not always been a model pupil, Amelia Courtnay."

Amelia hung her head, her cheeks burning with guilty shame and disappointment. It seemed so unfair that she was to be punished. She had tried; tried so hard to be good and please all her schoolmistresses, really she had.

"No, ma'am. I am sorry, ma'am."

"As indeed you should be." Miss Catherstone's eyes swept the classroom with a steely, all-seeing glare and the giggles were instantly silenced, the girls hardly daring to breathe for fear of incurring their headmistress's wrath. "As should any girl who is foolish enough to defy me." Her gaze flicked back to Amelia. "And for goodness' sake, stand up straight, girl. Have you so little regard for correct deportment that you must stand like a slattern on a street corner?"

Trembling, Amelia forced herself to straighten up and return Miss Catherstone's gaze. What could she possibly have done to offend her? Why, she hadn't even been able to get out of the school compound for the past week, to visit the bazaar or go for walks with Mary Bates—her housemistress, Miss Rodway, had been watching her like a hawk. Amelia looked up into Miss Catherstone's face and, to her surprise, saw that a half-smile was playing about her thin lips.

"However, over the past few days I have heard much-improved reports of you, Amelia. Your housemistress has been quite favourably impressed by your obedient behaviour."

"Th-thank you, ma'am."

"I cannot impress upon you too highly—any of you—that a girl who lacks training and the proper education, as well as wanting a dowry, will find life extremely difficult once she leaves the sheltered precincts of the academy. But those of you who are obedient and tractable... Well, let us just say that I shall undertake—out of the goodness of my own heart—to make suitable arrangements for your future lives."

Her eyes were firmly fixed on Amelia now, and for one horrible moment Amelia thought that the moment had come—the moment when Miss Catherstone would announce that an "offer" had been made for her. Her heart was in her mouth, her pulse racing.

"But that is, of course, in the future," continued Miss Catherstone, much to Amelia's relief. "The reason I have called you out of class, Amelia, is because I have a task for you to perform. Not merely a task—a considerable privilege. One which I am relying upon you to accomplish with honour."

"Ma'am?"

"We have an important visitor to our town, girls—an envoy sent by Queen Victoria herself. Dr. Dorothea Strong is an eminent archaeologist who has come to Jainapur to study its native history and customs. And she has today sent me this communication." Miss Catherstone picked up a sheet of paper from the desk. "She has requested that I send one of our girls to show her around the town this afternoon. Indeed, Amelia, she has requested that that girl should be you."

"Me!" Amelia stared blankly at her headmistress, beyond comprehension.

"Yes, my dear. Having spoken at length with your housemistress, she has specifically requested that you should be sent as her guide. Of course, we must not disappoint our honored guest, must we? Go immediately to the dormitory and put on your best Sunday dress, Amelia. Dr. Strong will await you in the town square at two o'clock this afternoon."

It was just before two when Amelia emerged from the front gates of the academy and stepped into the shimmering heat of a Jainapur afternoon. Normally, at this hour she and her schoolfellows would be sleeping in the dormitory, taking their daily siesta, but it appeared that Dorothea Strong had been most insistent about the time of their meeting. She, like Amelia, was accustomed to the vagaries of the climate, and she wished to take a tour of the district whilst the town was relatively quiet.

Beneath her parasol, Amelia felt small, vulnerable, and just a little excited. How could it be that this woman—the very woman she had so admired through the barred window of the dormitory—had discovered her name and even persuaded her headmistress that she should be released from afternoon school in order to show her round Jainapur?

And another question, more pressing still, burned

within her. Not how, but why Dorothea Strong had gone to such lengths to track her down. Could it be that she, too, had felt the electricity passing between them?

Mary Bates watched from the scullery window as Amelia stepped through the front gates of the academy. She looked so pretty and so vulnerable in her pale yellow muslin, buttoned high at the neck but blown against her by the hot wind, so that it molded itself to every budding curve of her young body. Her fair, wavy hair was piled up on top of her head in a loose knot, revealing the oh-so-caressable nape of her neck, smooth and white and inviting kisses.

As usual it was suffocatingly hot in the scullery, but Mary did not feel the heat of the sun through the thick glass of the windowpane; the heat within her was far more intense—the blistering furnace heat of jealous love. Hadn't she staked her claim to Amelia's affections? Hadn't they shared intimacies and made each other promises? She felt the hurt of loss with a desperate keenness.

She saw Dorothea Strong even before Amelia had spotted her. A tall, slender figure dressed all in black with striking touches of white, she was leaning up against the central fountain, her head thrown back and her parasol lying unheeded on the dusty ground beside her. Her cropped, pomaded hair glistened in the fierce sunlight, and even jealous Mary could not help admiring the masculine grace of her athletic form, the clean, handsome lines of her aristocratic, quintessentially English features.

Dorothea turned at the sound of Amelia's approach and welcomed her with a smile that filled Amelia with confusion. Mary watched from the window, her hands tightly gripping the stone ledge and her heart thumping in her chest.

"Amelia. Amelia Courtnay. How charming."

Dorothea held out her hand and Amelia—not quite sure what she ought to do—took it and kissed it, bobbing a respectful little curtsey in the dust.

She blushed at Dorothea's husky laughter, but the archaeologist seemed delighted rather than irritated by her confusion.

"Such sweet innocence—that quality is indeed rare in an English girl in these imperfect times." Dorothea took her hand and pulled her to her feet, scrutinizing her slender form from head to toe with those large, dark eyes. "Your headmistress keeps you in strict seclusion?"

"Miss Catherstone is most insistent that we remain pure and untainted by the world."

Dorothea smiled.

"But you have amours? Surely you have your diversions and your flirtations? Oh, do not blush so prettily, my little one—it only makes my heart race faster. Of course you have amours—small, innocent flirtations with the other girls at your school. It is the same with all schoolgirls. I, too, had a very special friend—a dear, faithful friend with whom I shared everything." She paused for effect. "Even my bed."

Her gaze never wavered, and Amelia felt the hairs rise on the back of her neck as she shivered, suddenly burning hot and freezing cold, all at once. She recalled how she had felt when Mary Bates had kissed her the very first time, and how it had felt when she had run her cooling tongue over the throbbing flesh of her buttocks. She had felt like this then—overtaken by a hunger she could scarcely describe and still less understand.

"Come," said Dorothea, picking up her parasol and tucking it under her left arm, disdaining such effete, girlish protection against the sun. She revelled in even the fiercest, most metallic heat, quite unashamedly allowing it to bronze her skin—something which nicely bred young English ladies and their mothers considered quite unthinkable, mused Amelia as she tucked her small, gloved hand into the crook of Dorothea's right arm and they set off across the square.

Dorothea Strong was not like anyone she had met before. She was bold, unconventional, perhaps just a little cruel and so, so sensual. Even in her unsullied innocence, Amelia could sense the pulsing need within her strong and supple frame; feel the heat of her desire, far hotter and more powerful than the heat of the Indian sun. Up here in the foothills of the Himalayas, the sun lacked the brassy heat that made the plains so unbearable in summer, but even in the breeze that blew her dress against her body, Amelia felt suffocatingly hot. Beneath the parasol, she sweltered in her thin muslin gown, but Dorothea Strong seemed to soak up every ounce of heat like a lizard, deriving new strength and new energy from its power.

They strolled together across the square toward the ancient gateway. At this time of day there were few people to see them—one or two ancient spice sellers and an old fakir, sitting in tranquil immobility on his bed of razor-sharp nails. Dorothea glanced at him and turned thoughtfully to Amelia.

"Self-control—isn't that what they teach you at the academy? Discipline and self-control?"

"I...yes, it is one of the things we learn. Miss Catherstone feels it is most important for young ladies to have control over all their…appetites," parroted Amelia, half-suspecting that this whole thing might be a test dreamed up by Miss Catherstone to find out how well she had learned her lessons.

"Indeed!"

Dorothea chuckled and disengaged her arm from Amelia's chastely gloved hand. She slipped her arm loosely about Amelia's waist, in the attitude of a very dear friend and confidante. Amelia was not quite sure if this was permissible, or even entirely decent, but it felt very agreeable, and besides—who was there to see them here? She began to relax a little into Dorothea's embrace.

"Yes, Dr. Strong."

"Please—call me Dorothea. I am sure we are going to be such good friends." She let the flat of her hand skim Amelia's backside very lightly—so lightly that the touch might almost have been accidental, but Amelia knew that there was purpose in it. She blushed a deeper crimson, and this seemed to please the archaeologist as she continued speaking.

"My dear Amelia, we Englishwomen are all such innocents when we speak of self-control. In our knowledge of the sensual arts we are as children compared to our Hindu sisters. I, for example, have spent ten years and more studying the Eastern ways of love, but I am as much a novice compared to them as…as you are, compared to me. Is that not so, Amelia?" She squeezed Amelia's backside with a loving insistence, and in spite of her apprehension, Amelia found the sensation delightfully provoking.

"I…I suppose so; but I really wouldn't know. I'm afraid I don't know very much about anything."

"So pure and so delightfully polite. What a pretty mouth you have, Amelia. How moist and pink those lips are." Dorothea paused and her face was very close to Amelia's—so close that for a moment Amelia thought she might kiss her. "It seems such a pity that you must waste them in chanting rote learning."

"I must do as I am bidden. I am an orphan—if I do not do as Miss Catherstone tells me, I shall have no future. I shall be quite alone in the world."

"My dear Amelia, a girl as pretty as you are always has a future."

They walked on, arms linked once more, the silk tassels of Amelia's white parasol casting dancing shadows on the dusty red earth. Dorothea's skirts swirled around her ankles as she walked and Amelia made out the mirror-smooth surface of her patent leather boots, the spikey heels that left deep indentations in the soft roadway. Amelia felt curiously excited by the sight, as though she had caught a glimpse of something very alluring and very forbidden.

"Now, where are you going to take me this afternoon, my dear?"

"Do you wish to see the rest of the town? I could show you the English quarter and the new church where we go each Sunday, and the ancient temples by the river."

"No, Amelia, you may show me the rest of the town tomorrow. Today is rather hot and stuffy, don't you think? I have a fancy to go walking higher in the hills."

"But Dr. Strong…"

"Dorothea."

"The hills are dangerous, Dorothea, Miss Catherstone is always telling us so. We are not allowed to go there. All sorts of terrible things happen…"

"With me, Amelia, you are allowed to go anywhere. Anywhere I choose to go. Didn't your headmistress entrust you to my charge?" Dorothea quickened her pace and Amelia found herself climbing the dirt track which led up the steep side of the valley. "Besides, Amelia, there is nothing to be afraid of in the hills. Nothing at all. And there..." She smiled at Amelia, feeling her nipples stiffen with the anticipation of some unimaginable pleasure. "There, we shall at last be alone."

After an hour's hard walking, they reached a pass which ran between two high mountain peaks. A deep lake half-filled the hollow, its waters clear and pure as the mountain snows which melted into them every springtime.

"It's beautiful," whispered Amelia, a little breathless after her climb.

"Beautiful, yes," agreed Dorothea, "but scarcely as beautiful as you, Amelia Courtnay."

Her hands seized Amelia with a sudden, impetuous passion that caught her completely unaware. Dorothea's kiss was resolute and intense, demanding a response no less passionate. Her lips forced themselves against Amelia's, her hard, corseted breasts pushing against the softer corsage of Amelia's yellow muslin dress. Her tongue pushed between Amelia's lips, which at first were unwilling, then relenting, as though instinct overcame caution and instructed Amelia in the sweet art of surrender.

The kiss was something new and terrifying to Amelia; something wonderful also, for the sensation of Dorothea's tongue, winding and flicking inside her mouth, filled Amelia with the most delectable shivers. She could not help but respond to the knowing caress of that engine of pleasure, rubbing itself so lewdly over the surface of her own tongue, awakening her to a new world she had only dreamed of.

"You are so lovely, Amelia," murmured Dorothea, crushing her body against the schoolgirl's breast. "And I mean to have you—I must and I will have you, my beautiful one."

"No, no...please," whimpered Amelia, no longer at all certain if her protests were sincere or simply the product of years of relentless conditioning.

"Hush, child." Dorothea ran her fingers down Amelia's back, soothing away the tension, willing her to admit to the pleasure of the touch, to relax into her arms. "Just let me..."

"I can't. It's not right," gasped Amelia, but Dorothea was no longer paying any attention to her protestations of wronged innocence.

"It is exactly and wonderfully right," Dorothea told her, her hands moving lower down to massage Amelia's arsecheeks, plump and firm beneath the light covering of yellow muslin and fine petticoats. "You know that it is. That morning, when you looked down and smiled at me from your window, I knew you wanted me as much as I wanted you. As much as I want you now."

Amelia shuddered at Dorothea's touch, fighting the pleasure but losing as her resistance ebbed away. She felt as fragile as a rose petal blown by the mountain wind; as helpless as a butterfly captured in a net, never to be set free.

With an effortless skill, Dorothea set to unfastening the long row of buttons which ran up the front of Amelia's gown.

"You are young, Amelia. Young and pathetically ignorant of love, just as I was at your age. Let me cure you of that ignorance—let me become your mistress."

Amelia made no reply. Her body was answering for her, her pelvis gently pushing against the front of Dorothea's dress as her suitor began undressing her, little by little exposing the budding apples of her breasts, veiled only by the rough linen camisole.

"Have you ever had a woman's tongue in your arse? A woman's hand inside your quim, stretching you so hard that you scream with the pain but you want it to go on forever and ever and ever?" Dorothea laughed as she cupped Amelia's breast through the linen of her camisole, her thumb rubbing approvingly across the hard nut of her erect nipple. "No, of course you have not. But today, Amelia, if you will permit me, I shall take away the foolish impediment of your virginity and make you a woman. I know that is what you really want..."

"Oh, oh, oh." Amelia's voice was no more than a series of little gasps of pleasure as Dorothea rucked up the yellow muslin and crisp cotton petticoats, and thrust her hand straight into the wet furrow between her thighs.

"Sopping wet for me already? Oh, Amelia, I do so love to feel a young girl's sopping quim. Open your thighs wider for me, sweetheart, and let me in..."

Crack!

The rifle shot rang through the air, the bullet ricocheting off a rock only a few yards from Amelia's head. Suddenly, everything seemed to be happening in slow motion, though Amelia knew at the back of her mind events were actually moving very fast indeed. But everything seemed jumbled up, incomprehensible, terrifying. She pulled away from Dorothea, taking a few unsteady steps backwards, the open bodice of her muslin dress clutched tight over her breasts and her eyes wide with fear.

"Foolish Englishwomen. Foolish and arrogant, as are all your kind."

The bandit chief spoke in heavily accented English. He and all his band were swathed in loose headdresses and flowing robes which concealed all but the dark, glittering jewels of their eyes. A dozen rifles—no doubt stolen from the garrison arsenal in Jainapur—were trained on the two women, their muzzles glinting in the afternoon sunlight.

"I should kill you both now, strip your bodies and send you back naked, as the worthless English bitches you are."

"But beautiful," broke in one of the other bandits, his voice light and husky. "Beautiful enough to give pleasure. Perhaps before we kill them we should enjoy them first. It has been a long time..."

"Never!" shrieked Dorothea. Suddenly galvanized into action by the imminent threat, she lunged forward and attempted to knock the rifle out of the brigand chief's hand.

He parried her blow with consummate ease, seizing her wrist and twisting it so sharply that she shrieked with pain though her dark eyes flashed fire.

"This one's a spirited bitch," he observed. "I shall enjoy fucking her before I slit her throat."

"Leave her alone!" cried Amelia, and in that second all eyes were on her. "Whatever you must do, do it to me, but leave her alone."

This unexpected diversion was all the opportunity Dorothea needed to struggle free from her captor and run for cover, stumbling over rocks and tree roots as she rushed headlong down the hillside, half falling, half sliding as she went.

"Kill her!"

A second shot rang out, but it hit a pile of rocks, splintering off little chips of stone that scattered all over the mountainside. The third shot was aimed with greater accuracy, and this time Dorothea was not so fortunate. Amelia heard her shriek with pain as the bullet penetrated the flesh of her right shoulder. But the Englishwoman did not fall; Dorothea Strong was not so easily deterred. Half turning as she ran, she shouted back to Amelia: "I will get help. I will be back, I promise."

And then she was gone, slipping and sliding down the scree-covered hillside until she was out of sight.

"Let her go. This little bitch is much more to my taste."

Tears streamed down Amelia's face. Not only was she at the mercy of these ruthless bandits—her companion had been wounded and now she, Amelia Courtnay, was all alone. Behind her she heard the water lapping gently in the mountain lake. How could such terrible things happen in such a peaceful place?

"A pretty little prize," observed the first rider, getting down from his horse and handing its reins to one of his companions. Once standing beside her, he seemed little taller than Amelia, but powerfully built. His eyes glittered darkly beneath the colorful wrappings of his headdress and robes. "Perhaps I shall not kill you after all. There may be other purposes for you to serve."

He took off his glove and Amelia was surprised to see how slender his hand was, the second finger weighed down with a heavy silver ring in the form of a Hindu goddess.

"Please...please don't touch me," gasped Amelia, backing away. But she came up against solid rock and found her escape barred. All about her were the sounds of mocking laughter. She was surrounded, all chance of escape now gone.

"My dear, how can I take my pleasure of you if I do not touch you?" inquired the bandit sarcastically, forcing away Amelia's protecting hands so that the unbuttoned front of her muslin gown fell open, revealing the camisole beneath.

"No! No, get away from me..."

The bandit laughed.

"Whatever is the matter with you? Don't you desire me? I desire you, little English girl."

He seized the front of her camisole and for a moment Amelia feared that he would tear it down, leaving her naked and utterly, utterly exposed. But instead he let it go, and she sank to her knees, trembling. What was going to happen to her? What was going to become of her in this terrible place? If only she had obeyed Miss Catherstone's strict instructions to the letter....

"Poor little English girl." The bandit's voice was suddenly softer and silky. He reached up and pulled away the swathe of material that covered the lower part of his face.

Amelia gasped in astonishment and the chief laughed as the rest of the outlaws followed suit.

"Perhaps we are not entirely what you had expected?"

It was true. For, whilst everyone knew that bandits roamed the hills above Jainapur, who could ever have guessed that they would reveal themselves to be women?

Chapter 4

While the maiden is lying on her bed, the mistress should loosen the girdle and the knot of her dress, and when the maiden begins to dispute with her, she should overwhelm her with kisses. Having gained this point, the mistress should loosen the knot of her undergarments, and turning up her lower garment should massage the joints of her naked thighs.

—The Rosebud Sutra

Miss Catherstone's face was like thunder, her thin, bony fingers twisting and untwisting the knot of her lace-edged handkerchief.

"This cannot be," she gasped, but her face was white with the shock of realization. "You have betrayed me!"

Dorothea Strong, still weak from loss of blood, lay

stretched out on the couch, her normally smooth dark hair ruffled about her tanned face.

"I...am sorry," she said quietly.

"Sorry!" snapped Miss Catherstone. "That seems scarcely adequate in the circumstances. The understanding between us was that you would enjoy the girl's company for the afternoon, and if you were satisfied with her, you would pay me the sum of two hundred pounds to engage her services as your...travelling companion.

"I entrusted the girl to your care. She is a valuable asset, and yet you saw fit to lead her into danger! And having done so, you then chose to abandon her to her fate...."

Dorothea raised herself up on one elbow. A white bandage, stained with red, was wound around the flesh wound in her upper arm.

"Miss Catherstone, I had no idea... There was nothing I could do..."

"You foolish, stubborn woman. You knew very well that the hills are full of outlaws and brigands, and yet you led an innocent girl into their very arms. They have stolen her away from me. Do you know what they will be doing to her now? Sullying her virginal purity with their filthy hands..."

"I...I will try to find her. As soon as I can, I will ride into the mountains to look for her and bring her back. I swear it."

"Yes, Dr. Strong. You will. Or you will never be received at the academy again. Never, do you hear?"

Without waiting for a reply, Miss Catherstone turned and stalked out of the room, leaving Dorothea to tormented thoughts of what she had done, of what might have been.

Out on the landing, Mary Bates listened with mounting anger. She had not trusted Dorothea Strong the first time she saw her, and she certainly did not trust her now, with all her promises and her apologies. Mary thought tearfully of her lover Amelia, and of the terrible things that might be happening to her—all because of some convenient financial arrangement between Dorothea Strong and Miss Catherstone.

As soon as Dorothea had raised the alarm, a search party from the Jainapur garrison had ridden out in search of Amelia, but that had been three days ago, and there was still no news of Amelia. Still nothing to say if she was alive or dead. Mary looked through the doorway at Dorothea Strong and felt a surge of bitter rage. In that moment she made her decision.

If Dorothea did not go to look for Amelia, she would.

Amelia had lost all track of time. For two days—or was it three?—she had been led higher and higher into the mountains towards the distant, snow-capped peaks. Her wrists bound and tethered by a long hemp rope, she stumbled behind the lead horse, her yellow gown torn and muddied by the red dust that kept getting into her eyes and lungs.

They travelled mostly by night, when the air was so cold that it made Amelia shiver uncontrollably. In the daytime, they rested in the shade of the rocks, but still the sun beat down on her half-naked body with a vengeful intensity. She was far from home, far from friends. She even missed the stern face of Miss Catherstone, chiding her for some minor transgression.

Here, with these tall, hard-faced tribeswomen, the

prospect of one of Miss Catherstone's beatings held no fears for Amelia. She feared that in her captivity her treatment would be far more severe than anything she had ever suffered at the academy. And she dared not show her fear, for each sign of weakness was punished with a blow across the shoulders from a flexible leather thong. Even protected by the material of her dress and camisole, her flesh stung from the blows.

On the morning of the fourth day, as dawn turned the sky blush pink over the high Himalayan peaks, she saw the encampment: an untidy jumble of tents and horses, sheltering around a series of caves hollowed out of the bare rock.

At first the camp seemed deserted, save for a few scrawny goats and chickens and a piebald pony tethered beside the stream. But as they approached, figures emerged from the tents: young women clad in coarse woolen tunics, their dark hair falling loose and glossy about their shoulders. They ran forward to greet their lovers, who leapt down from the saddle and gathered them into their arms, embracing them with hunger.

Tears sprang to Amelia's eyes as more curious fingers explored her body, running over the silky skin of her arms and throat, loosening the tangles in her golden hair and spreading it out in a shimmering curtain that fell below her waist. She listened to the women chattering amongst themselves, understanding their dialect because it was so similar to the speech of the ayah who had cared for her as a child.

"Look at her skin—it's soft and juicy as a mango. Would it taste as sweet if I tried to bite it…?"

A hand insinuated itself between the buttons of Amelia's torn camisole and fingers pinched her breast, making her squeal in protest. She wriggled and tried to pull away, but other hands were exploring her more intimately still—girlish fingers pulling up her skirts, discovering the bare secret of her sex through the split crotch of her linen drawers.

"She is bare and wet!"

"She is ready for sex. Let us enjoy her now. Please, Mistress, we have been so long without fresh slaves..."

Nails raked the skin of her breast and she gasped with the exhilaration of sudden discomfort, astonishingly pleasurable through the sense-dulling mist of her exhaustion and fear. Another hand, stronger than the first, pried the fingers away, and she saw that the chief of the raiding party had intervened.

"No—you must not mark her. She is not for us. She is for Khara."

Little murmurs of disappointment filled the air.

"But why? We have waited so long. Our breasts ache for love, our cunts are so empty..."

The outlaw chief spoke again, her sonorous voice full of authority.

"She is a virgin."

The murmurs were instantly silenced, and the women drew away, as though in awe. Amelia stood stock-still, afraid to move or speak, terrified that if she did anything that offended the tribeswomen she would instantly be killed.

"She is a virgin, and therefore must be given as a gift to Khara. Come, slave."

A jerk on the rope that bound her hands together forced Amelia to move forward, half walking, half dragged across the stony ground which cut cruelly into her bare feet. She was being led toward one of the tents, by far the most magnificent, which stood in the center of the camp. It was made of dozens of multi-coloured blankets and tapestries, slung Bedouin-style over ropes and sticks which formed a large, boxy framework with an overhanging canopy.

Beneath the canopy sat a naked woman in an attitude of meditation, with her legs in the lotus position and a wickedly sharp dagger lying on the ground before her. Her outspread thighs displayed the shameless secret of her sex: the plump love-lips, that seemed to pout in a kiss of welcome; the glistening pink heart running with secret dew.

Despite her fear, Amelia looked at the girl with interest. She seemed very young, yet utterly self-possessed. Her neck was stretched into a slender column by dozens of solid gold rings, her arms and ankles encircled by many jeweled bracelets, her nose pierced by a jeweled chain which ran to a headdress of gold and rubies. Her eyes closed and her hands outstretched, she seemed oblivious to the world around her, but as they approached she spoke, her voice as unearthly and distant as an automaton's.

"Who approaches?"

"Makhani and a slave girl."

"What do you desire?"

"To make humble supplication to our queen."

"You may pass."

The outlaw chief Makhani jerked on the rope again and Amelia stumbled forward into the interior of the tent, blinking as her eyes gradually grew accustomed to the half-light.

There, on a bed of silken cushions, sat a beautiful woman dressed in the garb of a man, her full-breasted yet slender form attired in the rich, close-fitting finery of a maharajah. Her slim hips were encased in tight silver breeches which hugged the curves of her small, taut asscheeks. Her large breasts strained for release from the blue silk tunic, their size emphasized by the broad cummerbund wrapped tightly about her tiny waist.

Instead of the turban, she wore a plain gold toque on her long black hair, which was drawn back into a tight plait braided with multi-coloured silks. On either side of her stood naked girls, their firm young breasts slick with sweat as they cooled their queen with long-handled fans fashioned from gilded wood and peacock feathers.

"What gift have you brought to amuse me this time, Makhani?" Her voice was sweeter than Amelia had expected, yet it held a note of steel.

Makhani knelt before her queen and pulled on the rope so violently that Amelia was forced to follow suit, tumbling to her knees on the carpeted floor of the tent.

"I have brought you a new slave, your Highness," replied Makhani. "We captured her in the hills near the town of Jainapur."

"She is a fine enough English bitch," observed Khara coolly. "But I have many fine bitches to relieve my boredom."

"She is a virgin, your Highness. Tight as a child, hot as a tigress. I wager she will give you pleasure."

"A virgin! How quaint. And the girl must be all of eighteen, nineteen years old! How jealously the English guard the useless trinket of their virginity."

Khara got to her feet and Amelia noticed that she was wearing brocade slippers with curled toes. She looked like a picture from the Arabian Nights book Amelia had been given for her tenth birthday.

"You have verified her virginity?"

"Not personally, your Highness. The girl tells me

that she is a virgin and from her fear I judge that she speaks the truth."

Khara laughed.

"These English fillies are full of willfulness and deception. I shall examine the girl myself."

"No!" Amelia tried to scramble to her feet but Makhani caught her, winding the rope from her wrists around her throat, so tightly that she could scarcely breathe.

"Silence, slave!"

"I am not your slave," gasped Amelia. "I am…"

"Slave!" Makhani struck her with the side of her hand and she fell to the ground, fat teardrops trickling down her cheeks, all her spirit spent. "Do you dare defy your queen?"

"She is indeed a willful and spirited filly," observed Khara, with a degree of satisfaction. "Breaking that spirit might perhaps prove an agreeable diversion."

"Shall I prepare her for your examination?" Makhani looked up adoringly into her queen's face. It had been many moons since she had last been honoured to share Khara's bed, longer still since Khara had allowed her the joy of tonguing her beautiful hard clitoris. She burned with longing, praying that her gift would find favour in Khara's eyes.

"Strip her and make her lie down on the bed," Khara instructed her. "And light more lamps. I want to see every inch of this proud little filly's body. She must be taught that she can hide nothing from our eyes."

Amelia struggled in Makhani's arms, finding resources of strength she had thought long since lost on her grueling journey. She bit and spat like a she-cat as Makhani wrestled to remove her clothes. Khara watched and laughed, evidently delighted by this battle of wills.

"Restrain her." Khara clapped her hands and the two naked fan-bearers glided to her side. "I hunger to see the girl naked."

With three pairs of hands holding her, Amelia gave up her struggle. It was futile. Everything was hopeless. She had been carried off into a life of slavery and not a soul in the world knew where she was—not even Dorothea Strong, who had led her to this terrible fate.

Makhani unfastened Amelia's belt and drew it off, running the plaited silk with satisfaction over the palm of her hand. It would make a fine instrument of discipline to redden this filly's white skin and teach her the meaning of obedience. Then she turned her attention to the dress—the yellow muslin soiled and torn now from the long days' journeying through the mountains. The single button holding the waistband yielded easily and the remnants of the dress fell in a sighing whisper to the ground.

The petticoats proved a more difficult problem. Stiff with starch, their drawstrings were tightly knotted and impossible to untie. Not in the least daunted, Makhani took the knife from her belt and slit the crisp cotton from waist to hem, tearing it away to expose the knee-length bloomers beneath.

Amelia could scarcely believe that this was happening to her. It was all like some dreadful, surreal dream. And the worst of it was that something deep inside her—something shameful that no one should ever admit to—was pleased to be a slave, happy to become the victim of these women's lust. Even Makhani's ungentle touch awoke sensations of pleasure in her yearning flesh, so long deprived of the means of its own satisfaction.

"Such inexplicable garments these English girls

wear," commented Khara, circling Amelia so that she could observe her from different angles. "They primp and preen themselves with dresses and jewels, but underneath they are wearing these...these abominations." She plucked at the coarse linen of Amelia's camisole. "It is almost as though they are ashamed of their bodies, afraid of the pleasure that they can give."

"It is rumoured that the English take no pleasure from the sports of the flesh, your Highness," replied Makhani. "They are cold-blooded, sexless as eunuchs."

Khara tweaked the fabric of Amelia's drawers and the vent bulged open, exposing the golden curls at her crotch.

"Is that so? And yet, for all their pretended modesty, they expose themselves with such vulgarity," mused Khara, running the tip of her silver ferrule down over Amelia's belly and pushing it up against the soft wet flesh of her bare sex. Amelia moaned and instinctively pushed down against the cold silver-tipped cane; when Khara slid it out from between her thighs, it was wet with her juices. She breathed in Amelia's scent and licked a drop of juice from the silver tip. "Terrible garments. Remove them."

Makhani obeyed, first unbuttoning the camisole and sliding it off over Amelia's shoulders, then slitting the drawstring of her bloomers and pulling them down over her rounded hips.

"Step out of them," snapped Makhani. When Amelia hesitated for just one moment, she felt the cold hardness of Khara's ferrule slicing down onto her exposed buttocks. "Now."

Completely naked now, she shivered, suddenly cold in the chilly mountain air. Khara stood behind her, her strong hands toying with the matted veil of her golden hair.

"A charming enough gift," she conceded, "though a little travelworn. Make her lie down on the bed. I wish to examine her more closely."

Amelia made no attempt to resist as hands seized her by the arms and made her lie down on the wide, soft-cushioned couch which served as Khara's bed. Indeed, after so many long days and nights in the mountains, she yearned for the softness of a bed, for the gentleness of sleep.

But sleep could not have been further from Khara's mind as she stood over her helpless victim. She began by examining Amelia minutely from head to toe, stroking and pinching her skin, forcing open her mouth to examine the regularity and whiteness of her teeth.

"Hmm. She has a good form, though it is not yet fully developed. Her breasts are a little small for my taste, but the nipples erect quite adorably to the touch." She pinched and squeezed them with such skillful cruelty that Amelia felt a trickle of juice well up from the deepest heart of her, emerging from her swollen love-lips to stain the ruby red bed covering beneath her. Even this indignity did not escape Khara's attention.

"Ah, I see the slave has a certain aptitude. I can smell her hunger. That is good." Khara returned to her examination. "The umbilicus is deeply sunken, and that also is an auspicious sign. How pretty it would be if pierced for a ruby or an emerald…"

She pressed the tip of her long-nailed finger into Amelia's navel, and the English girl gave a yelp of surprised pleasure. She had never imagined that such a touch could be so discomfiting and yet so sensual. To her profound shame, she felt her clitoris swell with blood between her pouting love-lips, its engorged stalk the certain betrayer of her carnal lust.

Khara's hands moved slowly over the surface of Amelia's taut belly, tracing the slight downward curve from navel to groin, then the plump swell of her mount of Venus, garnished with a tangle of bright gold curls.

"Her maidenhair is of a pleasing silkiness; the sex-lips are full and plump, and the inner lips protrude slightly…that is a sure sign of a well-developed sexual sense. Ah…" She pulled apart Amelia's outer cunny-lips and peered inside. "I see that the fruit of her sex is juicy and a fine, deep pink. And see, Makhani—her love-bud is round and glossy as a fine freshwater pearl."

Her fingers were cool, the nails long and sharp as knife blades, and Amelia held her breath in fear and excitement as Khara ran the very tip of her index finger along the deep, wet groove of her sex. It was the sweetest torment, and Amelia let out a long sigh of pleasure as the hood of her clitoris slipped over the hard, round head. Syrupy sex juice was welling up inside her, oozing and dripping from between her gaping cunt-lips at each new and skillful caress.

"Good. Very good." Khara's voice became a low purr of satisfaction as she scooped up a little of the sex fluid and smeared it over the head of Amelia's clitty. "The English filly has a natural instinct for the ways of pleasure." She rubbed a little harder, and Amelia gave a cry of despair. Her body was no longer her own, each nerve ending crying out for the bliss she had felt that morning—it seemed so long ago now—when Mary Bates had teased her to her first orgasm. "So much so that I begin to doubt her purity."

Amelia sobbed her distress and her shameful longing as Khara's finger left her clitoris and traced a slow, lingering path toward the entrance to her vagina.

"No…please, don't touch me there." Her cunt muscles clenched instinctively as Khara's fingertip pressed a little way in to her sex. "You'll hurt me…"

Khara laughed.

"There are worse things than the pain of love, slave," she replied, good-humoredly. "In time you will come to understand that pain is an inextricable part of that love."

The index finger of her other hand rubbed hard on Amelia's clitoris, and the girl writhed in a torment of guilty lust, her hips bucking as though trying to take this new lover deep inside her. She could not break free; Makhani and the two naked girls were holding her down, pinning her shoulders to the bed so that she could only look up at the gently moving canopy of blankets that formed the roof of the tent. She could no longer see Khara, but only feel her as her cunt grew wetter and more welcoming and her crisis approached.

As Amelia's cunt muscles relaxed, Khara slid her finger smoothly into the wet tunnel of her sex, so tight that even her slender finger seemed to stretch its walls. With a wicked delight, she jabbed her sharp fingernail a little further in, and was rewarded with a sharp cry of pain.

"Please…please! That hurts!"

"Well, well." With as much brutality as it had entered, Khara's finger slid out of Amelia's cunt. Khara licked it clean with a reflective enjoyment.

"She is a virgin, your Highness?"

"She is indeed a virgin, Makhani. Tight as a bird.

So, so deliciously tight, and with a hymen as thick and as tough as glove leather."

"You intend to keep her and deflower her yourself, your Highness?" Makhani amused herself by taking Amelia's nipples between finger and thumb and pinching them long and hard.

"It is a tempting thought, Makhani, but no. I have other plans for this delicious English slut." Khara looked down at the bed, where Amelia's body was still writhing in the spasms of frustrated lust, her thighs spread wide and the pink oyster of her sex running with honey-sweet juice. "I shall sell her to the merchant, Indhira. With her golden hair and her beautifully tight cunt, she will fetch an excellent price."

"Indhira, your Highness? But she takes only those who are fit for training. She will take no virgins…"

"Very true, my dear Makhani." Khara's eyes gleamed as brightly as the gold toque on her glossy hair. "And so she must be relieved of her troublesome virginity, and initiated into the first stages of her training. When the merchandise is presented to Indhira, we must be able to show her that the filly has an aptitude for the sensual arts.

"Tonight, Makhani, when we have celebrated your return with food and wine, you and five of your sisters shall deflower the girl. I shall observe. I am sure that it will make an excellent and stimulating spectacle."

The moon rose slowly over the mountains, its fat white disc gazing down blankly from a sky of blackest velvet, sprinkled with stars. It was a beautiful night, filled with moonlight and the scent of flowers, but Amelia scarcely noticed its beauty. The sweet, thick wine she had been given to drink had made her brain muddled, and yet she felt curiously alert, as though all power of rational thought had been taken away from her, leaving only the hypersensitivity of touch, of taste, of smell.

Her whole body felt alive to the wealth of sensations around it. As she moved across the stony ground, her white silk robe brushed lightly over the buds of her breasts, already erect, already filled with the need to be sucked, licked, stroked, bitten. It felt as though a million eager tongues were running over her flesh, a million soft and skillful fingers stroking her wherever the silken fabric flowed and touched.

She heard Khara's voice, but it seemed a long way away.

"Bring her into the circle. Into the very center, where I can see her."

She felt hands closing again about her arms, and she moved forward obediently, forced to trust the hands because she could see nothing but a host of dancing, dreamlike images, images of things that she had never even imagined before and could scarcely believe were real.

There were naked women with painted breasts, and others moving about them in a slow and sinuous dance, their bodies heavy with jewelled chains that hung from pierced nipples and cunt-lips. Coloured and scented smoke rose from incense burners placed all around the margin of the wide circle, and between them burned flickering fires in copper braziers, orange and yellow flames rising up from the white-hot coals.

For a moment, Amelia quite forgot where she was, losing all sense of time and space as her eyes fought to focus on the chimerical dancing pictures—figures that moved so close she thought she could touch them, but when she reached out they were gone.

A nagging ache of memory kept drifting back in waves, like waves of sadness—yearningly real for a few moments, and then gone. She was Amelia Courtnay, a proud English girl who had been stolen away by brigands—savage, ruthless women who intended to sate their lust on her defenseless body. She must find some way to resist…

But it was futile. The thought lingered only a moment, and then it was gone, so far away that she could scarcely glimpse it any more, just one more dancing figure in the circle of leaping flames.

"She has been prepared?"

"As you instructed, your Highness. Her body hair has been shaved and she has been massaged with sweet oils."

"Then the ceremony may begin."

Khara clapped her hands, and at once a sweet, strange music filled the air. Amelia did not recognize the instruments, but the woody, rippling sound of pipes mingled with the clamor of strings, bowed and plucked. In the darkness beyond the circle of fire, a woman began to sing as the drummer's supple hands set the beat.

The rhythm was elemental and compelling, the woman's voice low and sensual, rising from time to time to a passionate crescendo that echoed the need in Amelia's aching body. The massage which the two naked girls had given her had left her warm and hungry, her breasts tingling and the tight amber rose of her asshole twitching and stinging where the scented oil had been rubbed into it.

She felt strangely naked beneath the white silk robe; almost childlike now that the hair of her cunt and axillae had been shaved away, leaving her helpless and pure. The shame had faded away as the sweet wine had done its work, the mulled spices kindling a low heat in her belly whilst the alcohol annihilated all her inhibitions. As the music swooped and soared around her, she let her instincts lead her into the dance.

Slowly she began to move, her body swaying in time to the chant, her feet shifting on the bare earth as the drumbeat called her to her destiny.

"Take off your robe, Amelia. Show your nakedness to me."

Automatically, with no pause for thought, Amelia took hold of the white silk robe and pulled it over her head. The night air was chill in the mountains, but she did not notice it. A furnace of desire was burning inside her, far brighter and far hotter than the leaping flames of the fires around her. She wanted to be naked; wanted to exorcise the terrible need within her.

"Now touch yourself, Amelia. I want to see how you give yourself pleasure."

Khara's voice seemed like another theme in the symphony of sound around her, and it seemed the most natural thing in the world to obey it. Yet how could she tell her mistress that she did not know how to give herself pleasure, that until Mary had kissed her and caressed her, her lewdest touch had been to stroke her nipples gently, in the dark seclusion of the dormitory?

"Put your hands on your breasts and touch yourself, Amelia."

She let her hands wander to the small, firm mounds of her breasts. It felt as though she was touching them for the first time, discovering them as a lover would. She had become her own lover, her fingers innocent yet knowing as they roamed over the bare flesh. Beneath her palms, the pink cones of her nipples were puckered and fiercely erect, so hard that it seemed impossible that they could be part of the same, soft flesh that made up the body of her breasts. They seemed alien in their hardness—not soft like flesh, but tough like rubber or wood, love-buttons that could be touched to turn on her desire.

Inspiration guided her fingers and she moved the palms of her hands in a sweeping, circular motion over her breasts, so that the nipples ground gently against them. The effect was electric, sending lingering aftershocks of pleasure right through her body from breast to cunt, from her nipples to the exposed pink triangle of her pubis.

"Very good, Amelia. But I want to see more. I want to see what else you can do."

Amelia drew her fingers up so that they were like pincers and fastened them on the twin buds of her nipples. At first she touched them only gently, her supersensitive body hardly able to bear even such a light caress; but as her flesh grew more accustomed to the touch, her hunger burned more fiercely and her body grew greedy for more piquant sensations.

She pinched and rolled the breast flesh with an almost brutal intensity, discovering with a child's delight how wonderful it could be to take herself to the narrow margin between pleasure and pain. The slight discomfort of the stinging, burning sensation seemed to intensify her sensual hunger, and as she pinched a little harder she felt an answering wetness grow between her thighs.

In her innocence, she had never caressed herself between her legs, never stroked herself to orgasm. Only Mary had ever taken her there—poor, sweet Mary, so many miles away in another world, or so it seemed now. Instinctively she pressed her thighs together more tightly and was rewarded with a burst of the most exquisite sensation. She rubbed her thighs together, and discovered that this stimulated the sensual hot spot between her cunt-lips to a burning frenzy of pleasure. If she kept on doing it, would she reach the same peak of ecstasy that she had enjoyed on that one ecstatic morning in Jainapur?

"You feel pleasure, Amelia; that is good." Khara's syrupy voice penetrated Amelia's brain and, like a child rewarded for good behavior, she felt the pleasing warmth of satisfaction. "But I want to see more. I want to see you touch yourself, Amelia. Open up your legs and touch yourself for me."

Amelia slid her feet a little farther apart on the soft earth and felt instantly bereft. All the wonderful warmth in her clitty seemed to ebb away, leaving only the terrible yearning for release. She felt so ignorant, so angry to have been kept so long in innocence. What must she do to please her new mistress—and to assuage the unbearable longing within her belly?

Keeping the fingers of her left hand on her nipple, she slipped her right hand over her smooth, shaven pubis and down between her thighs. She was amazed at the hot wetness she felt when she touched herself there, between the twin lobes of her plump pussy-lips. They seemed so swollen, so fat with juice that she scarcely recognized the feel of them.

What was this, this long, hard stalk that pushed against her hand and sent electric shocks through her body whenever she touched it? Could it really be the pert little clitty she had sometimes touched when she was washing herself? She had never known it could be so huge and hard. She pressed on it and the touch was almost painful in its intensity. It was too dry, too sensitive, its little pink hood forced right back so that the whole shaft of her clitoris was exposed.

She must be gentle, answer the cravings of her body with the lightest, the softest of caresses. She pushed her finger into the tight, wet tunnel of her sex and loaded it with the clear, slippery pre-come, then smeared it over the head of her clitty as Khara had done. The sensation was blissful, and somewhere, very far away, she heard her own voice moaning softly in harmony with the music.

"She is a born slut," observed Khara, drinking from a silver goblet as she watched Amelia stroking her own clitty. The girl seemed in a world of her own, lost to reality as she focused on the intensity of her need, her quest for the ultimate pleasure that still eluded her clumsy fingers. "Innocent of course, but then that is to be desired in one who is to be trained as a slave. She will learn quickly, and since she knows nothing, there are no bad habits for her new mistress to break."

Amelia trembled at the new, unknown pleasure of her fingers on her clitty, learning by touch the pathway to purest delight. Even now she could feel the sensations building inside her, the mounting excitement as the heat spread from her breasts and clitty to fill her whole body. It was as though her entire being was caught in time, waiting, breathless, for the moment of release. A few more strokes, a few more sweet caresses on her pleasure-bud and she would be there. She could feel the ecstasy almost upon her, feel the muscles of belly and ass and cunt beginning to tense in the seconds before the spasm overtook her.

She screamed out her pleasure as her cunt blossomed into orgasm, releasing a flood of fragrant nectar which dripped like honey from her nether-lips, anointing the barren earth on which she stood. All control had left her, all consciousness save the consciousness of overwhelming pleasure.

It was too much, the pleasure too powerful for her to bear; Amelia sank to the ground in a swoon, her body white and quivering in the dancing firelight.

"Excellent, excellent." Khara clapped her hands in delight. "I had not expected her to be such an apt pupil. I feel sure that her defloration will make an entertaining spectacle." She parted the folds of her robe to reveal her bare, shaven cunt, the left lobe of her outer sex-lips pierced by a silver ring set with emeralds. "Bring me the instrument of her initiation."

A serving girl, naked except for a filmy veil which obscured the lower half of her face, approached and knelt before the queen, holding out a cushion of dark blue velvet. On it lay a dildo of yellowed ivory, about seven inches long and its surface carved with lascivious scenes from the Hindu holy books: women kissing and stroking each other's breasts, massaging each other with sweet oils, masturbating with long, smooth sticks that distended their vulvas.

Khara picked up the dildo and kissed it—once on the shaft, once on the tip.

"It is yet fragrant with the spendings of our last slave," she observed with a nostalgic pleasure. It had been most agreeable, initiating the last girl. Although only a simple peasant from a village in the hills, she had proved both apt and willing. But her cunt had been a little large, and Khara felt sure that Amelia Courtnay would prove a still more interesting pupil.

She slid the dildo over her belly and placed its head at the entrance to her shaven vulva. Then, with a single thrust, she forced it inside her cunt, so deep that its entire length vanished between her love-lips, and she gave a sigh of satisfaction. As the outlaws' queen, she had many lovers—as many pretty virgins and knowing sluts as any woman could wish for—but none had the power to pleasure her as beautifully as she pleasured herself.

The dildo slid, glistening, out of her cunt and in the next second disappeared inside her once more, forced in by a second powerful thrust.

"You may masturbate me, Makhani," said Khara, her eyes closed as she slid the dildo into her cunt and held it there with tightly clenched cunt muscles. "Place your lips upon my rosebud and bring me swiftly to orgasm."

Makhani knelt before her queen and opened her lips, putting out the tip of her tongue and wriggling it into the deep pink furrow between Khara's thighs. She lapped like a she-cat, teasing and tormenting the little pink stalk with her lips and teeth whilst her tongue flicked repeatedly across its head. Khara sat with eyes closed, her face betraying no trace of her excitement, but her breathing quickening as her cunt walls gripped the carved dildo, sucking it into her as though it alone could give her the release she craved.

She came with the merest sigh of contentment, the walls of her cunt rippling with wave after wave of pleasure, and the dildo slid slowly out of her onto the ground, its carved surface wet with her sex juice.

"Take it, Makhani. The honour shall first be yours this night." Khara smiled as she handed the dildo to Makhani, laying it across her hands as though it were some precious, sacred object. "The girl is prepared. I wish to see you enjoy her."

Amelia, waking from her swoon, felt strong arms holding her down, pulling apart her thighs, making her draw up her knees so that her sex was shamelessly displayed between her outspread legs, a coral pink seashell at the base of her creamy belly.

"Hold her still," commanded Makhani. Amelia tried to focus on the woman's face, but it blurred and merged into dream images in her head, images of painted dancing girls, whirling and laughing, their hands touching and caressing each other's bodies as the music bubbled and swirled to a climax.

Her body ached. She longed for a release from this torment of frustration, this burning, itching ache that racked her whole body and made her clitoris throb to the pulse of her insatiable desire. Hands touched her, some holding her down, others stroking and pinching her breasts and belly, producing little starbursts of pain that served only to intensify her longing.

"Please, please, please...," she heard herself gasp. What was she pleading for? She no longer knew—only that she wanted the touching to go on, to become deeper, stronger, more extreme.

The pointed tip of the dildo nudged between her love-lips, seeking out the white-hot heart of her desire. At the first touch, Amelia arched her back and let out a shuddering gasp, the surrogate dick of carved ivory teasing and stretching the tight entrance to her hole.

"No!" The first twinge of pain brought with it some distant remembrance of fear. This could not be. There was not room, she was too small...

"Your Highness, she is very tight," observed one of the serving girls. "The initiation may pain her."

"In all pleasure there should be an element of

pain," replied Khara with a shrug of serene indifference. "In time, the pain will heighten her pleasure. Proceed."

Makhani pushed the dildo into Amelia's wet haven, but she moaned and twisted, trying to escape its inexorable advance. Her cunt was so tight that it felt as though she would split in two.

"Harder," commanded Khara, a note of excitement entering her voice. "Do not let her fight you. Push it deep inside her."

As the tip of the dildo met the unyielding membrane of Amelia's hymen, she gave a little sob of discomfort. But she no longer struggled. There was a terrible inevitability about the pain, the fear. And her whole body throbbed with the desire she was ashamed to admit, the desire that she could no longer conceal, for the juices were running freely from her cunt, anointing both the dildo and Makhani's relentless hand.

"Now!" Khara's voice summoned up the moment of her immolation, and—pressing on Amelia's love-bud with a skillful finger—Makhani gave the dildo a violent thrust. Amelia's back arched and she gave a shuddering cry as the dildo tore through her hymen, possessing her, releasing her at last from the prison of her virginity into womanhood in a shattering, breathtaking orgasm.

As one of the serving girls lapped at the scarlet pool of Amelia's virgin blood, soothing her hurts with the soft wet tip of her tongue, Khara sat back and smiled to Makhani.

"Such an apt pupil," she sighed. "She is sure to fetch an excellent price—now that she has been relieved of her virginity—for no virgin may ever enter the Temple of the Rosebud Sutra.

Chapter 5

When the slave is to be brought to her mistress, her dress should consist of many ornaments, various kinds of flowers, a robe decorated with different colors, and some sweet-smelling ointments or unguents. —The Rosebud Sutra

Dawn came up early over Jainapur, casting a dusty, rose pink light over the old wooden shacks of the bazaar and the elegant villas of the English quarter nestling in the wooded foothills.

Jainapur awoke sluggishly from slumber. One or two water-carriers were walking down to the wells through the silent streets, balancing huge earthenware jars on their heads, and in the whispering grove of trees to the north a small boy whistled to his flock of scraggy goats.

The heat that would form a shimmering haze over Jainapur at noon was still many long hours away, and behind the bars and shuttered windows of the academy the girls slept on in their crisp white nightgowns, their pale limbs chastely interlaced as they dreamed of desires they were too innocent to understand.

Miss Catherstone slept, too, her mind no longer overly disturbed by the loss of one rather troublesome, motherless girl. It was an irritation, of course, to lose such a valuable asset, but once sullied the girl would be of little interest or value to prospective purchasers anyway. If the soldiers failed to find her and bring her back, Miss Catherstone was quite prepared to let the matter rest. No one would greatly miss Amelia Courtnay.

Or almost no one. In the cool of the early morning, a solitary figure walked along the banks of a mountain stream, a light Indian shawl thrown around her shoulders. Mary Bates could not sleep. In fact, she had been unable to sleep soundly for many nights, tossing and turning in her attic room as she thought of poor dear Amelia, stolen away from her by treachery and now abandoned as though she were of no more value than some unloved pet.

A search party had, of course, been sent out from the garrison by its commanding officer, Brigadier General Waverley, but it had returned several days since, exhausted and empty-handed. Apart from a minor skirmish with Afghan tribesmen in one of the high mountain passes, they had made no contact with anyone who might have been responsible for Amelia's disappearance, and it was certain that the prisoners they had taken knew nothing of the girl.

Golden-haired, blue-eyed, and as innocent as a child—what chance had poor Amelia in that mountain wilderness, without so much as a friend beside her? A week ago, apparently recovered from her slight wounds, Dorothea Strong had left Jainapur for the mountains, declaring that she intended to find Amelia and bring her back. Miss Catherstone had publicly approved of Dorothea's solo expedition, praising her for her courage and devotion to duty, but Mary was not so certain of Dorothea's honourable motives.

A few days before Dorothea's departure, Mary had seen her in the marketplace, deep in conversation with one of the village girls—a dancer and handmaid in one of Jainapur's oldest houses of pleasure. Naturally Mary had been curious about what might bring these two unlikely companions together, and she had moved a little closer, intending to eavesdrop on their conversation.

Unfortunately Dorothea and the girl had seen her and immediately ceased talking—but not before Mary had heard the words "Rosebud Sutra" and "Citadel of Heaven." Mary had no idea who or what this *Rosebud Sutra* might be, but she could see from Dorothea's expression that it was of great interest to the archaeologist. And when Dorothea announced that she was setting off, alone, into the Mountains of Heaven, Mary could not help wondering if there was some other reason besides a selfless desire to rescue Amelia Courtnay.

There was only one thing to do, mused Mary as she watched a young girl bathing in the shallow stream, pouring dish upon dish of cool, clear water over her nut brown body. If she could not trust Dorothea Strong to do what was right, then she must make sure that she did it herself. She, too, must head into the mountains in search of Amelia Courtnay.

The pack mules wound their way slowly along the steep-sided mountain pass and Amelia swayed on the back of the fat piebald pony, gripping onto its mane to keep her balance.

At least she no longer had to walk behind the horses, mused Amelia. Now that Khara had decided she was of some commercial value, the outlaw women had developed a keen interest in safeguarding their asset. Two days ago they had set out on a long, winding trail through the mountains, in search of the merchant known as Indhira, a woman who made her living by buying and selling slaves.

Slaves! Amelia still could not quite believe what had happened to her in the last few weeks. First kidnapped by brigands, then kept at their queen's encampment to be "initiated" into the sensual skills she must learn if she was to survive.

It struck Amelia that she had grown up very quickly over these last few days and weeks. From the night when Makhani and her sisters had drunk her virgin blood, she had no longer been the silly, innocent child who had dreamed of desires she could neither describe nor understand. She had at last crossed the threshold into womanhood—and the transition was both terrifying and exciting.

There was so much to be learned, and she had hardly begun. But she knew that if she was to live, she must do as she was bidden, feigning obedience until the moment when she could escape and return to the world she had left. She thought to herself how strange that world would seem when—if—she returned. Linen camisoles and scratchy, knee-length bloomers were a whole world away from the robe of sky blue floating silk in which she had been dressed today, its borders embroidered with the finest gold thread. She looked down at her feet, balanced in the stirrups of the side-saddle, and could not help smiling at the scarlet-painted nails, so striking and shameless in the pretty open-toed sandals she had been given to wear.

She was under no illusions about why she had been dressed in such finery. Khara had not chosen to beautify her for any altruistic reason, but simply to increase the value of her investment. That morning, at their mountain bivouac, she had been awakened at dawn and forced to bathe in the freezing-cold stream before being massaged with oil of bergamot and coriander, an orange-spiced essence with the musky sweetness of cinnamon. Next, her blonde hair was washed and sun-dried, then braided with plaited silk cords of blue and scarlet, interwoven into a waist-length plait that ended in a long, swishing, silk tassel.

Her lips were painted with a scarlet dye, and her blue eyes rimmed with thick black kohl. Then her finger and toe nails were stained scarlet, and the palms of her hands and soles of her feet decorated with intricate patterns in a reddish brown henna dye which was stenciled onto the skin. The same patterns were traced with infinite care onto the plump mound of her pubis, freshly shaven and powdered to render it smooth as a child's; her nipples were painted with a deep scarlet to match the dramatic curve of her lips.

"She is an agreeable confection," concluded Khara, standing back to admire the creation. "Innocent and yet redolent with lust. How could any red-blooded woman resist her?" She cupped Amelia's pubis in her hand and let her long-nailed middle finger slide upwards into the deep, fleshy groove of her sex. "See how she trembles at my touch. Even with only a few days' schooling, she has begun to understand the skills she must learn. She will make a most able slave. Why..." She squeezed Amelia's sex-lips in her fingers and watched her blue eyes close in mute yearning. "I almost wish that I had chosen to keep her for myself. One so rarely finds a girl with the soul of a true-born slut."

She turned to Makhani with a satisfied smile.

"You may put on the harness. It is good that she becomes accustomed to it now, for she must wear it until she reaches the citadel. None must sully her until the mistress's touch is upon her."

Amelia listened in confusion. The mistress? Who could she be? She had heard Khara and Makhani speak of her in hushed voices, and had at first thought they were talking about the merchant woman Indhira, but she now sensed that they were discussing someone much more important; someone with a truly awesome power. Could it be that the woman they were speaking of was to be her mistress?

One of the serving girls emerged from the tent with a curious creation of leather straps and beaten silver. It jingled as she handed it to Makhani, and Amelia followed it with her eyes, curious and excited through her apprehension.

"The harness, my lady."

Makhani took it from her, handling it with the greatest care, and as she held it up Amelia saw that it was sewn like a little jacket of straps, running from shoulder to thigh.

"Stand still, slave."

Amelia could do little but obey, since her arms were held in a vicelike grip by two of the serving maids; in any case she felt little inclination to resist. In just a few days, her body had learned to respond to Makhani as to the touch of a mistress.

For Makhani's skill had quickly awakened her innocent desires, brought them many times to the peak of pleasure, yet left her hungry for more and still more games of lust.

Makhani unfastened two tiny buckles and slipped the harness over Amelia's head. Two sewn leather straps fitted snugly over her shoulders and criss-crossed beneath her tender young breasts, squeezing them and throwing them into relief. The leather was soft but the beaten silver plate that pressed against her belly felt hard and cold, raising little bumps of gooseflesh where it touched. Makhani buckled it so tightly across her torso that she could scarcely breathe, but the purpose was quickly clear: The hard silver plate pushed up her breasts, emphasizing the twin globes of flesh so that they looked much larger than they really were.

Two more straps hung down between her thighs, and between them was slung a smaller silver plate, slightly convex in shape, with little ridges on its inner surface. There was a small hole in it towards the front, but other than that it was quite solid, quite impenetrable. As soon as she saw it, Amelia began to understand what it was for, and the thrill of delicious apprehension ran through her body.

"Open your legs," Makhani ordered her.

She hesitated for a brief moment, then felt a sudden sharp pain between her shoulder blades as one of the slave girls struck her with a supple leather thong.

"Quickly now!" snapped Makhani. "Your mistress will not hesitate to have you killed if you disobey her, even for a second. You are worthless, my dear; a worthless little trinket. You must earn your mistress's favor—or die."

Shivering, Amelia let Makhani push her thighs apart, and waited for the inevitable pain. But there was no pain, only a strange and disturbing pleasure, as the small silver plate was strapped tightly between her legs. Its cold, ridged surface forced apart her love-lips, so that the many ridges were pressed hard against the inside of her vulva and the small hole was directly over her urethra. Although she knew that the ridges on the silver plate were very small, they felt enormous as they pressed against her sensitive cunt flesh, and if she made even the smallest movement, they rubbed with brutal accuracy across the head of her clitoris.

Makhani laughed to see her confusion, and strapped the disc a little tighter, enjoying the little moans and yelps of frightened pleasure that she was producing from her victim.

"You are indeed a slut by nature, my dear Amelia," she announced. "But this pretty toy will both stimulate and control your impulses. The torment of your pleasure will be with you always, but you will be unable to give your favours to any woman save your mistress." Taking a tiny silver key she padlocked the harness so that there could be no escaping from it. "Only your mistress will have the key." She laughed, evidently enjoying the joke immensely.

"Dance for me, Amelia," laughed Makhani. "Dance for me and show me your gratitude."

Amelia tried to move, but the ridged silver plate pressed so insistently against her clitoris that she let out a sob of agony. How could pleasure be so tormentingly close to pain? And how could that pleasure be ignored?

"Dance! I command you," repeated Makhani, and Amelia began to move her body, at first cautiously, and then with increasing sinuousness as the pleasure impulse grew stronger and her clitty swelled under the constant pressure of the silver disc.

"Even when you are spent, the hunger will never leave you," said Makhani with satisfaction, watching Amelia weep tears of torment as her cunt clenched and unclenched in never-ending spasms that led not to the warm afterglow of pleasure, but to an instant rekindling of need. "Never, do you hear? Not until your mistress chooses to release you. You must pray that that will be soon."

And so it was that she found herself on the little piebald pony, being led along the winding mountain pass in fine silk robes that concealed the shameless secret of her sex. She tried hard to sit still in the saddle, but was forced to adjust her position continually to avoid the greedy, insistent caresses of the metal chastity disc between her thighs. Beneath the silver her cunt felt lonely, bereft. She could feel it pulsing gently like the mouth of some hungry sea creature, opening and closing in an empty embrace. How she longed to be freed from this prison, to engulf a lover's finger, a lover's tongue, to shower her lover's face with slippery love-juice.

"Our journey is almost over, slave," announced Khara, turning in her saddle to look back at Amelia. There seemed almost a touch of regret in her imperious voice. "The citadel lies before us."

They rounded a bend in the pass and she saw it, still quite far away and yet so dazzlingly beautiful that it seemed to fill the horizon, drawing the eyes like a magnet. The citadel lay high above, in the secret hollow between two mountain peaks, a walled city of great antiquity, its white walls reflecting the morning sunlight like polished glass.

"The Citadel of Heaven," murmured Makhani. "The sacred place. The forbidden city."

"You are a fortunate slave indeed," observed Khara, "for you shall be travelling where we cannot follow—no, not even I, though I am of the blood royal. Those who pass beyond the gates of the temple shall never return. And those who have set eyes upon the *Rosebud Sutra* must keep its secrets for all eternity."

The merchant woman Indhira observed Amelia with a critical eye.

"I will give you five hundred rupees for her," she announced.

Khara's eyes flashed a warning.

"I advise you to think very carefully before you cheat me," she snarled, and she withdrew the ivory-handled dagger from her belt. "The girl is no ordinary slave. I will kill her rather than sell her to you for such a pittance."

"Then she must prove her worth," retorted the merchant, spitting on the ground, apparently unperturbed by the prospect. "I will not pay above the odds for exotic merchandise such as this."

"You are a wealthy merchant," snarled Khara. "The wealthiest slave merchant in the whole of northern India."

"And I owe my wealth to caution," replied Indhira. "If you wish to negotiate a better price for the filly, she must show me her mettle. Perhaps if you were to allow me to fuck her..."

"Impossible," snapped Makhani, lifting Amelia's

robe to reveal the tormenting leather and silver harness. "As you see, the slave has been properly deflowered and prepared for the temple."

"She has a good, tight cunt?"

"As smooth and tight as a bird's," smiled Makhani. "Turn round, slave." Amelia obeyed and Makhani pulled apart her asscheeks. "See the tightness of her virgin ass. None has penetrated that fragile membrane, and her cunt is even more blissfully tight."

"You whet my appetite for the bitch," conceded Indhira. "But she must give some proof of her worthiness for the temple."

"Then she shall bestow pleasure upon you in another way," replied Khara. "On your knees, slut. She has a divinely sensitive mouth and a long and muscular tongue."

"Which is as it should be," smiled Indhira, pulling up her rough woolen skirts and tucking them into her belt. Underneath, her cunt was thickly covered with glossy black curls that could not quite conceal the prominence of her inner cunt-lips, which projected like the tip of a deep pink tongue from between the outer lobes of her vulva. "Let her therefore demonstrate her skills, if skills she indeed has."

Amelia knew what she must do, though she had only been allowed to lick Makhani's cunt once—and had been punished with a beating for not drinking all the juices of her spending. She put up her white, trembling hands and touched the margin of Indhira's love-lips. They felt very hot to the touch, her fleshy pubis so thickly forested with hair that it felt like the pelt of some wild creature.

As she pulled apart Indhira's cunt-lips and pressed her face into the wild thicket of curls, the merchant's fragrance wafted into her nostrils; the strong, heavy tang of an unwashed pussy, wickedly sensual and so powerful that Amelia reeled from its intoxication.

"Drink deep, little one," murmured Indhira, stroking Amelia's golden head as her tongue penetrated the inner sanctum of her sex. "Drink every sweet drop. I want to drown you in juice."

Amelia held apart Indhira's cunt-lips with her thumbs, whilst her face burrowed deep into the soft, wet furrow between. The cleft was already running with moisture, a potent melange of stale and fresh juices, fermenting to a heady liquor that seemed to Amelia the essence of pure sex. Her questing tongue sought out the stalk of Indhira's clitoris, and her thumbs slipped a little further in, pressing their nails into the soft flesh, scratching and stretching the elastic walls of her cunt.

Indhira rewarded her diligence with a copious draught of sex fluid, which seemed to flow more quickly than Amelia could drink it down. Her mouth was filled with it, her face sticky with the sweetness, her lips glossy and fragrant.

"Suck harder, slut," Indhira commanded, slightly out of breath as she pressed her pubis more insistently against Amelia's face. "The girl is willing, though a little clumsy."

"She was but lately a virgin," pointed out Khara coolly. "She has much to learn, but she is an apt pupil. And an innocent slave is so much more malleable, don't you think?"

Indhira looked down at Amelia, her pretty henna-patterned hands almost in an attitude of prayer between her thighs as her tongue flicked again and again over the secret heart of her sex.

"Stroke my ass, slave. I shall not be able to come unless you stroke my ass."

Amelia remembered how good it had felt to have Mary's tongue between her asscheeks, the cool, wet slipperiness skating over the tight membrane. How much more blissful it would have felt to have had Mary's tongue right inside her arsehole, opening up her forbidden gate with the same gentle insistence that had driven her caresses on Amelia's virgin pussy. How she regretted her shyness now, wishing that she had given in to Mary's gentle seduction. She slid her right hand from between Indhira's thighs and around their sides, enjoying the feel of the plump, yet firm flesh under her fingers.

Indhira's asscheeks were full and round, like two clouds of soft flesh which Amelia longed to squeeze. How would it be, how would it taste, to sink her teeth into that juicy backside, as soft and yielding as a baby's? Surprised at her own audacity, Amelia felt her excitement heighten at the very thought, and she shifted position on the hard earth so the metal disc strapped between her thighs moved almost imperceptibly across the head of her clitoris, sliding back the fleshy hood.

She gave a little moan of need at the welter of sensations and shivered with pleasure as her fingers delved deep into the crease between Indhira's fat asscheeks. Her puckered hole was surrounded by a little coronet of wiry hairs, and Amelia amused herself for a few moments by plucking at them and winding them about her fingertips. Indhira seemed much taken with this, for her cunt began oozing even more copiously, and Amelia felt half-drowned in the floodtide of her pre-come.

Indhira's sphincter seemed quite loose and relaxed,

as though she were very much accustomed to the touch of a lover in this most secret of places. Even as Amelia touched it, it seemed to blossom and open to her fingers, inviting her to yet more daring caresses.

Feeling very bold and intrepid, Amelia pushed quite lightly with her index finger and was astonished to feel it swallowed up to the first joint in the soft flesh of Indhira's backside. It was a curious sensation, not quite like anything Amelia had experienced before. The muscular ring of Indhira's sphincter gripped her rather firmly, but the portion of her finger that was inside Indhira's ass felt utterly unconstrained. She tried moving it around whilst she sucked and licked, and sure enough, Indhira started gasping and moaning with pleasure.

"Little slut. Oh, you beautiful little slut..."

Emboldened by this success, Amelia pushed her finger in deeper, this time right up to the knuckle. By now, Indhira was going crazy, her body heaving against Amelia's face as though it wanted to be swallowed up by her kisses.

"Harder. Do it to me harder."

Amelia began sliding her finger in and out of Indhira's ass, winding it round with a spiral motion which brought her fingertip into contact with the soft, elastic walls and stretched them so deliciously that Indhira's cunt became a rushing river of juice.

Pushing her face greedily between Indhira's thighs, Amelia darted her tongue into Indhira's haven, the long muscular probe sliding easily into the well-lubricated love-tunnel whilst the tip of her nose rubbed across the head of Indhira's clitoris.

"Such lewdness. Such an instinctive skill," gasped Indhira, her crisis very near. "I can scarcely believe the girl was but lately a virgin, and yet she is so succulent and pure...."

With oohs and ahs of rapture, Indhira welcomed the pleasure that rippled through her, delighting in the fluid gushing out of her, filling the eager mouth between her love-lips.

Amelia, too, moaned and writhed, for the ridged metal disc was cruelly tormenting her, scratching and rubbing on her clitoris with each tiny movement she made, making her mad for the touch of the other woman's curious tongue, the other woman's skillful fingers.

"See how the little slut tries to masturbate herself to pleasure," observed Khara with a certain satisfaction. "See how she sways her hips and tries to rub her thighs together." She put her hand on Amelia's shoulder and pulled her away from Indhira's still-parted thighs. "Stop that at once!"

"But your Highness," sobbed Amelia, the need burning and throbbing at the apex of her tight squeezed thighs. "I need it so much. I can't bear it any longer...."

"You must learn to control yourself," broke in Indhira, releasing her skirts from her belt and letting them fall modestly to her ankles, veiling the fat mound which Amelia so longed to taste again. "If you are to become a favored slut, you must attend to all your mistress's commands."

Khara's lips curved into a smile. "I knew you would want her," she said, "once you had tasted the fruits of that pretty pink tongue."

"Seven hundred rupees," said Indhira, reaching into her horse's saddlebag to take out a fistful of gold coins.

"One thousand, no less."

"Eight hundred, and that is my last offer."

"Nine."

Amelia could scarcely believe what she was hearing as the voices bartered calmly for possession of her, body and soul. What was happening? What was going to become of her, friendless and so far from home? She drew her knees up to her chin and hugged them, determined to ignore the insistent throb of her clitoris as the silver disc ground firmly against its fleshy knob.

"Eight hundred and fifty."

Indhira hesitated for a few moments, her dark eyes travelling over Amelia's hunched form, taking in the slender curve of breast and backside, the ivory skin, the bright blue eyes, and the waist-length braid of bright blonde hair. Finally she reached into the saddlebag and counted out another handful of gold pieces.

"Done."

"Go to the merchant, Amelia," Makhani commanded her, grabbing her under the arm and hauling her roughly to her feet. "And mind that you are obedient and serve her well. Indhira is going to deliver you to your new mistress."

The road to the citadel was long and tortuous, and the pony often stumbled on loose scree. Amelia hung on to its mane for dear life, fixing her eyes on the road ahead, mortally afraid to look down. On one side of the mountain track was an almost sheer rock face, so high that even if she craned her head all the way back, she could not see the top. It was scabbed and scaled with yellow-grey lichen that dripped with moisture like the tongue of an unclean lover. If she turned her head to the left, the road—at best six or eight feet wide—fell away sharply into a vertiginous drop, what the inhabitants of Jainapur called a khud.

There could be no question of escape, not here and not now. For the time being, Amelia decided, she must simply go along with whatever was demanded of her. Perhaps what lay ahead of her would not be as bad as she had imagined. She supposed mistresses could be good as well as bad, kind as well as cruel. It might not be so terrible to be kept as the pampered pet of some soft-hearted maharanee....

But even as they approached the massive wooden gates of the fortress, Amelia knew in her heart that her destiny would be not be one of simple comfort. In the days she had spent at the brigand camp, she had been shown some of what she must learn: the sensual skills she must try to master if her life was to be spared. And it was no use deluding herself—should she fail, her new mistress would scarcely think twice about having her killed.

The dirt track widened into a stone-flagged road which led up to the heavy gates of the citadel. These were set into tall, thick walls of a smooth white stone that reflected the ever-changing colours of the sunlight—sometimes pink, then grey, orange, or blue. As Amelia dismounted and walked with Indhira toward the gates, the sun came out from behind a cloud and the stone shimmered like white sand on a tropical beach, radiating a secret inner heat.

A powerfully built woman in the garb of a warrior stepped from the shadows and drew a wickedly sharp, curved sword from her belt.

"Declare yourselves."

"I am Indhira, the slave merchant. I bring new merchandise for the high priestess."

"Show me this merchandise."

Indhira pushed Amelia forward and she did as she

had been bidden, raising her bound hands to her forehead and bowing slightly in an attitude of humility and respect.

The guard slid the sword back into her thick leather belt and walked slowly around Amelia. "A European slave. How exotic."

"English. She is sure to please the High Priestess," said Indhira, hoping that she was not mistaken.

"She has been prepared?"

"According to the sacred scriptures." Indhira turned to Amelia and snapped: "Lift your robes, girl."

Amelia tentatively raised the hem of her gown, but Indhira dealt her a stinging blow across the cheek.

"Higher, you stupid slut! Bare your cunt."

Amelia obeyed, lifting her skirt waist-high so that the extent of her shame was clearly visible—the tightly strapped leather harness and the silver plate covering her belly, leading down to the straps that ran between her thighs, holding the ridged metal disc hard against her tormented pussy.

The guard nodded.

"She has been deflowered in the accepted manner? You know that no virgin may enter the citadel, upon pain of death?"

"Of course. But as you can see, the child has such a sensual aptitude that I have had to harness her to prevent her from offering herself to all who desire her. She is raw and untutored but she will learn quickly." Indhira smiled knowingly. "You may be very sure that I have prepared this very special merchandise exclusively for your mistress, and for no other..."

"You may enter." The guard clapped her hands and the huge wooden gates swung inward on silent hinges.

Indhira pushed Amelia forward, and she took her

first, faltering steps into the world beyond the gates of the fortress. At first all seemed quiet, even deserted, as she walked into a large central courtyard, but then figures began to emerge from the surrounding buildings—beautiful young shaven-headed women in saffron-colored robes; older women in black; naked dancers with silver rings piercing the lips of their hairless cunts. No one spoke. They collected around the margin of the courtyard and stood in silence, watching, waiting…for what? Or for whom?

A cymbal struck: once, twice, three times, the sound lingering on the thin mountain air like a shimmer of ripples on sunlit water.

"On your knees, slave," Indhira hissed between clenched teeth, and she pushed Amelia to the ground, kneeling beside her with bowed head. "On your knees if you value your worthless life."

A whispering sigh ran through the assembled women as soft footsteps sounded nearby, and Amelia raised her eyes just long enough to glimpse a tall woman on a wooden balcony above the courtyard, looking down on the women below.

"Kneel before the High Priestess of the Temple," a high, clear voice intoned, and the cymbal sounded again: once, twice thrice. "Kneel before the High Priestess of the Rosebud Sutra, the Goddess upon earth."

The sound of footsteps came closer as the high priestess descended a narrow wooden staircase which ran from the balcony to the courtyard. Through her modestly lowered eyelashes, Amelia saw white skirts swirling, the dazzling robes hemmed with gold parting to reveal small, coffee-coloured feet in golden sandals.

"The Goddess is good," intoned the unseen voice.

"She is the source of all desire," replied the assembly of women, their voices hushed and reverential.

"Praise the Goddess with the softness of breast and the sweet fragrance of yoni."

"For she is thrice-blessed and walks among us."

The woman in the white and gold robes walked into the center of the courtyard and all the women of the citadel fell to their knees, touching their foreheads on the stone floor.

"And so you come to visit us again, Indhira."

"Yes, high priestess." Indhira bent low to kiss the high priestess's feet. "I have brought merchandise which I am certain will amuse you."

She raised herself up and sat back on her haunches, savoring the uncommon beauty of the woman: her tall, aristocratic bearing, her shaven head tattooed with sacred signs, and the globes of her breasts, their succulent flesh pierced with innumerable tiny rings that glittered like stars when she walked. She was naked from the waist up and wore around her long and slender neck a chain bearing the symbol of the goddess Akhtar, of whom she was said to be the living incarnation.

"Indeed, Indhira?" The high priestess's eyes travelled over the crouching figure before her, the golden plait bright as ripening corn in the sunshine. "Is she worthy of the Goddess?"

"Worthy of the Goddess and of the temple, your Highness," replied Indhira eagerly. "She has the makings of the finest temple slave I have ever encountered."

"Do I require any more slaves?" mused the high priestess to herself. "I have but lately received the gift of three sisters from a mountain village, brought here for initiation."

"This one is special, your Highness."

"Very well. You may show her to me."

"On your feet, slut!" Indhira got up and dragged Amelia with her. Amelia stood bewildered and afraid beside her, yet curiously enchanted by this strange place, this ancient city of women, hidden high in the mountains, far from the eyes of the world.

"Hmm." The high priestess took Amelia's pointed little chin in her hand and forced her to look deep into her eyes. The unswerving gaze made Amelia tremble, not only with fear but with the instinctive realization that those coal black eyes were windows to a soul of such sensuality that it was beyond her girlish understanding. "An English girl. I think not. I have often found them too cold, too unresponsive."

"She is hotter than a bitch in heat, your Highness, I swear it."

"And what knowledge does she have of the sexual arts?"

"She is but a novice, your Highness, but a skillful and eager pupil. I myself have felt the soft heat of her lips upon my yoni. And being such an innocent, she is capable of being instructed in the ways of the temple without the need to eradicate unsuitable behavior."

The high priestess regarded Amelia in silence for some moments, as though weighing the advantages and disadvantages of this new proposition. Amelia felt her gaze like a caressing hand smoothing over her face and body with an expert's touch, awakening hunger where, only moments before, there had been exhaustion and fear. For the first time, Amelia began to hope that she would not be turned away, that the high priestess would find her worthy of whatever fate might lie in store for her.

"Have her stripped and brought to the Temple," the high priestess announced. "I cannot take her on trust. If the girl is to become a temple slave, she must first accept the service of my body's sacred desires."

Chapter 6

"In the citadel many priestesses may enjoy a slave belonging to the high priestess, either one after the other, or at the same time. Thus one of them holds her, another enjoys her, a third uses her mouth, a fourth holds her middle part, and in this way they go on enjoying her several parts alternately.

—The Rosebud Sutra

From the journal of Dorothea Strong, June 1885

Yesterday I began to feel both fear and doubt for the first time. Of the fate of Amelia Courtnay, I still knew nothing; nor yet of the whereabouts of the *Rosebud Sutra,* despite the hopeful indications given to me by the dancing girl in Jainapur. I was almost at the point of losing heart.

Why, I was unsure even of my precise location, for this area of mountainous country to the north of Jainapur is uncharted and reputedly very dangerous. I have my pistol and hunting knife to protect me, but the nights are lonely and cold, and my dreams are filled with the dark shapes of murderous brigands riding down out of the hills to rob and kill me.

Last night I was fortunate indeed in happening upon the small mountain village of Punjinoor. The village is high in the hills, and virtually unknown to all but the merchants who travel the trade routes to Kashmir through the mountain passes. At this time of the year, the village is deserted save for the women and children, for the men have climbed higher still in the mountains, taking with them their flocks to graze on the sweet grasses beneath the snowline before the monsoon rains. And so it was that I was welcomed with some curiosity and excitement by the womenfolk of Punjinoor.

They are a comely race, these northern women. Their features are noble and regular, their skin a light honey colour suffused with a rosy glow at the cheeks and breast. They wear quantities of bright jewelry, made from local polished stones and irregular pieces of amber strung together on silver wires or fine leather thongs to form necklaces, bracelets and anklets; their noses and ears are pierced to carry single bright semi-precious gems, in the traditional Indian manner.

Their dialect is that of the northern hills, but they speak with a light, lilting accent, their voices turning up at the ends of each sentence so that they sound forever cheerful, forever warm and welcoming.

And my welcome was indeed warm. As soon as I dismounted from my horse, a crowd of children surged out of the little wooden shacks, rushing around me and chattering as their small hands plucked at my clothes. I judge that, in this remote place, they have seldom encountered Western women with our tight-laced dresses and our sensible boots. What bliss it must be to live one's life unfettered by such nonsense! As the women of the village walked out to greet me, I admired the lightness of their garments, the tempting way in which the sinuous lines of their bodies may be glimpsed even through the layers upon layers of gauzy fabric that they wind about themselves.

"I greet you in peace," said the chief of the village, a middle-aged woman with a broad, sensual mouth and the smallest, prettiest feet I have yet seen, bare yet immaculately manicured beneath the legs of her wide silk trousers. What can compare with the sight of a well-turned ankle and small, painted toes, unless it be the equally arousing spectacle of a young woman unwinding herself from her sari, exposing little by little the secrets of her nubile body?

I offered her gifts—a few small tokens which she accepted with good grace—and in turn her womenfolk garlanded me with flowers. It was almost dusk, and as night falls quickly in the mountains, I was happy to be invited to remain at the village for the rest of that night.

Imagine, then, how much more delighted I was to be offered the chief's daughter as my companion for the night! A doe-eyed creature of eighteen years, she was the most willing and obliging of young women; quite unlike our English maids, who simper and flirt but who are too ashamed of their bodies to become expert lovers.

Jaghira—for such was her name—made me a soft bed from blankets and cushions, over the top of which she laid a great rug of sewn animal skins.

"I am bidden to serve you," she told me, pressing her hands together and inclining her head in the traditional attitude of respect. "You may command me to do anything for your comfort and pleasure."

"And what of your pleasure, Jaghira?" I replied, my appetite keen and my curiosity roused. "Are there things it would please you to do this night?"

"My pleasure is unimportant," she countered, her eyes modestly lowered but her bosom heaving with emotion beneath her simple cotton tunic.

I got up from the soft bed where I had been reclining, and took both her hands in mine.

"Jaghira, I command you to reveal to me the secrets of your pleasure," I declared, as sternly as I could, for truly I burned to know what desires lurked in the breast of this ingenuous young girl.

"Memsahib, I am ashamed to tell."

"Tell me—or I shall punish you."

Jaghira's cheeks colored, and she half turned her face away.

"Oh, memsahib…," she whispered.

"That is it!" I cried in triumph. "It pleases you to be punished, doesn't it, Jaghira?" I drew her near to me and squeezed her broad, firm ass through her tunic. Beneath it, her wide-legged pants of fine cotton slid invitingly across the juicy cheeks.

"Oh, memsahib…yes, memsahib," she sighed. I felt her body stiffen with excitement as I squeezed her ass a little tighter. "I so love to feel the cane and the strap. Sometimes one of the women uses the wedge and the piercing instrument on my breasts, or the pincers with their sharp teeth—I so love to feel them biting into my flesh."

Such talk made me think of the little box of toys I

kept in my rooms in London, and with which Floss and I had enjoyed such inventive games. I thought of the hand-made silver clips from Turkey, with the exquisite engraving and the needle-sharp teeth, fashioned to fit with perfect snugness over a pair of juicy pink nipples. Of the wooden paddles I had brought back from a house of pleasure in France; the carefully oiled and polished paddles that had so often reddened Floss's breasts and bumcheeks. Of the finely woven silk cords I had brought back from Venice, cords that made Floss's breasts bulge so attractively when I bound them and pulled them tight…

Jaghira's fingers fluttered to the buttons on the front of my riding shirt, but I pulled her hand away and dealt her a hearty blow that made her fat, fleshy breasts wobble quite adorably. Jaghira's sob of pleasure inflamed me further, and I feigned an anger which truly I did not feel in the least.

"How dare you touch me!" I cried. "For that insult, you must strip off your trousers and offer up your backside to me."

Jaghira complied with a speed which I found most pleasing, lifting up her tunic to unfasten the white cotton pants. They were cut in a traditional pattern, with wide legs gathered into a yoke which was stretched tight across the hips and backside.

Jaghira unfastened the button that held them up and slid them down over her thighs, revealing her bare skin beneath. Such kissable skin it was too, smooth and golden with a little dimple in the center of each fleshy globe.

"Brace yourself against the wall," I instructed her, unbuttoning the cuffs of my dress and rolling my sleeves up to the elbow.

She complied with my every command as meekly and silently as a nun, accepting everything I chose to inflict upon her—every punishment, every blow, every caress. But I could hear her breathing in the silence—a low, staccato sound that grew almost imperceptibly quicker as the game progressed. Her enthusiasm was infectious, and I looked around the hut for some instrument worthy of the deliciously creamy little ass that she was presenting to me.

On a low table beside the entrance lay a broom—a sort of home-made besom fashioned from bundled-up, springy twigs bound together with twine. I picked it up and weighed it in my hand; it felt nicely balanced, light, but with just enough weight to make it easy to wield. I took a few practice strokes with it, and it cut the air with a satisfying swish. Yes, this would do; it would serve the purpose very nicely indeed.

Beneath the fine white tunic, now pushed up above her waist, Jaghira's shoulders were heaving with emotion, and her breath was coming in great stuttering gasps as anticipation and apprehension mingled. It was almost as if I were watching her bringing herself to orgasm before my very eyes with but the thought of her chastisement—for I had not yet even struck her once.

I raised the besom and swung it sharply through the air so that it struck home in the very center of her right buttock. Jaghira's body leapt at the cutting stroke, but she made no sign except for the faintest sigh imaginable—the sigh of perfect contentment.

The first stroke had produced a rather agreeable mottling effect on Jaghira's buttock, and I proceeded to match it with a hard swipe at the left asscheek. Again Jaghira's rump leapt into the air, and this time I saw her fingers clawing at the rough wood of the wall in the paroxysm of her agonized pleasure.

My own pleasure was not slow in coming. Since I had arrived in India, I had been rather starved of the piquant pleasures that I had so enjoyed at my London home. Indeed, I had almost forgotten how marvelous it felt to have a pretty girl's bare ass beneath my hand and an inexhaustible supply of energy in my strong and eager right arm. Jaghira was an excellent tonic for my flagging spirits, her appealing meekness combined with an obvious enthusiasm for what scholars are apt (erroneously) to term the "English vice."

Rather than try to escape the ferocity of my onslaught, Jaghira seemed to wish to offer herself up to it more completely, thrusting out her backside further and further as her hands slipped down the wall, until her body formed an almost perfect ninety-degree angle and her bumcheeks were splayed in a shameless and most enticing manner.

My fingers tightened about the rough handle of the besom and I raised my arm for an even more violent stroke. The sharp, flexible twigs had already made their mark on Jaghira's flesh, mottling the honey-gold with criss-crossed stripes of pink, dotted here and there with spots of darker pink and red where the twigs had penetrated her skin.

Now that she was bending with thighs apart and head down, her backside was in an unrivalled position to receive the full force of my blows. The asscheeks stood proud and slightly apart, so that I caught tantalizing glimpses of the deep amber furrow between. With a malicious delight I aimed the besom carefully at the entrance to that secret garden and brought it down ferociously on her flesh.

At last I heard her cry out—a tiny, high-pitched whimper as the bundle of twigs forced its way between Jaghira's bumcheeks and struck the very epicentre of her secret pleasure: the small, puckered rose that blossomed pink and dewy in the heart of the amber crease.

Her cry of passion seemed to galvanize my own lust and I felt a tremendous burning between my thighs as my clitoris swelled into a turgid stalk. My mouth felt dry, my throat parched, and I knew that I must drink from the wellspring of Jaghira's sex or expire for lack of sustenance.

Flinging myself upon her, I threw her to the ground and seized great handfuls of her flesh. Wrenching apart her asscheeks, I buried my face in the long furrow between cunt and ass, lapping and teasing with tongue and teeth.

She wept freely now, her backside no doubt smarting furiously from the beating I had given her, and my caresses rough and insistent on her raw, red skin. But her cries served only to inflame me still further, and as I lapped at her cunt I thrust first one finger, then two, then three into the forbidden palace of her ass.

Impaled upon the unforgiving spikes of my fingers, Jaghira twisted and turned and bucked, all to no avail. I had her helpless, crying out for more, and that very helplessness excited me to the point of no return. As I lay between her thighs, the gusset of my drawers rubbed over my clitoris and that slight touch was enough to spark off a tremendous climax. We spent together, her juices filling my mouth whilst mine soaked the chaste white cotton of my drawers.

Afterwards I stripped her and laid her down beside me on the bed of rugs and furs. Lifting my skirts, I graciously allowed her to put her hand inside my drawers and masturbate me whilst she talked to me of her village and of the pretty games played by the girls.

"You have a certain skill in your fingers," I remarked as Jaghira brought me very close to the point of orgasm, holding me there for many moments in a state of delicious apprehension. I joked, "One might almost think you had been taught the ancient arts of the *Rosebud Sutra*."

At these words, all the color seemed to drain from Jaghira's face and she froze, her fingers for an instant immobile on my throbbing clitty.

"Whatever is the matter?" I demanded, a little peevish that the girl should cease from her ministrations without so much as a by-your-leave.

"*The Rosebud Sutra*," she whispered. "You must beware, memsahib. Danger lies there."

"What do you know of it?" I demanded, my curiosity suddenly overtaking my lascivious desire.

"Only that it is death to look upon it," she replied in hushed tones. "It must surely be—for those who enter the citadel are never seen again."

"Tell me," I urged her. "Tell me of this citadel. Where is it? How may I find it?"

"I...I must not tell you," she said, drawing away. "I have spoken too much already."

"You must tell me! I have to know."

"It is better that you know nothing. It is better by far that you forget that you ever heard the name of the *Rosebud Sutra*."

She tried to run out of the hut, but I recaptured her easily and threw her back down onto the pile of furs. Kneeling astride her, I pulled apart her thighs and worked my fingers roughly over the soft pink heart of her sex. She closed her eyes and moaned, and I knew my victory was assured.

"Tell me," I repeated. "Tell me all you know about the *Rosebud Sutra.*"

Amelia shivered in the sudden chill. The temple was not as she had imagined it would be. It was not a gloomy, churchlike building filled with silent worshippers. Rather the Temple of the Rosebud Sutra was filled with the light from dozens of windows and with the sound of music.

She looked around but she could not see the musicians. It was as though the music were a creation of the scented air in which she moved, or perhaps even of her own imagination.

The temple was filled with statues of the many-headed, many-breasted goddess Akhtar, her thighs splayed and her fingers pulling apart her pussylips to reveal the huge, distended clitoris within. Between and among the statues were carved wooden couches covered with soft cushions and drapes in different shades of red and gold. A light breeze blew in through the open door and caught the huge, soft drifts of flower petals that lay across the earthen floor, blowing them into lazy swirls of pink-white snowflakes that fluttered down softly onto the altar.

The high priestess greeted them from her chair beside the altar. Amelia noticed how ornately it was carved with the faces of demons and the entwined limbs of lovers, coupled for eternity at the height of their passion.

"Welcome to the temple, Amelia. I trust you will not disappoint me. If you do, I may have to amuse myself by having you killed."

"I...I will try to please you, your Highness," replied Amelia, very conscious of the danger facing her, and yet excited also; excited because she had been chosen. For the first time in her life she began to feel just a little important—something that she had never been allowed to contemplate before, certainly not in the presence of the awesome Miss Catherstone.

"I am sure you will," replied the high priestess with an air of serene malice. "Few of your kind have the spiritual strength to welcome death." She got up from her chair and two shaven-headed priestesses glided forward, anonymous and yet somehow alluring in their robes of saffron-coloured cotton. "Take my cloak."

She unfastened it and slipped it off her shoulders, handing it to one of the priestesses. Underneath, she was entirely naked, the tiny breast-rings glittering and sparkling in the light from the many windows. Amelia noticed for the first time that the high priestess also had a pierced navel, from which hung a small chain bearing an enormous diamond, so heavy that it distended the flesh.

Amelia felt uncomfortable and rather shameless in the encasing harness, now no longer covered by the sky blue robe. Her bare breasts seemed huge, squeezed by the tight leather straps and pushed up by the constricting silver plate. But by far the worst torment was the silver disc between her thighs, its cruelly ridged surface now soaking wet with the juices of her frustrated longing.

She shifted her feet a little in the drifts of flower petals and felt the disc grind inexorably against the inside of her sex.

Her small sigh did not go unnoticed.

"If you are to remain here and become a servant of

the temple, Amelia, you must learn greater self-control. Much greater self-control, is that clear, slave?"

"Y-yes. Yes, your Highness. I am sorry, your Highness."

"Nevertheless, Indhira tells me that you have potential, and on a first acquaintance I am inclined to agree with her assessment. You are an unusually pretty wench, and the Goddess has a taste for variety in her servants..." The high priestess's voice trailed off into a snapped command: "Stand still, slave!"

"I am sorry!" Amelia held her breath, certain that she would be beaten—or worse—for daring to move, daring to pleasure herself with the silver disc whilst her new mistress was speaking to her.

"You *will* be, Amelia, if you do not quickly learn obedience." The high priestess clapped her hands and one of the saffron-robed priestesses brought forward a small vial of a golden liquid. "Take it, child."

Amelia reached out and grasped the glass vial. It felt slightly warm in her hands, and she wondered what it might be.

"As I told Indhira, your first task must be to accept the service of my desires, whilst renouncing and denying your own. You shall anoint my body, Amelia, with the sacred oil. And whilst you are pleasuring me, one of my priestesses will endeavor to excite you with her kisses and caresses.

"You must not respond to her, do you understand? Your only care is my pleasure—your own is of no importance. No matter how desperately you yearn for sensual release, you shall not allow yourself to climax unless and until I give you permission. Do you understand?"

"I understand, Highness."

The high priestess laid herself down on a pile of soft

rugs before a statue of the Goddess, her eyes closed and her hands by her sides.

"You may commence."

With uncertain fingers, Amelia eased the cork stopper from the little glass vial, and a pungent scent rose to her nostrils from the golden fluid within. She tilted the vial and a few drops fell into her palm. The oil was warm and quite viscous, like sugar-syrup, but when she folded her fingers into her palm and touched it, it felt as slippery-smooth as ice.

Kneeling down on the edge of the rugs, she laid her hand on the high priestess's belly, and began moving it very lightly over the surface of the taut skin. For the first time, she had an opportunity to appraise the fine lines of her body, the strong musculature beneath the pale amber of the skin. Despite her shaven head, she radiated a quintessentially feminine power that made Amelia feel quite drunk with excitement. The high priestess's lips were a plump bow of deepest pink, her dark eyelashes long and silky, and Amelia felt a sudden impulse to kiss that haughty, aristocratic, sensual face.

The high priestess made no sound as Amelia began the sensual massage, but Amelia felt her belly tense and then relax as her hands began moving together, sliding easily over the firm flesh on a thin film of scented oil. She had no learned skills in massage, but the technique seemed to come naturally to her, imbuing her fingertips with an unconscious power.

Her hands moved upwards, toward the crested hillocks of the high priestess's breasts. They seemed alien and terrifying, with their many jewelled rings passing not only through the tough, dusky brown nipples, but also through the delicate breast flesh. Amelia touched one of the rings with wondering apprehension, and it moved slightly, slipping easily through the pierced skin. The high priestess's body jerked momentarily at the touch, then relaxed, and Amelia felt a silent sigh whisper through the priestess's body.

Suddenly she wanted very much to please the high priestess, not simply to protect herself from further danger or hurt, but because to have the high priestess's favour would in itself be a supreme pleasure. She worked her hands more boldly over the small hummocks of tit-flesh, and they wobbled and quivered obligingly, the small silver rings slipping round and round faster as the oil lubricated their rims.

Bending over and rubbing harder, Amelia was so absorbed in her new task that she had almost forgotten what the high priestess had told her about what was to happen. It was not until she felt the saffron-robed priestess's hands on her backside that she remembered the high priestess's words: "She will pleasure you but you must not climax. You must not give in to your desire unless and until I give you permission."

At first it was not too difficult to resist the lure of the pleasure offered to her. The priestess's hands clutched and pinched her asscheeks, pulled a little apart by the encircling leather straps, but that small stimulation could not compare with the delight of stroking and caressing the high priestess's firm, globular breasts. How could any caress compare with the feeling of having this powerful woman's tits in her hands, the feeling that she had been given sole charge of the high priestess's pleasure?

But her sense of triumph was short-lived, as the high priestess had known it would be. The English girl knew just enough of the ways of lust to make her overconfident and foolish. Seconds later, the priestess's hands climbed up her waist and fastened on her breasts, cupping them so that the long, hard nipples protruded between the priestess's fingers.

Amelia's breasts ached for caresses, already stimulated by the leather and silver of the harness which pushed them forward and apart, turning them into hard white spheres. She gave a little yelp of astonishment at the skill of the priestess's touch, the lewd and knowing way in which her cupping fingers drew tightly together, so that her trapped nipples were pinched in between them.

Kneeling there, her knees wide apart and her back arched over as she massaged the high priestess, Amelia felt suddenly very vulnerable. The harness was incredibly tight around her body, and even the slightest movement seemed to provoke unimaginable sensations as leather and metal pressed into her most secret places. She began to understand the fiendish cleverness of the mind that had designed this subtle instrument of torture. Who could have imagined that the pressure of a silver plate beneath the breasts could be so exciting or the chafing of a roughened leather strap along the groin so desperately irresistible?

The silver disc between her thighs felt wet and slippery, a smooth-tongued intruder into the soft pink heart of her sex. As she sank lower over the high priestess's supine body, she felt the disc's rippled ridges press more insistently against the moist, sensitive flesh. Her clitoris was pushing its swollen head against the curved metal plate, and the sensation was excruciatingly brutal, taking her breath away.

She let out a strangled sob and sank a little lower, her breasts cupped and supported in the priestess's hands. Her whole body seemed to offer itself up to that touch, the promise of those skillful, pinching fingers, their caresses as piquant as a serpent's bite.

For a second she stopped massaging the high priestess's breasts, frozen in time as she felt the surge of delicious sensations pulsing through her helpless body, the sting of her tormented nipples, the throb of her clitoris, so ungently tortured by the silver plate pressing between her love-lips.

But then the high priestess's words flooded back to her: "You must resist. You must not allow yourself to climax. You must forget your own pleasure, forget it utterly..."

She forced herself to go on, moving her hands from the high priestess's pierced breasts, back down the smooth curve of her belly toward the slight swell of her shaven pubis. The right lobe of her pussy-lips was decorated with a dark red jewel, so heavy that it distended the flesh, pulling apart her pussy-lips to reveal the deep red heart within.

Amelia's head was spinning, her clitoris pulsing with need, her nipples incandescent with the sacred fire of her longing. Yet two longings burned within her: the longing for her own release from this torment of lust and the longing to please the high priestess, this enigmatic, powerful woman whose lust was her command.

She forced herself to keep on stroking the high priestess's pussy-lips, though she yearned to slip a hand between her thighs and press the silver disc just a little harder, forcing it against the throbbing love-bud that was so very close to blossoming. She slipped a finger between the high priestess's sex-lips and, picking up the vial of scented oil, upended it over the soft heart of her juicy fruit.

For the first time, she felt the full intensity of the

high priestess's lust. Her body arched on the bed of soft rugs and, although she did not open her eyes, Amelia saw a smile of pleasure play about the corners of her large, sensual mouth. Slowly she drew up her knees, parting her thighs to receive the warm, scented tribute.

Encouraged by her success, Amelia let her fingertip stray into the large, warm pool of oil filling the high priestess's sex. It spilled out of her, mingling with the sweet ooze of her sex juice, blending its own pungent scent with the compelling fragrance of her desire. Amelia pressed her finger deeper into the soft red fruit, and it slid effortlessly into the silky wet heart of the high priestess's cunt.

Behind her, the priestess's body was hot and hard through her saffron robe, her kisses light but relentless, her fingers cruelly pleasurable as they cupped and pinched and massaged. She tried to shut them out of her mind as she bent to kiss the high priestess's cunt, thrusting out her tongue with a gauche enthusiasm that delighted her prospective mistress. But the throb in cunt and breast served only to intensify her thirst for cunt juice, setting the rhythm as she lapped and sucked at the burgeoning stalk.

She could feel the high priestess's body growing tense: hotter and harder and full of anticipation. Her breathing was harsh, her breasts rising and falling in rapid, shallow gasps, so that her breast-rings caught the light and glittered like the facets of some precious jewel.

It was coming; she could feel it. The high priestess was on the very brink of orgasm, and her own crisis was breathtakingly close. Amelia gave a sighing sob, a little shuddering cry that was the expression of a dreadful pain—the pain of frustrated ecstasy. Just one small movement, a slight swaying of the hips, a pressing of her breasts into the priestess's hands, and she would come. She could almost feel it now, could prefigure the intensity of the sensations, and she wanted them so, so much.

Forbidden. It was forbidden. She must be strong. She must put her mistress's pleasure above her own. But it was so very difficult to ignore the treacherous warmth between her thighs....

Suddenly, when Amelia was on the very edge of despair, the high priestess's body grew rigid and a tiny gasp of air escaped from her lips. Her beautiful, almond eyes opened wide and she smiled. A moment later, Amelia felt the powerful clenching of her vaginal muscles as the high priestess reached the peak of orgasm.

Spasm after spasm racked the high priestess's body, her cunt muscles tensing and untensing around Amelia's finger and her love juice flooding out like a tide of sweet nectar, filling Amelia's mouth. The bliss of her mistress's pleasure seemed to overwhelm the aching need in Amelia's cunt, making her think only of the joy of the high priestess's come on her tongue.

"Indhira was right. The girl does have potential," observed the high priestess, getting to her feet as coolly as if nothing at all had happened.

Her naked body was still glossy with oil, and a heady fragrance surrounded her—the blended fragrance of incense, exotic flowers, and sex. Amelia hoped that her own sexual scent was not as strong as it seemed to her—it filled and surrounded her, betraying her desperate attempts to appear unmoved, in control of her own desire.

"You are satisfied with the girl's powers of self-control, your Highness?" inquired the priestess who had been stimulating Amelia's helpless body. There was a note of surprise in her voice.

The high priestess laughed.

"No, of course I am not satisfied! Do you not see how the little bitch is sweating and trembling with lust?" She reached out and drew Amelia to her feet, squeezing her breast so hard that Amelia gave a little shriek. Her nipple stuck out like a hard, pink finger, the betraying finger of her lust. "Her cunt is dripping juice—can you not smell it? She is like a bitch in heat. One moment longer and she would have climaxed in your hands. Only my own pleasure saved her from disgrace."

Amelia hung her head in shame. She had failed. She had failed in the task she had been set, and now she would be killed. But it was the pain of the high priestess's displeasure that most distressed her. She had so longed for the high priestess to be pleased with her.

"That being said," continued the high priestess, "she is young and supremely innocent. Her body is untutored, and yet she shows an unusual aptitude for the sensual acts. Her performance of the Auparishtaka upon my yoni was quite exceptional in one so naive."

Amelia's heart soared.

"Then you will accept her as a postulant to the temple, your Highness?"

The high priestess hesitated.

"I am not yet wholly certain," she replied. "There must first be one more trial—the trial of endurance."

She clapped her hands, and two more priestesses appeared from the shadows. Amelia looked from them to the high priestess and back again, her expression questioning and fearful.

"I must divine the depth of your sensuality," the

high priestess told her. "Here, in the Temple of the Rosebud Sutra, each temple slut must perform many and varied sexual acts with the priestesses and—on the occasions of greatest ceremony—with the high priestess of the Goddess herself."

She took a sharp knife from the hands of one of the priestesses and—disdaining the buckles and the little silver padlock—she used it to slice through the leather straps holding the harness tight around Amelia's body. Amelia let out a sigh of release as the harness fell away; of release and also of loss, for her body still yearned instinctively for the unforgiving caresses of the little silver disc between her thighs, the straps buckled so tightly between and around the small white globes of her breasts.

"You have a pleasing body, Amelia," commented the high priestess, laying the knife upon the temple altar. "But is it open to all the sensual excesses? Will you welcome both the pleasure and the pain of each new encounter, each new joining, each new worship?"

"I...I will try, your Highness," whispered Amelia.

"Then let the trial begin."

She stood back and let three of the priestesses come forward, shedding their robes as they did so to reveal hard, shaven bodies tattooed with serpents and fantastical flowers. As she looked on, wide-eyed and fearful, Amelia saw that two of the women had dildos of polished black stone strapped between their thighs, and instantly she knew what was going to happen to her.

A wild thought ran through her mind. She could run; she could run through the open door and try to get away. But how—and why? Even if she did escape, how long could a naked English girl survive out on the inhospitable mountainside? And the more she thought about it, the more she became convinced that, no matter how far she ran, the priestesses of the temple would find her and bring her back.

Hands touched her, stroking, cajoling, reawakening her desire and kindling it furnace-bright. Hands pried apart cunt-lips and asscheeks, opening up secret places that were shamefully willing to be displayed. The cold black stone of a dildo nudged into the virgin-tight tunnel of her vagina, so wet and slippery that it welcomed the intruder without protest. Amelia found herself clutching at the priestess who was invading her, impaling her on the spike of her surrogate dick and hoisting her aloft in strong arms, making her wrap her thighs about her waist so that her delicious little backside was thrust out like a juicy fruit. Oh, she wanted this; she wanted it so very much.

The second dildo touched her ass and she squealed in sudden terror. It felt so huge and she was so very tight down there, a hot bitch in her cunt but still a timorous virgin in her ass. But there was no space for fear, and still less for refusal. There could be no denying the hardness of the dildo between her asscheeks or the way Amelia's body seemed to offer itself up to the sharp pain that knifed through her at the first thrust against her virgin hole. Almost fainting from the pain, Amelia felt a great surge of elation as, at the third thrust, the dildo penetrated her ass and was swallowed up by the tight sheath of flesh.

She was a prisoner—a prisoner of her mistress's lust, and of her own. She was afraid, she was in discomfort, and yet the pleasure was exquisite and she wanted it never to end.

The third priestess's hands and lips roamed all over

her body, her greedy tongue roaming into exposed folds of flesh, intensifying both pleasure and shame as the fucking became an all-consuming, almost hypnotic pleasure.

The high priestess, watching from the altar, nodded her approval to her priestess.

"Tell the merchant Indhira that I shall take her. She has the makings of a more than passable temple slut."

"And the price, your Highness?"

"The price?" The high priestess smiled at her own private joke. "The price is a high one for us all, Bheli, and higher still for the little English slut. For once she is initiated as a slave of the temple, she will never see the outside world again."

"Miss Catherstone?"

The headmistress turned, her hand still tightly clenched around the handle of the riding crop. Before her, securely tied to a wooden sawhorse, was a doe-eyed brunette who had been reported to her for missing lessons. The girl's skirts and petticoats were flung up over her head, and her coarse linen drawers had been pulled down to her ankles, leaving her fleshy buttocks quite bare.

A few angry red stripes already criss-crossed the white skin, but Miss Catherstone had barely started the punishment. She was most displeased at this interruption to her pleasure.

"What is it, Miss Grahame? Can you not see that I am occupied in chastising this wretched girl?"

"Indeed, ma'am." The youthful housekeeper shuffled her feet uneasily on Miss Catherstone's highly polished parquet floor. "But I would not have disturbed you if it were not a matter of some importance."

"Then pray be swift."

Miss Catherstone turned back to the errant girl. She doubted very much that Evangeline Grahame had anything of great importance to say. She had always considered her a woolly-headed little flirt, though admittedly quite attractive. Indeed, Miss Grahame might herself benefit from undergoing a course of discipline at the hands of her headmistress.

"It is one of the school servants, ma'am."

Miss Catherstone let out a gasp of irritation.

"The servants are your concern, Miss Grahame. You must deal with them as you see fit. I cannot be expected to discipline them for all their petty indiscretions—not when I have a hundred pupils whose welfare must be my primary concern."

She regarded the girl's trembling rump with a pang of lust and aimed a well-judged swipe at the bare flesh. As the riding crop hit home, the girl's backside leapt up, and a little hissing sob emerged from the heap of skirts and petticoats that covered the girl's head.

"Silence!" snapped Miss Catherstone. "How are you ever going to accept discipline if you will not make any effort at self-control?" She turned back to Miss Grahame with a bored expression. "You were saying?"

"It is Mary Bates," began the housekeeper, uneasy about Miss Catherstone's reaction.

"That slatternly creature! If she has been caught stealing food again..."

"No, ma'am, nothing like that. But when I went down to the kitchen this morning to find out why the breakfast dishes had not been collected and washed..."

"Yes, Miss Grahame? What did she have to say for her miserable self?"

"Nothing, Miss Catherstone. That, I fear, is the crux

of the problem. You see, there was no sign of her. And when I checked her bed in the attic, it hadn't been slept in. I fear she has run away, Miss Catherstone. Where, I have not the faintest idea."

Chapter 7

The women of the temple harem cannot see or meet any outsiders, for they are strictly guarded. Also, they do not have their desires satisfied, for their only mistress is common to all of them. And so the women of the harem, when they are amorous, do the acts of the mouth on the yonis of one another.

—The Rosebud Sutra

In the seclusion of the temple harem, the days seemed to blend into each other. Amelia had lost all track of time. Was it days or weeks or months since she had come to the Temple of the Rosebud Sutra?

There were more than a hundred slaves in the high priestess's harem, each one dedicated to the will and sensual service of the Goddess. Since the high priestess Ishtar was believed to be the Goddess's earthly incarnation, this meant that all the homages and ceremonies due to the Goddess must be made to her.

Amelia was placed in one of the harem's twelve "training houses"; a beautiful, almost circular hall of white marble, in which the slave women would live their entire lives except when called to the temple or to the high priestess's bed. Curtains of gossamer-fine lace and gauzy tulle hung over little alcoves where beds had been strategically placed, and there were heaps of downy-soft cushions all over the elaborate mosaic floor, which portrayed a young slave girl in an attitude of prayer, her love-lips grotesquely distended by a huge carved dildo.

In the middle of the hall was a large oblong sunken pool, filled with pink, rose-scented water warmed to an even temperature by underfloor furnaces kept burning night and day. Beside it was a smaller, circular pool, filled with water so icy that even the stone walkway surrounding it was inhospitably chilly to the touch.

As soon as she arrived at the training house, Amelia was put in the charge of a group of senior slaves and quickly inducted into the routine of harem life.

"Her skin is so white!" exclaimed one of the eunuchs, a young boy with the intricately painted face of an exquisitely beautiful girl. "She looks so fragile... almost as if she would break if you touched her."

He put out his hand but Amelia backed away, uneasy and afraid in this strange, cloistered world. At the academy, she had grown accustomed to barred windows and regular punishments, but in this exotic setting everything seemed alien and frightening. And if the windows here were barred and the doors guarded by eunuchs and fierce warrior women, how could she ever hope for a chance to escape?

If, of course, she still wanted to escape. She felt so confused, hopelessly uncertain about what she really did want. A big part of her wanted to be back at the academy and in the reassuring arms of Mary Bates, but an almost equal part yearned for the high priestess Ishtar to summon her to her bed and fuck her to the point of exhausted ecstasy.

"Hush, stupid boy," snapped the head slave, Bheli. "She is an English girl and there are some who consider them handsome. Although personally," she looked Amelia up and down with a critical eye, "I have always found them rather displeasing to the eye. But one must not question the high priestess's tastes, her sacred name be praised." She turned to her assistant, Shakhira. "Undress her. It is time we set to work on her preparation. From what I hear, she has a great deal to learn before her initiation."

Amelia submitted meekly to the impatient hands that stripped her of the thin robe and sandals and unfastened her still-braided hair. Shakhira wrinkled her nose.

"She stinks of sweat and sex," she said. "And she is filthy after her long journey."

"Then she must be bathed," replied Bheli with cool common sense. "I doubt that even an English bitch will smell too offensive after she has been thoroughly washed."

Amelia's cheeks burned with shame and anger, and she did not quite know whether to laugh or to cry. But she remembered what Mary had always said—that nobody was any better than anyone else, and that everyone had a right to their pride. Curiously enough, she also remembered Miss Catherstone, purse-lipped and stern, not caressing but beating pride into her pupils. Even Miss Catherstone had believed in the superiority of Academy girls over the ordinary hoi polloi of army daughters in Jainapur.

"Please, ma'am, I only want to do as I am bidden," she hazarded, and was rewarded with a hefty slap across the buttocks.

"Be silent, slave!" exclaimed Bheli, outraged. "Do they teach you no respect in your English schools?" Her voice softened, but only the merest hint. "Here, slave, you will quickly learn only to speak when you are given permission to do so."

"Otherwise," interjected Shakhira with relish, "you will feel something far worse than the weight of Bheli's hand."

Silenced for the time being, Amelia waited to see what would happen next. Bheli took her by the shoulders and made her turn round slowly, so that she could examine every aspect of the new slave's physique.

"She has a strong, well-defined body," conceded Bheli. "A little skinny perhaps, but the Mistress likes her fillies lean. The hair is a rather diverting color. The hands and feet are regular and small, the features not too coarse or common." She gave Amelia's backside a ringing slap, and enjoyed the spectacle of the girl's reddening flesh, quivering like a blancmange. "You have my permission to bathe her and shave her straight away."

"Shave me!" exclaimed Amelia in horror, quite forgetting Bheli's prohibition. In the time since she had been captured and deflowered by the outlaw women, her golden pubic curls had almost grown back, and she dreaded having to go through the same ordeal all over again. A half-second later Shakhira's hand fell across her breasts, and she gasped at the ferocity of the onslaught.

"Stupid, empty-headed girl!" hissed Shakhira. "How much pain will it take before you learn elementary obedience?" She threw a disgusted glance at Bheli. "This one will never learn. She is far too unintelligent. The high priestess might as well have her killed now and give us all better sport."

"Be quiet, Shakhira," said Bheli with a calm firmness. "I shall deal with the wench as I see fit." She turned her eyes on Amelia. "You are a slave now, child," she announced, "and quite undeserving of any explanations. However, you are young... In this place, all body hair is considered unclean, and it must be shaved off. Why, the priestesses are so holy that they must also shave their heads, but you..." She laughed dryly. "You need have no fear on that score. You are destined to become only a plaything, a pleasure-toy—not a holy priestess of the Goddess."

The pretty, girl-faced eunuch produced a cut-throat razor of the sort that Amelia remembered her father using when she was a small child. Its blade was sword-sharp, and she felt quite faint as the boy plucked a hair from his immaculately groomed head and sliced it neatly in half along its length.

Shakhira held a bowl of soft soap to which Bheli added warm water and a few drops of rose essence, mixing the whole concoction to produce a thick, pinkish lather.

"Lift up your arms," Bheli instructed her, and Amelia raised her arms waist-high. "No, no, above your head—do you want me to risk cutting you?"

Hastily Amelia raised her arms higher, and Bheli

began smoothing handfuls of lather into the hollow of her axillae, covering the golden hairs that had sprouted there like corn-stubble. The sensation was rather a ticklish one, but she knew that to laugh or wriggle would provoke the most fearful punishment; besides which, the eunuch boy was examining the oiled blade of the razor, turning it round in the morning sunlight. It looked breathtakingly sharp.

"Give me the razor," said Bheli, taking it from the boy and wiping it on the hem of her robe. "Stand still, slave, and this will not hurt you."

She ran the blade over the skin beneath Amelia's arms, and the sensation was surprisingly pleasurable, so light that it was a little like being stroked with a bunch of feathers. The creamy lather trickled in thick, cooling gobbets down from her underarm and onto the jutting curve of her flank.

The second armpit shaved, Bheli replenished her stock of lather and set about anointing Amelia's lower belly and pubis. Now Amelia began to feel very uneasy. This was such a sensitive and intimate place; as the soap moistened the tufts of wiry golden curl, she dreaded the feeling of cold steel on naked flesh.

"Open your legs and stand still," Bheli commanded her. This time, Amelia did not even contemplate disobedience. Bheli was crouching down in front of her, the blade of the razor flat against her belly. It felt a little cold against her overheated skin, and she sensed beads of sweat breaking out on the nape of her neck, trickling down into the small of her back.

The razor's blade slipped down from navel to pubis, lifting away the fine trail of blonde hairs that pointed the way to the heart of Amelia's sex. Moments later, it was scraping through her pubic hair, pressing quite hard on her mount of Venus as the golden curls were lifted away, one by one. Then Bheli took hold of her pussy-lips and pulled them taut, making a smooth surface for the razor to glide over.

She could not repress a tiny gasp of fear and surprised pleasure as the razor skimmed the very margin of her cunt-lips, pressing not hard enough to break the skin, but firmly enough to tease and redden it. The blade passed so close to her clitty-stalk that it responded as to a lover's touch, springing up and pushing its head past the pink fleshy hood that had covered it.

"Oh. Oh, aah...," gasped Amelia, and this time Bheli did not bother to silence her. Wiping a soft towel across Amelia's now-shaven pussy, she regarded her handiwork with some satisfaction.

"See how she responds, even to the blade," said Bheli. "Even at the moment of greatest danger, this little filly will sing for the touch of a tongue on her yoni, the bite of a silver clamp on her breast." She opened up Amelia's cunt-lips and surveyed the hot, wet interior. "Her clitoris is large and well formed. See how delightfully erect it is. She has a slut's appetite for pleasure. Now turn her round, Shakhira. I must shave her ass."

Amelia held her breath, more afraid and more excited than ever because she could not see her tormentor, only feel the cold kiss of the blade as it glided over the generous curve of her buttock and into the well-soaped interior crease where her secret rosebud lay.

Secret no more. For since that day in the temple, when she had been enjoyed by three of the priestesses in the approving presence of Ishtar, Amelia had come to understand that there could be no secrets, not from these new mistresses and companions. All that had been shameful and secret before was now to be open and unashamed, an offering to the greater glory of the high priestess.

The lather felt warm and liquid, like a long, luxurious trail of saliva; the blade felt cool and hard, like a lover's eager fingernail, scraping down toward the puckered heart of her ass. As it slid across the tight sphincter, scraping away the few golden hairs surrounding it, she felt it open like the mouth of a starfish, welcoming in this new intrusion.

"She will suffice," announced Bheli, wiping away the last of the lather and parting Amelia's asscheeks with her strong fingers, to survey the secret garden within. "Such a tight little ass." She amused herself by wriggling her fingertip the merest fraction into Amelia's asshole. "She will afford much pleasure."

"Shall I bathe her now?" demanded Shakhira. "She stinks like a street harlot."

Bheli gave a faint smile.

"You may conceal your desire as scorn, Shakhira," she said, "but you do not convince me. I'll wager you want the little bitch for you own bed—isn't that so?"

Shakhira affected outrage.

"Me? Want a dirty little slut like her?"

"Yes, Shakhira. I think you do. Look at these." Bheli pulled aside the front of Shakhira's robe and her two fat breasts bobbed out, hard-tipped and eager. "Your nipples are hard as betel nuts, and I can smell the ooze from your cunt."

Shakhira turned her head away, just a little, so that Bheli could not see the confusion in her eyes.

"Shall I bathe her now?" she repeated.

"You may proceed."

Shakhira gave Amelia's rump a rough prod.

"Get down the steps into the pool. And hurry—we have better things to do than wait for you all day."

Amelia entered the rose-scented pool with a perfect willingness. The water was a little warmer than body temperature, and its warmth felt deliciously soothing on her aching body. She had forgotten how long it had been since she had slept soundly or felt a gentle touch on her poor, misused flesh.

Six white marble steps led down into the sunken bath, and as Amelia walked down them the water rose slowly up her legs to her thighs, lapping at the bare skin of her shaven cunt before engulfing it in an ocean of warmth. With a sigh of pleasure, she took the last step and walked into the bath. Its waters came just above her waist, lapping at the underside of her breasts as she walked, making little wavelets with her arms and legs.

This tranquil idyll could not last, for Shakhira had followed her into the bath, and she was carrying a large, rough-sided loofah.

"Come here and let me wash you," she sneered contemptuously, but Amelia could see how stiff her nipples were, heard the huskiness in her breathing. "Dirty little sluts must be washed thoroughly."

"I'm not...," began Amelia, and then remembered that she must not speak. Her heart thumped as she saw the look of glee on Shakhira's face.

"Will you never learn, slut?" Shakhira's hand smashed down across her breasts, making them leap and wobble. Amelia's breath escaped in a convulsive gasp, and tears sprang to her cornflower blue eyes.

"I...am sorry."

The second blow reddened her breast flesh and her nipples puckered in a torment of pleasure-mingled pain.

"You will address me as Madam at all times."

"I am sorry…Madam."

"Hold on to the edge of the bath and bend over. You are to be cleansed."

Having little option, Amelia obeyed. Wading toward the side, she grasped the smooth metal rail that ran round the edge of the pool and bowed her head.

"I said bend over, slut. Properly. Like the little bitch you are."

Shakhira gave her a hard shove and she bent lower, pushing out her backside and sliding her feet further back on the smooth marble floor of the bath. Her small breasts hung down like juicy fruits now, their roundness slightly distorted so that they became ripe pink pears or sweet mangoes ready to drop from the tree into a hungry lover's mouth. Their firm yet soft flesh shifted and swayed in the moving currents as the water both supported and caressed them.

She could feel Bheli's eyes upon her, appraising the spare, firm lines of her youthful body, feasting greedily on the ripe fruits of her breasts, exploring every nook and cranny of her body through the shifting veil of warm, rose pink water.

The loofah felt hard and scratchy on the skin of her back, but the sensation was not unpleasant, and Amelia found herself pushing herself slightly against it, prolonging and strengthening the sensation as the stiff implement rubbed up and down the length of her spine. She arched her back so willingly and so well that her face was only a fraction above the water, and as Shakhira moved, the water was stirred up into little pink waves that lapped like tongues at her eyes and mouth.

It was a dreamlike state, and the warmth and scent

of the water made Amelia feel languid, even drowsy. If this was some kind of discipline, then perhaps discipline was not so bad after all. Even the roughness of the loofah on her bare bumcheeks only served to make her sway her hips with guilty pleasure.

Shakhira's fingers felt flame-hot on her backside as she pried open the deep crease to inspect the treasures within. Amelia felt the single closed eye of her anus blink open and then close again as Shakhira's sharp nail grazed down over the long furrow between her ass-cheeks.

"She is a filthy minded slut," observed Shakhira with relish, and Amelia was not so naive that she misinterpreted the satisfaction in Shakhira's voice. She knew enough of the world by now to understand the tones of desire, the little low notes in Shakhira's breathing that betrayed the depth of her lust. This slave woman might be feigning disgust, but everything about her screamed desire. "This English girl is a filthy minded little slattern who will give up her body to any woman who desires her."

And you desire me, thought Amelia, with her own thrill of satisfaction. There was something very exciting about knowing that a woman like Shakhira wanted her body, wanted to do things to it—things that would give both of them an unspeakable, inexpressible pleasure.

"Then cleanse her of her wickedness," said Bheli with studied disinterest. She, too, was clearly enjoying the novelty of the game. "We must do all that we can to make the girl worthy of the temple."

Holding Amelia's buttocks apart with the fingers of one hand, Shakhira pushed the loofah into the enlarged space she had created. Instantly Amelia bucked and wriggled, her body both fighting and welcoming this harsh new intrusion.

"Hold still, or you will be taken to the Chamber of Correction," Bheli chided her. "There you will be shown no gentleness, I can assure you of that."

Amelia could hardly conceal her excitement. A shameless, once-secret part of her almost wanted her to be sentenced to the this mysterious, terrifying chamber. She had seen some of the temple slaves taken away to it, and brought back to the harem a few hours later, bloody and bruised yet smiling and weeping with joy, as though they had glimpsed celestial bliss. Whatever lay beyond the stout wooden doors of the punishment chamber, Amelia was beginning to think it might be worth the pain of incurring Bheli's displeasure.

But she held fast to the metal rail and submitted to Shakhira's will. Perhaps in pleasing these new mistresses, she would earn herself a greater pleasure still. And how could she even contemplate the Chamber of Correction, when she was so weak in body and spirit that she could not even withstand the simple torture of a loofah being pushed between her asscheeks?

On the skin of Amelia's back and buttocks, the loofah had felt scratchy and not at all disagreeable. But as soon as it penetrated the hidden sanctum between her asscheeks, the sensation kindled to a terrible inferno of torment. The harshness of the loofah, so agreeably stimulating on the more resilient skin of her back, was like the points of a thousand daggers, the biting of a thousand serpents' tongues on the hypersensitive membrane of her anus.

"No, no, no. No, please," she whimpered, but no one paid her protests the slightest attention. In the water, inches below her, Amelia saw the reflection of her own face, wide-eyed and open-mouthed, and behind it the moving silhouette of Shakhira.

The loofah worked back and forth, up and down, its long, fat shaft coarse and sharp as a thorn bush. It reddened the flesh, drawing a few drops of blood where it had punctured the skin, and soon the individual tortures of each scratching, piercing point had blended to form a single furnace heat.

Just when Amelia feared she could bear no more, Shakhira withdrew the loofah and inspected it. As she drew it through the water, little feathers of dissolved blood floated away, mingling with the rose-scented waves lapping at Amelia's wounded backside.

"She will suffice," announced Shakhira.

Amelia's body burned, not only with pain but with an agony of frustrated lust—the pain of Shakhira's torture had awakened deep, dark desires that she scarcely dared confess.

"Turn around, slut. I wish to inspect and cleanse you further."

Tremulous, yet her pulse racing with excitement, Amelia let go of the smooth metal rail and turned around to face Shakhira. Behind and above her, on the rim of the pool, stood Bheli and the eunuch boy, his girlish face a picture of perverse desire. He leered at her and Amelia blushed and turned away her face.

The rose pink water felt soothing as it rose about her backside, insinuating itself between her nethercheeks and tingling as it flowed over the raw, abraded skin.

"Her nipples are very erect," observed Bheli. "Clearly the filly has a taste for pain."

"I have heard tell that such is the English way," butted in the eunuch, biting into a mango and lapping at its cloyingly sweet flesh with his small, neat tongue. "They are sent away to school when they are tiny children, and their teachers and governesses beat them regularly, so that they learn to enjoy the pain."

"Be silent," Bheli scolded him. "It is not your place to have opinions. It is your place only to give your dear sisters pleasure with your pretty mouth." Her attentions returned to Shakhira. "Inspect her clitoris manually. I want to know the depth of her lust."

"Open your legs, slut." Without waiting for Amelia to comply, Shakhira pushed her hand roughly between Amelia's thighs and pressed the side of it up hard against the fat fleshiness of her freshly shaven pussy. "Open, damn you!"

Amelia shuffled her feet apart, secretly happy to have Shakhira's touch, however ungentle, on her throbbing slit. Her clitoris was like a little ball of flame between her love-lips, and she longed to show her need by bending her knees, so that it would grind down against the hard side of Shakhira's hand. But that would surely be unforgivable. So she held herself as still and as passively as she could, praying that there would be a speedy release from the terrible torment of her lust.

Shakhira's hand sliced between the pouting lips of Amelia's sex and slid back and forth a few times, testing the long furrow which ran from cunt to ass.

"She drips with her own wetness," she announced. "I should not be surprised if she had already spent during the cleansing. Is that not so, slut?"

"No, no, Madam! I would not dare..."

"Quite so." Bheli passed her slender, ringed hand down over the front of her robes, tracing the plump swell of her breast, pushing the thin material taut against her flesh so that the erect crest of her nipple stood out clearly. "For if she dared to do such a disobedient thing, she knows she would be severely punished, is that not so, Amelia?"

"Y-yes. Yes, Madam."

"Feel her clitoris, Shakhira. Is it hard?"

"Hard and swollen, Madam. Unyielding as carved ebony."

"And the hood?"

Shakhira's fingers worked unforgivingly at the hard nubbin of Amelia's clitty, discovering all its secrets, demanding a response which the English girl knew she must not give. She began trembling, in that same way she had trembled when the priestess had tried to shame her by making her climax. She must not give in, must not let it happen.

"It is pushed back, Madam. The head of the clitoris is fully exposed."

"As I surmised. The girl is indeed gifted with an unusually strong degree of sensuality."

"She is a slut, Madam. A simple English slut, with no more self-control than..."

"Beware you do not accuse the girl of faults which you also share, Shakhira," said Bheli quietly. "It seems to me that you too have been endowed with a troublesome sensuality which you have not always found it easy to control."

She looked hard at Shakhira, and the slave turned away her face, not wishing her senior slave to see the anger and shame on her face.

"Yes, Madam," she replied with a deceptively submissive quietness. But she pressed very hard, very suddenly on Amelia's clitoris, and the girl yelped with painful longing, almost climaxing at that very moment.

"I seek only to do my duty."

"We all do, Shakhira," assented the senior slave. "And it is our duty to prepare this unruly girl for the temple. You may proceed with the next stage of her preparation."

Amelia stood stock-still, not so much fearing the pain or discomfort which might ensue, but the uncertainty, the awfulness of just not knowing. It had been a little like this with Miss Catherstone sometimes, she remembered, in that other, faraway life at the academy at Jainapur.

Whenever the headmistress had wished to punish her girls with particular severity, she would tell them that they were to be punished, but conceal from them the time and place and even the nature of the punishment. Sometimes it had been whole days before they had been punished, and they would spend all of the intervening time in a state of anguished uncertainty. That was exactly how Amelia felt now: like a guilty schoolgirl awaiting some unknown punishment, not knowing where, or when, or how.

"There are skills you must learn, Amelia," said Bheli. "Many skills—and so little time. On the night of the horned moon, when the brightest star sits in the crook of the crescent moon, you shall be initiated as a slave of the Temple of the Rosebud Sutra. From that time on, your life shall be dedicated to the service and protection of the sacred book. It is slavery, Amelia, but it is a blessed and honorable servitude, and your life will be filled with the joy of serving our high priestess Ishtar, blessed earthly incarnation of the Goddess.

"But Amelia, mark me well, if you have not learned both skill and self-discipline by then, your initiation will not be pleasing to the Goddess. If you fail in the pleasure tasks set for you, you will be cast out of the temple and killed."

"Mark your lessons well, Amelia," continued Bheli. "Heed all that is taught to you, and practice the sternest self-discipline in all things, for an undisciplined slave is a blasphemy and an abomination. Accept everything that is done to you, for in the heat of the most excruciating pain, there lies the source of the greatest pleasure."

Amelia was still trembling, afraid of failure, afraid of death. But most of all, afraid of the pain of her mistress's displeasure.

Shakhira closed her eyes, raised her hands as though in supplication to the Goddess, and began intoning the first of Amelia' s lessons:

"Pressing with the nails is of seven kinds, according to the forms of the marks which are produced. And these marks are called sounding, the half-moon, the circle and the line, the tiger's claw, the peacock's foot, the jump of a hare, the leaf of a blue lotus."

She opened her eyes and Amelia gazed for a few seconds into their depths: dark, deep pools of unfathomable need. What did it all mean? What lay in store?

She did not have to wait long, for Shakhira was stroking her neck and throat with her fingers—long, slender fingers with sharp scarlet talons.

"The circle and the line," she breathed, and Amelia felt a series of sharp, stabbing pains as Shakhira began pressing her fingernails into the skin, forming first a circle, then a line of half-moon-shaped impressions.

Amelia gave a little moan of protest, her body stiffening and her head jerking away, but Shakhira held her fast, hissing her displeasure at such rebellious behavior.

"If you dare move again, slut, you will feel far, far

worse than the pain of my nails in your flesh. I have the power to do that, you understand, don't you?"

"Y-yes, Madam." Amelia blinked away the unshed tears that threatened to burst from under her lids and run down her cheeks. She felt thoroughly ashamed of her own weakness.

Shakhira's hand had left her throat, but Amelia could still feel the impression of the five fingernails, like a dull, throbbing ache on the side of her neck. Shakhira stroked and massaged her shoulders and arms, and this time Amelia was not surprised when she felt the sudden sharpness of nails in flesh. She turned her head slightly and saw the circle of pink indentations in the skin, marking her with the sign of her servitude.

"It is a great honor to be marked by your mistress," said Bheli. "If you succeed in your initiation, your mistress, the high priestess Ishtar, will grace your skin with the permanent mark of her possession. This is merely a useful exercise to accustom you to the sensation and to teach you the first of the sacred skills." She sighed, a note of regret in her soft voice. "These marks and this pain, alas, soon fade…"

"The tiger's claw," ordered Shakhira, and Amelia could not suppress a sob of distress as the slave's knife-sharp fingernails jabbed and pressed into the soft flesh of her left breast. This time, the pain was almost more than she could bear, and her lips quivered with the tremendous effort of self-control. She would not, she must not cry. She must not—and yet the sob escaped from her, a tearing, echoing cry.

"Control yourself!" snapped Shakhira, pressing her nails more deeply into Amelia's breast flesh. When she took them away, Amelia looked down and saw a broad, sweeping curve of red half-moons, forming a half-ring around the areola of her breast. To her surprise, the after-sensation was not the same throbbing ache that she could still feel, albeit dimly, on her neck, but a warm, pulsing glow that seemed to spread out all over her body, rekindling the desire she had fought so hard to suppress.

Shakhira's fingers closed in a tight circle about Amelia's breast, hesitating for a brief moment before digging very hard into the soft pink flesh just beyond the margin of the nipple. Through eyes blurred by tears, Amelia saw Shakhira's lips curving into a smile, her eyes fixed on the fiendish work of her fingernails.

"The jump of a hare," whispered Shakhira, excitement making her voice husky and low. "Feel how it burns. See how it marks you for the lustful little slut you are, Amelia."

She took away her fingers and Amelia saw the tight ring of red marks around her nipple. She closed her eyes and she seemed to see them even more clearly, feeling the stabbing, burning intensity of a pain which sent shock waves right through her body, reaching even as far as the throbbing rosebud of her desire, so cruelly tormented by Shakhira and now reasserting its forlorn right to pleasure.

"That is most pleasing to the eye," concluded Bheli, admiring Shakhira's handiwork. "You have done well."

"I thank you, Madam."

"The girl has a yet imperfect command of her body, yet she strives to please. In time, I think, she will learn to deny her own pleasures and to care only for those of her mistress. Now, perhaps, I think we may proceed to a more advanced lesson in self-discipline."

Bheli snapped her fingers and the eunuch beside

her disappeared, returning moments later with a small rosewood box inlaid with ivory and mother of pearl. He opened it, and Bheli reached inside, taking out something Amelia could not see, something small and glittery as it caught the light.

"Take them, Shakhira." She handed the unseen objects to her assistant, who accepted them with a reverence that astonished Amelia, folding her fingers over them as though to keep them safe from impious eyes. "These, Amelia, are most sacred instruments of discipline. They will teach you to control your own impulses, to learn that a greater pleasure can be achieved by the satisfaction of your mistress's desires than by the fleeting gratification of your own lusts."

Shakhira opened her fingers and Amelia saw what lay in the palm of her hand. Two shiny silver clamps, elaborately engraved, with jaws as long and savage as a crocodile's, lined with a double row of sharp, glittering teeth. At first she did not understand what they were for and looked questioningly into Shakhira's face. She was smiling.

"It is about time you understood the true meaning of pain, slut," she said.

Suddenly the water swirling around her no longer felt warm and caressing. She felt a cold shiver run down her back, raising gooseflesh on her breasts and arms. She opened her mouth to speak, but no sound came out.

"You wish to speak, slut?"

Amelia shook her head soundlessly, unable to find the words to express her terror. Silver clamps. Clamps with predatory jaws that longed to snap shut onto soft and helpless flesh.

"Good. A well-trained slave never speaks unless she is given permission to do so. In fact," her smile grew broader, "a well-trained slave never makes any sound without her mistress's express permission."

She held up the clamps, one in either hand, gripped between finger and thumb. As Amelia watched, dry-mouthed, she exerted a light pressure on each of the clamps and the jaws opened a fraction, in a macabre smile of greeting.

Amelia wanted to back away, but the side wall of the sunken bath was right behind her, and the smooth metal handrail was already pressing hard between her shoulder blades. She stared, transfixed, at the silver clamps, already imagining the pain of their inexorable kiss.

"What is the matter, Amelia? Surely you are not afraid?"

Shakhira's voice was mocking, and Amelia suddenly felt very defiant and angry. She was as good as any girl here—better, even. She could withstand anything that might be done to her.

"No, Madam. I am not afraid."

She did not even convince herself, and certainly Shakhira's cynical smile did not wane.

"Do you want to leave us? Bheli and I could throw you out of the citadel into the empty mountains, naked and defenseless. Of course, if the bandits did not kill you first, you would quickly die of exposure..." She laughed humorlessly, and Amelia felt cold all over. Cold, then hot, then shivery and full of rage.

"Please, Madam," she replied, her voice steady and calm, though she felt anything but calm. "I want to stay."

"Good. Because truly, Amelia, you have no choice. Soon, you will become a slave of the *Rosebud Sutra*. And no slave may ever leave the citadel alive."

She pressed harder on the silver clamps, and their

jaws opened very wide, like the slavering maws of carnivorous beasts hungry for flesh. Amelia almost imagined that she could see little strands of saliva trailing from between the hungry teeth.

Amelia was expecting the pain and thought she was ready for it, yet the first clip snapped home with a suddenness that took her breath away. The hurt was as sharp as a dozen needles at first, then began radiating out from each central spike in long, pulsing waves that rushed through her from breast to abdomen to the soft wetness of her yearning cunt.

The second clip completed the circuit, forming an arc of delicious pain that ran from nipple to nipple, then spread out to take over the whole of her body. Her eyes closed. It was too much. Her clitoris was a burning brand between her thighs, and her nipples had turned to liquid fire, all-consuming and relentless. She could no longer cope with the welter of sensations piling in on top of her; she needed to shut out the world. But Shakhira took hold of the clamps and twisted them, stretching and squeezing her flesh until at last her eyes fluttered open and the tears began to roll down her face. Tears of pain; tears of ecstatic joy…

"Do you think she is ready?" Shakhira turned to Bheli, who was watching intently from the edge of the pool.

Bheli put her head on one side and smiled.

"She is ready."

Amelia was scarcely aware of what was happening to her as Shakhira's hands pushed her across the bath toward the steps, then pushed her up them, one by one. The only reality now was the intense overload of sensations, the tumult within her as pain met desire and mingled, defying her resolve.

She must resist. She must control these unruly impulses, which were threatening to destroy her.

Shakhira led her out of the pool and around its edge, toward the second, smaller pool, where lily petals floated on the surface of the clear green water. There were no steps down into this smaller pool, and Shakhira paused with Amelia on the edge, holding her there for a few moments, manipulating the tit-clamps to make her moan and writhe with suppressed desire.

"Jump, Amelia," she whispered.

Dizzy and disoriented with the piquancy of her torment, Amelia vaguely glimpsed the green waters in front of her through half-closed eyelids.

"No, no. I cannot," she gasped. "I cannot…Madam, please."

"Jump."

Amelia hesitated, no longer quite sure where or who she was. Should she jump as she was bidden, or should she stand fast and resist, as she was so valiantly resisting the insidious pleasure impulse between her poor tormented thighs? Which would gain her mistress's favor? Which would lead to more and greater punishments?

And which would she truly prefer: the pleasure or the pain?

She had hesitated too long, and Shakhira was not a patient woman. With enormous satisfaction, she seized Amelia by the arms and threw her headlong into the pool.

Amelia disappeared beneath the icy green waters with a scream of anguish, emerging moments later with her blonde hair straggling behind her in rat's tails and her blue eyes bright with alarm.

But not only alarm. For the icy water had a more

treacherous, more devastating effect. As it touched the silver clips and flooded the secret, yearning heart of her sex, it destroyed Amelia's resistance for one short, but crucial moment. And in that moment, she knew that the battle was lost.

Her cunt tensed and she drew in breath and held it; a moment later the sweet, irresistible spasms of orgasm overtook her, twisting and tormenting her body in the freezing water.

Bheli and Shakhira watched her in silence for a few moments.

"She spends," observed Shakhira. "See how the disobedient slut spends, in defiance of your will."

"It is as I surmised," replied Bheli, evidently unsurprised. "She has but a child's control of her body. She has a great deal to learn. It is for us to teach her what she must know."

"What do you wish me to do with her, Madam?" inquired Shakhira, secretly hoping that she would be given the postulant slave as a gift, ostensibly for the purpose of training her, but in reality as a toy to satisfy her own lusts.

"When she has recovered, have her pulled out of the water, dried, and her hurts tended to. And when you have done that..."

"Yes, Madam?"

"When you have done that, see to it that she is brought to the Chamber of Correction."

Chapter 8

Sexual congress may be compared to a quarrel, on account of the contrarieties of love and its tendency to dispute. The place of striking with passion is the body, and on the body there are certain special places. —The Rosebud Sutra

"Ensure that she is securely bound. I will not have her seeking to evade the sacred punishments which have been laid down for her correction."

Amelia blinked in the sudden darkness. How could she possibly have imagined that she might want to be brought here? The punishment chamber was dauntingly different from the brilliantly lit temple and the harem house with its sunken baths and soft couches.

The only light in here came from a few guttering oil

lamps hanging on the walls—walls that were grey and bare, and dripped with an unseen wetness. They glistened as the smoky yellow light flickered over their rough surface, picking out grotesque shadows which seemed to dance gleefully about the white-faced captive.

"You have, of course, brought this upon yourself, Amelia," Bheli told her as the two slave girls dragged her across the uneven stone floor toward the huge punishment frame.

It towered above her, formed from two rough-hewn tree trunks lashed together with rope to form an X shape. Amelia winced as her hands were seized and forced through leather straps which were buckled tight about her wrists. Next, the same was done with her ankles, and she found herself spread-eagled on the frame, her face pushed through a sort of leather hood which supported her chin but left her face free, staring ahead into the flickering gloom.

"Do you understand why you have been brought here, Amelia?" demanded Bheli.

"I…I have been disobedient, Madam." She tried to turn her head to look at Bheli, but the leather hood held her face in a vicelike grasp, forcing her to look straight in front of her. She did not know exactly what it was that she had done, but sensed that it had something to do with her weakness.

"Indeed you have, Amelia. You committed one of the greatest sins that a postulant slave may commit. You put your own pleasure before that of your mistress. In some harems, the slave girls are made to wear garments that preserve chastity and prevent self-pleasure, but the Temple of the Rosebud Sutra is served only by those who have the spiritual and physical strength to control their own sensual desires.

"In the days leading up to your initiation, you must learn a far greater measure of self-control. Your first rule must be never to pleasure yourself unless your mistress has given you permission to do so, do you understand?"

"Yes, Madam."

"And you must never allow yourself to climax unless the mistress permits it. After initiation you will be allowed to indulge in acts of gratification with other slaves of the harem—but with your mistresses you must always be submissive and deferential.

"It is for your own good that I have brought you to the Chamber of Correction, Amelia. Here you may learn the self-discipline which will not only please the high priestess, but promote your own greater pleasure."

Amelia heard a light swish, then gave a guttural cry as burning points of pain flared all over her back.

"Ten strokes to begin with, Shakhira. Then we shall see if she is more receptive to the lessons of the temple."

Amelia grasped the wooden staves beneath her hands and bit into her lower lip with such force that her mouth filled with the salty, metallic taste of her own blood. Even so, she was not ready for the second stroke, or the third: blows of a cruel cat-o'-nine-tails, each deceptively soft leather thong tipped with a little ball of lead shot that bit into the flesh, pitting it and making the blood ooze from the broken skin.

"Madam...," she gasped, desperate for the pain to stop.

"An extra five strokes, Shakhira." Bheli's voice was still soft and calm. "You see, Amelia, you only make things worse for yourself by being disobedient. If you keep silent, you will suffer less."

Amelia's white, naked body twisted in its bonds, her wrists and ankles jerking convulsively in an instinctive attempt to escape from this place of torment. Instinctive, but futile. There could be no possibility of escape from the punishment chamber.

Little by little, Amelia was coming to recognize the treacherous warmth which had always redeemed the punishments Miss Catherstone had given her. It started quietly, almost imperceptibly, a gentle undercurrent to the severity of the sharp, cutting pains in her back. It was as though, slowly but surely, the pain was dimming, like a gas lamp turned down very low, until at last she scarcely noticed the cat lashing down on her back, lost in her private dream world of burgeoning excitement.

With difficulty, she kept silent. She dared not betray the excitement she felt, the thrill that ran through her as the ache of lust joined with the kindling warmth in her belly.

"The pain is exciting her, Madam," announced Shakhira, with contempt.

"Good," replied Bheli. "It is excellent that she is responsive to the ancient ways of pleasure. But she must learn to control her arousal. Can you control it, Amelia?"

Amelia did not reply. Her eyes were tightly shut and she was trying not to think of the awful burning in her clitoris. She was terrified that at any moment something might touch her, stroke her, strike her—and the contact would trigger her orgasm. It felt so very close.

"Answer me, Amelia." Bheli took hold of Amelia's nipples, pulled them very hard, and then twisted them. Amelia yelped with the pain.

"I will try, Madam."

"Fetch the beads." Bheli signaled to one of the saffron-robed priestesses, and she melted away into the shadows. "Let us see if your determination can withstand these pretty little toys."

The priestess reappeared, carrying something on a velvet cushion, which she held out to Bheli. Amelia wished she could see what Bheli was picking up from the cushion, but it was just beyond her line of sight. Bheli must have seen her trying to sneak a look, because she gave a little dry laugh and walked round to the front of the punishment frame. She held her hands out, showing Amelia her prize.

"See, child. Here is the instrument of pleasure which I promised you. Is it not beautiful?"

"What…?" Amelia hadn't the faintest idea what the thing could be. It was black and semi-shiny, as though made of latex, and seemed to consist of six beads, the size of large marbles, strung on some sort of long, rubbery string. Was it for striking? For caressing? Or for some other purpose which Amelia, in her innocence, could not divine?

Bheli laughed again.

"You want to know what it is? You will know very soon." She turned and beckoned to Shakhira. "Here—take it, use it well." Turning back to Amelia, she smiled, stretching out a hand and pressing it quite hard against Amelia's belly, just above the pubic bone. Amelia winced and gave a little groan. "Ah, your bladder is full, as I knew it would be."

"Please, Madam. May I…?" She wished fervently that she had not accepted the long, cold drink of sweet cordial that she had been offered in the harem.

"No, Amelia. You may not. I told you when you came here—the Chamber of Correction is a place for instilling good discipline. And the pretty toy which Shakhira is about to use upon your body is another aid to self-control."

Shakhira was now directly behind Amelia, and she could not see anything of what she was doing. But she quickly began to divine Shakhira's purpose, for her hands were grabbing hold of her buttocks and opening them up, just as she had done when they were together in the warm, scented bath. Her ass was still red-raw from the violent scrubbing Shakhira had given it with the loofah, and she tried to resist, but to no avail.

"It pains her," observed Bheli.

"So much the better," retorted Shakhira.

"Use a little of the salve," Bheli directed her. "The purpose is to train and discipline her, not to cause gratuitous pain."

With evident reluctance, Shakhira rubbed a cooling salve into the crease between Amelia's buttocks. It felt soothing and for a moment Amelia almost forgot her fears. Even her raw, stinging back seemed to hurt less whilst Shakhira's fingers were smoothing cool ointment over her puckered nether mouth, and the ache from her full bladder felt duller, somehow less oppressive.

"She is ready now," decided Bheli.

The sudden discomfort which followed half maddened Amelia, and her backside twitched in frantic protest as the first of the round black beads slipped through the tight sphincter of her anus.

"Oh, oh, *oh!*" she squealed, and was rewarded with a second, harder thrust which took the second and third beads into the interior of her ass.

"If you struggle, it will be the worse for you," Bheli reminded her. "Acceptance is release. Obedience is the key to pleasure."

Amelia submitted tearfully to the rest of the black rubber beads. Despite the thick layer of slippery salve which Shakhira had spread between her buttocks, it hurt madly as each one pressed its way through the tightly clenched muscles of her ass and disappeared inside. At last they were all inside her, and she could feel the long rubber string hanging down between her thighs, swinging heavily from side to side as she twitched and swayed her tormented backside.

The beads in her ass felt huge, not like marbles but something much bigger, more intrusive. They were stretching the delicate walls of her rectum and, worse: They were moving around inside her, causing the most alarming tumult of sensations. From time to time they pressed against the heavy, water-filled balloon of her bladder, and she felt an overwhelming urge to relieve herself.

"Oh please, Madam. Please, I really need to…"

"No, Amelia. You will wait. You will wait until I give you permission. Do you understand?"

"Yes, Madam."

It was all very well saying that she understood. That was the easy part. It was so much more difficult to be what she pretended to be—strong, resilient, controlled.

"Now apply the clips. Let us see how well she performs this time."

Shakhira obeyed with a relish which chilled Amelia's blood. The crocodile jaws opened wide, then sprang shut on her nipples as Shakhira let them go. This time, Amelia was ready for the pain and at first she rode it out, breathing deeply and rising above the pulsing waves of discomfort.

But she had not reckoned with Shakhira's determination to humiliate her.

"Take this inside your yoni and hold it there until you are given permission to release it," snapped Shakhira, and Amelia felt something knobby and hard push its way up into her vagina. It was impossibly huge, impossibly heavy—much too heavy to hold in her cunt with her legs splayed wide apart—but she knew that she must.

Shakhira took her hand from the dildo and suddenly the full weight of it was inside Amelia's pussy, slipping very slowly downward, defying all her efforts to keep it inside her. With all her strength she clenched her cunt muscles and the dildo slid back into the heart of her, but now she was sweating with the effort and the discomfort—the discomfort which threatened so persuasively to become the onset of pleasure.

"You may now continue the punishment," announced Bheli. "You may stimulate her further."

More punishment! What more could they do to her, thought Amelia as she strained to keep the dildo in her cunt. Its knobby tip was pressing against her cervix, which in turn seemed to push against the heaviness of her full bladder. And all the time the black beads twisted and coiled on their rubber string, pushing out the walls of her rectum, making her fearful of losing all control of herself.

But of all the things that she might do, she must not lose control.

When Shakhira's fingers moved with terrifying accuracy to the exposed bud of her clitoris, Amelia stared defeat full in the face. Shakhira's fingers were so knowing, her nails so long and sharp as they grazed over and over the hard pink head, smoothing the slipperiness over it, moving away and then sliding quickly back to renew the assault. It was agony. Beautiful, exquisite, blissful agony.

"Good. Yes, that is really quite good." Bheli's voice sounded smooth as cream, patronizing and full of smug self-satisfaction. "Our little English filly is learning. But she must yet learn more. Do it to her harder."

Shakhira needed no prompting. Pinching Amelia's clitoris between her unforgiving fingers, she began pulling and twisting the long, hard stalk with a fierce eagerness which made Amelia gasp and sob for the pain and delight of it. At the base of her belly, her bladder sloshed and contracted, the muscles aching for release. Amelia gave a little moan of distress, knowing that she could not hold out much longer. And there was worse to come, for as she squeezed her vaginal muscles to hold in the heavy dildo, she drew the black rubber beads further inside her, producing the most terrifyingly pleasurable sensations.

"Harder," commanded Bheli, her voice a distant echo through the red mist of Amelia's tortured desire.

Shakhira gave Amelia's clitoris a long, hard squeeze, and suddenly the whole world seemed to stop on its axis. All was silence, save for the regular thud, thud of her own heartbeat, echoing the silent pulse of her tormented clitty.

Her body tensed, every nerve ending shrieking for relief as her muscles contracted, holding her whole body in suspense for an endless moment until the pleasure came crashing down upon her, unstoppable and so, so cruel.

"Oh, oh, oh..." Amelia heard her own voice but it sounded far away, as though it were someone else's: a faint, rhythmic moan of infinite distress.

She hardly noticed the pain of the sharp-jawed clips on her bruised and reddened breasts or the sting of her half-flayed asscheeks. All she knew was the incredible pleasure as her sex muscles clenched in the first huge spasm and then released their tension for a fleeting instant, letting down a flood tide of clear, sweet liquid which made the inside of her sex as slippery as an ice rink.

The dildo, now beautifully lubricated by this gush of juice, defied all Amelia's attempts to hold it inside her; with a soft sucking noise, it disengaged itself from her flesh, sliding slowly down until it freed itself from her body and fell to the bare stone floor.

And her humiliation was not yet complete—as the dildo slipped out of her, relaxing the pressure on her cervix, Amelia felt her bladder give a convulsive twitch. A moment later she felt the most exquisite mingling of shame and elation, as a great flood of fragrant liquid gushed out of her in hot spurts, dripping down the inside of her thighs and spattering the floor between her widely outspread thighs.

Somewhere in the distance a woman's voice was laughing—shrill, high peals that mocked and derided Amelia's distress—but she cared for nothing but the never-ending pleasure coursing and pulsing through her helpless body.

She did not see Shakhira's hands taking hold of the black rubber string that hung from her tightly puckered ass. She pulled on it so firmly that Amelia had no power to resist. All she knew was that the pleasure suddenly became ecstasy, great clenching spasms of sun-bright ecstasy as one by one the fat rubber beads emerged slowly from her ass.

"The girl has a pitiably small amount of self-control," sniffed Shakhira—ostensibly contemptuous, but concealing a pang of unsatisfied lust in her bittersweet tones. She had wanted to enjoy this postulant slave more extensively, but it seemed that Bheli had decided to keep her all to herself. How sweet it would feel to have the English girl's pouting pink lips on her sex-bud, sucking and biting her to orgasm whilst she beat the girl with the lead-tipped cat.

"She has done well enough for a novice," replied Bheli, her voice syrupy with satisfied desire.

Shakhira knew exactly what had happened, knew how it excited Bheli to observe the punishment of the youngest and tenderest slaves. Bheli's sensual powers were so highly developed that she had only to press her thighs together to make herself come. Shakhira did not doubt that Bheli was even now enjoying the afterglow of orgasm, and a pang of envious anger ate away at her heart. Why did Bheli not desire her, as she desired Bheli? Why did Bheli prefer the company of an untrained, artless English bitch to the skilled services of Shakhira's experienced mouth and fingers?

"What do you wish me to do with her now?" inquired Shakhira, still vaguely hoping for a chance to enjoy the girl alone, exacting from her tender young body a sweet vengeance for Bheli's cold-hearted indifference toward her.

"Cut her down and bring her back to the harem house," replied Bheli. "She has much to learn, and her training has only just begun."

The eunuch yawned, stretched his hairless, silken body, and popped another juicy grape into the perfectly painted O of his scarlet lips. Rolling over onto his belly, he adjusted his yellow silk robe so that it fell open at the side, exposing one perfect limb from ankle to thigh.

Life was good and he so loved to watch. Simply

adored to feast his girlish eyes on his beautiful sisters at worship and play, savouring each vicarious thrill as they took their pleasure from each other's bodies. He wished so much that he too was a slave girl and not an in-between creature fated never to feel the caress of his sisters' tongues on the scented inner folds of a coral pink sex.

He had imagined so often how it must feel to have that sacred touch that only a woman could experience. Here, in the temple harem, it was his sole duty to give his sisters pleasure, and he had learned every flick of the tongue, every long, smooth caress which would bring the slave girls to ecstasy.

He could not share their physical ecstasy, and yet after all this time he could almost believe that he felt everything they felt, shivering and moaning as his tongue darted into the soft, wet heart of a girl's pussy, as though he could feel it darting into his own. Knowing their bodies so well made him feel he possessed a certain power over them, and that in turn gave him great pleasure, but better even than that was the pleasure of watching.

Propping himself up on his elbows, he peeped around the edge of the gauzy silver curtain. The scene beyond was a diverting one, and he swallowed hard, his mouth filling with saliva as his hunger and thirst were stimulated.

The slave girl Premila was sitting on a pile of crimson cushions, frigging herself—not solely for her own pleasure, but for the amusement of the senior slave Bheli and the torment of the little English girl, Amelia Courtnay.

The eunuch grinned to himself as he pressed the grape against his hard palate and burst it, enjoying the sensation of the semi-sweet juice trickling down his throat. He wondered if Amelia Courtnay's juices tasted half as delicious, and guessed that they must, for Bheli could not keep her eyes off the girl, even though it was Premila who was doing all the frigging.

Premila was one of the adorably sweet submissives whom Bheli had trained to serve in the bedchamber of the high priestess Ishtar. But Ishtar had many such slaves, and it was, alas, rare that one should be called frequently to serve in her bed or in the Temple of the Rosebud Sutra.

And so the slaves must learn to satisfy their own and each other's lusts. The rules were simple: Once they had passed their initiation, they were free to accept pleasure from their own or another's touch, but whenever in the presence of a senior slave, priestess, or the high priestess herself, they must at once revert to the submissive role which they had been taught.

It was permitted that they should lighten the tedium of their lives in the harem with a little pleasure, but they must always remember that their own pleasure came a very poor second to that of their superiors, and that the greatest pleasure they could ever experience was in pleasuring their mistresses. That was one of the central teachings of the *Rosebud Sutra*, to whose secrets they were gradually admitted as they grew in knowledge and skill.

Premila had assumed her role of temple slave easily and instinctively. Brought up from infancy to serve the pleasure of her five older sisters, she had readily accepted the new dominion of the high priestess, the Goddess in human form. The eunuch knew that the girl was one of Bheli's special favorites, for she had the ability to withstand even the most intensive punishment without complaint, and her tongue was said to be the sweetest instrument of torture in all of the high priestess's twelve harem houses.

He laughed silently to himself as he watched, for the English girl was clearly in the grip of a tumult of emotions. Naked save for a rather exquisite slave collar of jewelled leather, Amelia was being forced to watch Premila's self-pleasure without giving in to her own lust, for Amelia was a mere postulant, one who must undergo a thousand torments and trials before she would be deemed worthy of her initiation to the temple. And even then, what if she should fail...?

"Watch Premila," Bheli commanded her, jerking hard on the chain which led from the jewelled collar to her gloved hand. "You will perhaps learn something of value."

With the utmost reluctance Amelia forced herself to look at Premila, watching the ringed fingers of her left hand spreading the shaven lips of her pussy whilst her right index finger explored the expanse of bright pink folded flesh within.

Premila's clitoris was a revelation to Amelia, and her eyes widened in a sort of terrified ecstasy as she glimpsed the long, reddish-pink stalk which emerged, glossy and swollen, from underneath Premila's massaging finger. Premila's clitty was not a pert pink rosebud like Amelia's, nor yet a fat, springy mound like the merchant Indhira's. This was a long—impossibly long—stalk, a good inch long, hard and flexible, and drawn out even further by the heavy gold ring which passed right through its bulbous head.

"It is a pretty jewel, is it not, Amelia?" Bheli cast Amelia a sidelong glance.

"Yes, Madam."

"Mark it well, slut. It is the mark and badge of complete submission. Perhaps, if you learn better manners, you will one day earn that badge. The badge of your mistress's possession."

Amelia felt quite dizzy with excitement as she watched Premila's fingers fluttering and caressing about the head of her clitty. Could that really be a clitoris? And how could a woman bear to have such a thing piercing the tip of her most intimate, most sensitive place of all? Amelia rubbed her thighs together surreptitiously, trying to assuage the tingling sensation that had sprung up in her pussy as in her mind she lived the experience of the needle passing through her clitty flesh, the sudden sharp pain, the pain-mingled bliss as the ring passed through the flesh and at last she wore the token of her mistress's sacred ownership.

If Amelia thought that her sly movements had gone unnoticed, she was very much mistaken. Bheli missed nothing. She had been watching Amelia more closely even than Premila, and retribution was swift and uncompromising.

"Bitch! Did I not tell you that self-pleasure was forbidden?"

"B-but, Madam, I wasn't. I was only..."

Bheli pulled the neck chain very tight, and Amelia's hands shot up to the collar, clutching and scrabbling at it in an attempt to slacken its choking grip on her throat.

"Do not lie to me, slut! I saw you pressing your thighs together, trying to give yourself pleasure. Your defiance is unbelievable—it is almost as if you are deliberately courting my displeasure."

Amelia did not reply. Deep in her heart, she could not help wondering if what Bheli had said was true. There was something shamefully thrilling about the novel punishments which Bheli dreamed up to discipline her for her omissions and transgressions. Perhaps more thrilling even than a reward…

"On your knees, slut." Bheli pulled the chain tighter still, forcing Amelia to slump to the ground until she was on her knees, looking up at her cruel but beautiful mistress. "Now, Premila: Frig yourself harder, my sweet, for I want our little English filly to know the true meaning of yearning."

Amelia wanted to close her eyes, turn her head away—anything to avoid the pain of watching this beautiful girl rubbing herself to unimaginable pleasure. But Bheli's eyes were on her, her gaze burning into her, demanding her obedience. She looked straight ahead of her, the collar a little slacker now but the chain wrapped about Bheli's hand in readiness for a more extreme punishment.

"There, see how beautifully she frigs herself, Amelia." Bheli's voice was once again smooth and syrupy, as though she were deriving some vicarious sexual pleasure from observing this pretty harem tableau.

Amelia could hardly fail to see. Premila's fingers were working to such good effect that her cunt was positively oozing honeydew. Even as she watched, it seemed to well up and overflow, like the gush of tears from a brimming eye, spilling over her fingers, making them glossy and slippery like polished glass.

"Such a pity that you too cannot share that pleasure, is it not?" Bheli was taunting her almost as Shakhira had, finding the very weakest point in her armory and insistently returning to it. "You'd like that, wouldn't you, slut? You'd like to be running your fingers over your own pussy."

"I…yes, Madam. I would."

"Or would you prefer to be licking out my dear sweet slave Premila? She has a very sweet cunt—sweet and spicy, like cinnamon and honey mingled together. I'll wager you'd love to take that golden ring between your lips and tease her to her crisis."

"Madam. Oh, Madam, please…"

Bheli gave a little chuckle, filled with the warmth of sexual satisfaction.

"Such a pity. But you see, Amelia, whilst you are a humble novice in this training school, you may only have pleasure when I give you permission to do so. And I do not give you permission, Amelia. Who knows how long it will be before I give you that permission?"

It was a deliberate taunt; a challenge to Amelia to resist the burgeoning desire within her. But even there, even kneeling on the cold marble floor beside her tormentor, Amelia could not resist trying to give herself a little pleasure. Her knees shifted slightly on the marble tiles, and as she did so her pussy-lips parted, opening to allow currents of cool air to waft over the erect bud of her clitoris.

It was the gentlest, the slightest of caresses, yet to her pleasure-starved clitty it felt like electricity. She might have succeeded in concealing her excitement but for the little trembling sigh which escaped her lips.

"Disobedient. Little. Slut."

The words exploded softly from her lips, each punctuated with a jerk of the slave chain which made Amelia dizzy and light-headed.

"It is no use pretending, Amelia. You cannot conceal anything from me. You are a silly, headstrong little filly and you think in your foolish innocence that you can deceive me.

"But I am wise in ways you will never understand,

Amelia. And what is more, I am doing all of this for your well-being. Can you not understand that? Obedience will be your salvation and your joy; disobedience will be your destruction."

"I am sorry, Madam. I will not do it again."

"Then crawl for me, like the hot little mare you are," Bheli instructed her.

Hastily Amelia complied, dropping to hands and knees on the cold, implacable white marble. Lifting her head, she saw Premila smile beatifically and heard her give the quietest, most whispering of sighs as she came, her inner sex-lips gaping open like the heart of an exotic flower unfolding its petals to the sun.

She tried to close her eyes to escape the dreadful longing that washed over her as she watched Premila's ecstasy, but again Bheli pulled on the chain.

"See how she pleasures herself, Amelia. She has magic in her fingers and tongue—magic which can prolong her crisis for many long moments. Perhaps, when you are a slave of the temple, you too will have an opportunity to learn some of her secrets."

"Yes, Madam," sighed Amelia, longing throbbing in the heart of her.

Bheli picked up one of the flexible punishment switches from a holder on the wall.

"Now crawl for me, bitch," Bheli commanded her. "Two circuits of the sunken pool, on your hands and knees."

Amelia began her journey around the edge of the sunken pool. Its rose-tinted depths looked so warm and inviting, like a lover's embrace, but Bheli was not offering her warmth or sensual gratification—only the pleasure of knowing that she was at last obeying her mistress's commands to the letter.

To her dismay, she found that the tiles near to the edge of the pool, habitually strewn with sweetly scented flowers, concealed a more sinister secret. It was not until a dozen pinpricks of pain shot through her bare knees that she realized that beneath the layer of pink and white petals lay a second layer—of thin branches and twigs cut from a thornbush.

Amelia winced and hesitated for a moment, unsure where to move to avoid the thorns and ease the pain in her knees. She lifted her right hand, and saw tiny beads of red where the thorns had scratched through the surface of the skin.

"Something ails you, Amelia?" demanded Bheli, her voice soft yet curiously menacing.

"Please, Madam—there are thorns."

"Of course there are thorns, Amelia. If there were no thorns, the exercise would be far too easy and painless, even for you. Proceed." She tightened the chain and the collar bit into Amelia's throat.

"But, Madam..."

"I said, proceed."

The switch cut through the air with a familiar swishing noise and struck Amelia full on the rump. Her backside leapt up but she made no sound save the rush of an indrawn breath.

"Good. Now proceed."

Amelia set off hesitantly across the floor, doing her best to pick her way through the thorn-strewn flowers. It was like crossing a minefield—sometimes her knees and hands would meet only flowers, at other times they were cruelly pierced by thorns. Whenever she hesitated, the switch would come down on her backside as Miss Catherstone's cane had once done, efficiently and with cruel precision.

She had almost completed the first circuit when there was a tremendous commotion in the harem, and even Bheli stopped, reining in her headstrong charge and turning around to see what was happening.

Lying on his belly on the carved wooden couch, the eunuch peeped through the gap in the silver curtain and his scarlet lips curved into the prettiest, most mischievous smile.

There, in the doorway to the harem, flanked by two of the citadel's fiercest warrior women, stood a disheveled captive. The crop-haired figure was dressed European-style, in a man's soft calfskin riding breeches and knee-length boots, a torn white linen shirt and broad leather belt.

"Get your hands off me! I demand it..."

But the guards held their captive securely. Intrigued, Bheli dropped Amelia's chain and walked across to inspect the new arrival.

"Here," she said softly, "you may demand nothing. If you are very fortunate indeed, the high priestess may perhaps decide not to kill you." She ran questing fingers over the soft leather of her captive's riding breeches.

"Get off me, damn you!"

Daring for the first time to lift her head, Amelia turned her gaze on the captive. There was something in that voice, something she recognized. As her eyes met the captive's, recognition flashed between them, and a name escaped from Amelia's lips. It couldn't be—but it was.

It was Dorothea Strong.

Chapter 9

A woman should have recourse to various means to excite her lover's passion. At the commencement she should rub her yoni with her hand or thigh and not begin to enjoy her until she becomes excited. —The Rosebud Sutra

Locked in a cell in the harem house, Amelia and Dorothea Strong spent the long night together, awaiting the dawn when the high priestess would pronounce Dorothea's future.

"Tell me again about the temple," Dorothea whispered to her in the darkness. Amelia could not help thinking how handsome she looked in the low gleam of starlight which filtered into the cell through the small, high window. "Tell me about the *Rosebud Sutra*."

Amelia shrank from Dorothea's insistence, almost too afraid to speak, let alone tell her about the *Rosebud Sutra*. Outside the door of their cell slumbered two guards, light sleepers both. If they suspected for a moment that Amelia was revealing the secrets of the temple to an outsider, Bheli's punishment of her would be swift and severe.

"No, please, Dorothea, tell me why you came here. You haven't even explained that to me yet," protested Amelia, still recovering from the shock of seeing Dorothea for the first time since they had parted company in such disastrous circumstances. "I thought you were dead..."

Dorothea laughed, putting her strong arm around Amelia's shoulders. It was chilly in the cell and they were both naked but, with Dorothea cuddled up very close, Amelia began to feel a reassuring warmth oozing back into her cold limbs and belly.

"It would take more than that to kill me, little one," she smiled. She put Amelia's fingers to her upper arm. "Do you feel that?"

Amelia probed the slight depression in the skin.

"Dorothea—your arm!"

"All is well, little one, have no fear. I was stupid enough to stop one of their bullets, but it was just a flesh wound. A couple of weeks and I was fully recovered, and here I am, just as I promised I would be."

"You came here just to find me and rescue me?" Amelia's voice was slow and cautious, as though she couldn't quite believe that this could be true.

"Of course I did!" Dorothea held her more tightly. "I've been travelling for days and days, trying to track you down. It was no mean feat, I can tell you. And then, this afternoon, when I finally came upon the citadel, I was so exhausted that I became foolhardy. That is when those amazonian guards caught up with me, damn them. And now we are imprisoned in this hole together, like rats in a trap."

"I'm glad that you came, Dorothea. But the danger. You really don't understand..."

"I have faced far worse than this," retorted Dorothea. "And what is more, I shall have us both out of here in no time, don't you worry. But now that I am here..."

"Yes, Dorothea?"

Dorothea planted a little kiss on the nape of Amelia's neck, then ran her lips down over her shoulder and round to the side of her breast, just under the arm. She seemed to know all the sensitive places, all the ways to awaken Amelia's latent desire. Her gentleness flooded Amelia with warmth after being so long starved of caresses.

"Since I am here, you might as well tell me about the temple and the *Rosebud Sutra.*"

"It is dangerous, Dorothea. Terribly dangerous."

"So you keep telling me." Dorothea curled the tip of her tongue about Amelia's nipple and savoured the ripples of delight which ran through the young girl's body. "But I am a very determined and very experienced woman, Amelia. I am not accustomed to letting anything—or anyone—prevent me from accomplishing my desires."

"Why do you want to see the *Rosebud Sutra*?" demanded Amelia, anxious and suspicious in spite of Dorothea's reassuring kisses. "I don't understand."

"Why, sweet creature, I do not simply want to see it. I want to possess it! I fully intend to take it back to England for the greater glory of Queen Victoria and the Empire."

"No!" Horrified, Amelia tried to draw away, but was prevented by Dorothea's encircling arm. "You cannot do that!"

"Listen, sweet child." Dorothea assumed her softest, most conciliatory tone. "These people, these women—they are no better than savages. Have they not treated you with a brutal cruelty?

"Do not misinterpret my words, Amelia, for truly I love India and respect its wealth of ancient sensual knowledge. But in the hands of these barbarous, secretive women, that knowledge is hidden away. I want to take it back to England so that the secrets of the *Rosebud Sutra* may be taught to all women. Think of that, Amelia—all women released from servitude by the ancient love lore of the *Rosebud Sutra!*"

"The penalty for even looking at the *Sutra* without permission is death," protested Amelia. "That much has been made abundantly clear. And they say that anyone who tries to steal it away will suffer a terrible fate, an agonizing death..."

Dorothea scoffed. "An ancient myth, my sweet, that is all. A myth dreamed up to frighten anyone who covets the *Sutra*. But I am not afraid, Amelia. I am not afraid to do my duty for Queen and country." She drew the young English girl toward her and pressed her lips on Amelia's. To her immense satisfaction, she felt Amelia's warm, scented breath escape in a long, shuddering sigh of sensual release.

The girl was far too innocent to resist her for long. "Now come, sweet girl, tell me of the *Rosebud Sutra*."

"It is kept in the temple, that is all I know," replied Amelia reluctantly. "It's in a casket of solid gold and rubies, guarded by gold statuettes of the Goddess Akhtar and the demons who serve her—but the book is locked away from prying eyes, and is only brought out from the temple on the holiest days. Even then, it is guarded, and only the chosen few may look upon its pages. Please, Dorothea—think again."

"I will find it, Amelia," replied Dorothea. "I will find it and I will take it from this place. But now..." She pressed her hard-tipped breasts against Amelia's plump young buds. "Let us comfort each other and lighten the darkness of this cold night."

Amelia could not fight the desire within her, although she felt a terrible ache of guilt. Would Bheli know if she gave into her powerful carnal impulses now with Dorothea Strong? Had she locked them together, in this cell, expressly to test her resolve, so that when she transgressed, she could be punished with greater severity?

It was all so confusing, and here, in the velvet darkness with Dorothea naked beside her, to give and receive pleasure seemed the most natural thing in the world. They embraced again and this time Amelia gave in to instinct, allowing her hands to roam over Dorothea's body.

This was the first time she had ever seen and felt Dorothea's nakedness. Back in the hills above Jainapur, she had only glimpsed the bounty of Dorothea's body. Here, in the gloomy half-light of the cell, she was discovering Dorothea's unique beauty as much by touch as by sight.

As they embraced, Dorothea mused over the day's events. Being caught by the guards had been dashed bad luck, and then to be dragged unceremoniously in front of some supercilious woman who was no more than a jumped-up slave...

To Dorothea's outrage, she had been stripped and

bathed, as Amelia had been, and then all her body hair was shaved off. The slaves of the temple harem had been most entertained and perhaps even a little shocked by what they had discovered beneath the glossy black triangle of Dorothea's pubic hair.

Amelia was even now discovering it for herself.

"What...?"

"Touch it, my sweet. It won't bite."

Wonderingly and half-afraid, Amelia ran her fingers over the smooth, shaven mound of Dorothea's pubis. Her sensitive finger tips discovered one, two, no many little raised bumps, forming a pattern on the skin. She tried tracing it in its entirety, following the lines and whorls of raised skin. It seemed to be an elaborate abstract, a pattern of great artistry and complexity.

"What—what is it?"

"It is African tribal art," replied Amelia. "Body-art, or body-cutting, as they call it. In the Dark Continent it is a great honour to have one's skin decorated in this way."

"How do they do it? You said body-cutting?"

Dorothea chuckled.

"Yes, child, I confess there was a certain pain in the piercing of the flesh, but some might say that the pain was a pleasure in itself. Besides, my dear Amelia, the pain was no more than a trial to be endured."

"But why?"

"Because, my dear, if I had not consented to undergo this ritual, the women of the tribe would never have permitted me to enter the sacred places where their secrets were kept."

"Tell me. Tell me about it." Amelia's palm smoothed over the raised skin, imagining the knife, the blood, the curious pleasure in the pride Dorothea must have felt at enduring this sacred ritual. "I should like to know what happened."

"Well," began Dorothea, "it was about three years ago, as I recall. I had been commissioned by the Royal Archaeological Society to travel to West Africa and study the sexual and initiation rites of the tribes. Whilst there, I heard rumours of the existence of a tribe of women; women who never met with men, and who perpetuated their tribe's existence by taking young women from neighboring villages and initiating them into their ways, as though they were their daughters. I determined at once to find these women, and I set out for the heart of the forest.

"Alas, after many long days of journeying through the forest, I was exhausted and almost ready to give up my quest. My bearers had left me, and I was utterly alone, sustained only by my dreams. At the moment when I had almost given up hope, I saw it—the heap of crumbling stones that might once have been the wall of some magnificent building, now half obscured by a thick growth of vines and creepers.

"I pushed on a little further, and the foliage around me began to grow less impenetrable. I passed many more fragments of stone walls, the broken remains of statues and hummocks of tangled leaves and branches marking the site of what might once have been a house or a temple. Intrigued, I looked around me. Surely these were the ruins of some ancient city, lost for centuries in this unknown and uncharted jungle land.

"As I stood there, gazing around the clearing, I heard a rustling sound and as I turned I saw two women emerging from the hanging curtain of creepers and tree branches. Very graceful and well-formed, they must, by my judgment, have stood almost six feet tall, and their moist skin glistened in the greenish light like polished jet.

"They spoke to me, but I understood nothing of their language. I am fluent in many African dialects, but this was like nothing I had heard before—almost classical in its intonation, yet melodious and rhythmic as a tribal chant. But they signalled to me and I followed them, grateful at last to have met with human company and filled with the excitement of knowing that I had at last reached the object of my quest.

"The women's village was some distance from the ruins of the old city, and consisted of the traditional circle of mud-and-grass huts. But there was something very remarkable indeed about this particular village, for there, at the very center of the circle, stood a magnificent statue, close on twenty feet high—a statue which bore the unmistakable features of the goddess Venus.

"Before it lay one of the prettiest maidens I had ever seen, thighs outspread and arms crossed on her chest. I saw that one of the tribal elders was licking eagerly at her cunt, and was given to understand—by signs—that this girl had been stolen away from another village and was now being initiated into the tribe.

"The sight was such a stimulating one that I began to feel quite aroused. Seldom had I seen such a delicious assemblage of womanhood: graceful, naked women gathering about me, plucking at my clothing, marvelling at the pallor of my skin. Their touch awakened my sensual need, reminded me that it was many days since I had enjoyed the touch of a woman's tongue upon my clitoris.

"The tallest woman stepped forward, naked save for a white sash worn toga-style in a drape from shoulder to waist, exposing the heavy, fleshy gourd of her right breast. On her oiled black hair she wore a circlet of gold set with large green stones which, I realized with a start, must assuredly be fine emeralds.

"She raised her hand in a clenched fist and drew it across her breast in salute.

"'*Salve.*'

"I could scarcely believe my ears! This woman was addressing me in Latin! Suddenly I began to understand. This village must be the descendant of some enclave of Roman occupation. Over the centuries the city had crumbled away into the encroaching jungle, but the women who lived here had carried on the beliefs and traditions of those who had come before them. Evidently the common language of everyday life was now a curious blend of Latin and the local patois, but the elders of the tribe had preserved the purity of the Roman language.

"'*Salve,*' I replied, copying her salute. And we began to talk—I, for my part, grateful for the classical education which had taught me the skill of conversing in this long-dead language.

"The woman—whose name was Florinda—clearly believed me to be some descendant of Roman stock, and because of this I was treated with the utmost respect. Together we watched the young girl's initiation into the tribal family, and it was explained to me that, in order to be admitted into the secrets of the tribe, the girl must first undergo a number of ordeals.

"The first were scarcely ordeals at all, for the girl was submitted to the most delightful trials of pleasure. I watched entranced as one of the tribal elders licked the inner lips of the girl's maiden cunt, running her tongue tip along the sides of her clitoris, as though savoring the sweet and spicy taste of the lubricating juice which trickled out of her sex, making it glisten like a ruby-fleshed fruit.

"As the girl climaxed, her spendings were captured in a small wooden bowl, and the women of the tribe made merry, celebrating the girl's admission to womanhood. The tribal elder lifted the dish above her head for all to see, then carried it across to the statue, laying it upon the stone plinth with a prayer of supplication to the goddess of love.

"The last ordeal was one of endurance, and I confess that I felt fear as I saw the tip of the dagger pierce the flesh of the young girl's shaven pubic mound. I saw her body tense, her hands clench tight, but she refused to make any sound despite the tears sparkling on her eyelashes.

"'When the scars heal she will be a worthy member of the tribe,' Florinda told me. 'She will wear her scars with pride, as though they were costly jewels. And now that she has passed the initiation rite, she will be permitted to learn the secrets of our tribe...'

"I begged Florinda to let me, too, discover these secrets. I burned to know all that these beautiful, noble women knew. I pleaded, but she refused to be moved.

"'Only an initiate may learn of the holy places,' she replied. 'Only by becoming an initiate yourself may you hope to share our knowledge.'

"There could be no question of refusing. Florinda had offered me a chance, and I took it joyfully. Her handmaidens stripped me and shaved my pubis with a blade of sharpened bone, and I prepared for my initiation the very next day."

Amelia listened in round-eyed fascination.

"Were you not afraid?"

"Of course I was afraid. But fear is no reason to deny

oneself the chance of greater knowledge." She took Amelia's hand and guided it back to her pubis. Amelia stroked it, marvelling at the thought that such a delicate pattern could be the result of such cruel torment. The little pattern of scars seemed to hold a new meaning for her now. "I was initiated the following day, and a week later, when my scars were healed, I was shown the path to the secret holy places."

"Tell me about them," breathed Amelia, warming to the tale. Dorothea was so brave, so indomitable. Perhaps she, Amelia Courtnay, had been foolish to be so timorous. Perhaps Dorothea was right after all, and things really would work out for the best in the end.

"Deep in the jungle, almost hidden by the overgrown foliage, lay a building untouched by the passage of years—a perfect Roman temple to the goddess Venus. Inside, within the cool darkness of the inner sanctum, stood an erotic statuette of the goddess. A statuette of solid gold, with an emerald set between her cunt-lips, signifying the pleasure-bud of her clitoris. I saw immediately why the tribeswomen guarded it so jealously, serving it with complete devotion.

"It was the most beautiful thing I had ever seen, Amelia. As soon as I saw it, I knew that I must have it."

Amelia drew away, astonished and suddenly alarmed. "You stole it from them?"

Dorothea shrugged dismissively.

"I tried to. But I was almost captured in the attempt. I was lucky to escape with my life." She sighed. "It was such a beautiful statuette. Bringing such a thing to London would have secured my reputation as England's foremost archaeologist. Perhaps, one day, I shall return to claim my prize."

Amelia fell silent for a few moments, then spoke.

"And now you want to steal away the *Rosebud Sutra?*"

"I have explained, Amelia; it will not be stealing—merely claiming it for the superior power and civilization of the British Empire. The *Sutra* will be of far greater use to humanity once it is available for study in the British Museum."

"Oh, Dorothea, you must be careful," pleaded Amelia. "You don't understand the dangers, really you don't." She hushed her voice to an even lower whisper. "There is a eunuch in the harem. He has told me the most terrible stories of what will happen to anyone who tries to harm the *Sutra* in any way."

"It will not be harmed, I promise you. I am an archaeologist, Amelia, not some ignorant treasure-seeker." Dorothea seized Amelia's hand very gently, and slid it down between her thighs. "Trust me, child. All I want is to give you pleasure."

"We mustn't!" Amelia wanted to resist but it was so difficult. All she wanted was to feel the gentle warmth of a soft caress, and Dorothea's haven seemed so hot and wet and welcoming to her touch. "If Bheli or Shakhira or the high priestess find out what we have been doing, we shall be punished."

"They won't find out, Amelia. How could they? We simply won't tell them."

"Oh. Oh, Dorothea…"

Amelia sank into Dorothea's arms with a low, shuddering sigh of submission, and Dorothea smiled at her easy victory.

"Let me show you how they make love in the South Sea Islands," she murmured, rubbing her pussy-lips hard against Amelia's willing fingers and inundating them with her powerfully scented juices. "Lie back and I shall do it to you. No, we shall do it to each other."

Amelia let herself sink back onto one of the straw palliasses which formed the sole furnishings of the cell. It rustled gently underneath her, the rough cotton covering making a light swishing sound as she slid over it, adjusting her position.

"Open your thighs just a little. Don't be shy, Amelia—you weren't shy that day when we walked into the hills together, were you? Don't you remember? You let me unfasten the front of your dress, and I saw straight away that you had the prettiest, the most kissable bubbies I had seen in many moons." Dorothea gave a low chuckle in the back of her throat. "But I never did get to kiss them, did I, Amelia? Won't you let me kiss them now?"

It was useless to feign any kind of resistance. Amelia was readier than she had ever been for Dorothea's caresses, and both of them were well aware of that readiness. She moaned quietly as Dorothea lay on top of her and ran her tongue round and round her breast, in a narrowing spiral which led gradually toward the aching crest of her nipple. But she dared not make any other sound, for the guards were sleeping only feet away, beyond the door of this makeshift prison.

Dorothea found her victory sweet, sweeter even than she had anticipated when first she had approached Miss Catherstone with her proposition. That proposition had been simple, and sound—exactly the sort of financial offer Miss Catherstone welcomed heartily. And when all was said and done, who could blame the headmistress of a charitable foundation such as the academy if she invited offers for her prettiest pupils? Was she not simply doing her best for her girls? They would have a home, a secure life of service, whilst she would pocket the not inconsiderable fee in compensation for her trouble.

The first time she had seen Amelia, looking down at her from the barred window of the dormitory, Dorothea had sensed a depth of sensuality which was rare in one so young. She had determined, there and then, to explore that sensuality, and if it proved sufficiently to her taste, to make Miss Catherstone a tempting offer for her charge.

Dorothea Strong was not an exceptionally wealthy woman—at least not yet—and as a general rule lived her life frugally, but she was always prepared to make an exception for a truly promising young woman like Amelia Courtnay. Once the girl was back in London, under the expert tutelage of young Floss, she judged that Amelia would quickly learn her duties and adapt to her new life as a "lady's maid." And Dorothea's learned friends would surely be charmed to be invited to the house to partake not only of Mrs. Graveson's excellent cooking, but of the sexual favors of Dorothea's latest acquisition.

Alas, that plan had not worked out quite as Dorothea had planned. But if she succeeded in getting away from the citadel with the *Rosebud Sutra,* why not achieve a double victory by also spiriting away the citadel's newest postulant slave? Dorothea felt confident that she could succeed in persuading Amelia to her point of view. Despite all that she had learned since that afternoon in the mountains, Amelia Courtnay was still a very naive and suggestible young woman.

Amelia closed her eyes and let Dorothea have her will. She was still convinced that retribution would fall upon them both at any moment, but she had almost ceased to care. Some unspecified future punishment seemed a small price to pay for the exquisite pleasure of this gentle lovemaking.

With her eyes closed, she could almost believe that it was Mary Bates, and not Dorothea Strong, who was kissing and licking her nipple. She reached out and slid her hands round Dorothea's waist, smoothing and stroking the firm flesh, enjoying the sensation of silky skin under her fingertips.

"Doesn't this feel better?" Dorothea let Amelia's nipple escape from her lips for a moment. Her voice was a whispered gasp. "Doesn't it feel better when I do it? Wouldn't you rather have your tit on my tongue and your cunt in my hand than that bitch of a slave mistress flaying your pretty skin with a whip?"

"Oh, yes, Dorothea. Oh yes."

Dorothea teased Amelia's nipple with her fingers, amusing herself by brushing them very lightly over its erect crest, so that the very tip barely skimmed the underside of her hand. She grinned to herself in the semi-darkness, secure in the knowledge that to Amelia she was just a featureless silhouette against the small, grayish square of sky which represented the high window.

"It feels good, does it not?"

"Good. Oh, yes, so, so good."

"But this feels better. Don't you think?"

Dorothea nudged her thigh between Amelia's, pressing it at first gently and then with greater pressure against the soft lower margins of her pussy-lips.

"Oh!" Despite her fears of being overheard, Amelia could not suppress a startled gasp of delight.

"Hush, sweet child." Dorothea soothed her with sweet words and caresses, silencing her with a kiss. "Just lie back and let me do it to you."

"Please, Dorothea. I can't bear it, it's too wonderful..."

"Hush. Trust me. I can make it feel even more wonderful, just you wait and see."

She worked her thigh back and forth a few times, quite gently, until she felt Amelia's juices smearing over the skin of her thigh and knew that all her resistance had gone. It would not take many moments to bring her young pupil to her first orgasm, but Dorothea had a fancy to make tonight's tutorial last a little longer. Besides, her own arousal was reaching an uncomfortably high level, and the throb of her lonely clitoris demanded to be satisfied.

"You'd like to give me pleasure, too, wouldn't you, Amelia?"

"Yes, yes, of course."

"You'd like to make it wonderful for me, too? Then draw your thigh up just a little, and slide it between mine." Still making sure that her own thigh was pressing lightly on Amelia's pubis, Dorothea straddled Amelia's slender limb, shivering with pleasure as the cool, silky flesh slid between her legs and into the wet groove between her sex-lips. "Oh, yes, sweet child. That feels good."

Amelia was in seventh heaven, her whole body relaxing into the pleasure as into a warm and sensual bath. The pleasure was all around her—inside her and surrounding her like lapping water, and Dorothea's thigh felt like a warm wavelet, ebbing and flowing at the margin of some tropical beach.

Happy and excited, she responded eagerly to Dorothea's skillful caresses. The flesh of her breasts became tauter and firmer, the small white globes crested with hard, pink spikes that delighted in the stimulation given to them by Dorothea's kisses. And all the time, the rosy-lipped mouth of her cunt kept on opening and closing in a sweet, secret welcome.

Dorothea too was half-crazy with pleasure. For all her innocence, Amelia Courtnay had already proved to be an instinctively sensual young woman—the perfect material to serve her in her London home, catering to her every small whim, ministering devotedly to the ache of lust which came so frequently to her loins. Eyes half-closed, she worked her thigh back and forth along Amelia's crack whilst Amelia reciprocated with eager, instinctive movements which brought her all too soon to the very edge of ecstasy.

"Slower, my sweet," she panted, but Amelia was beyond censure. The bucking movements of her pelvis were gathering pace, her lust burning with an irresistible intensity as she reached out for the climax her youthful body so craved.

With a sigh of longing, wishing that she could have prolonged the game for a few more minutes, Dorothea joined her new pupil in a joyous festival of unbridled lust, riding Amelia as hard as she rode her chestnut mare across the Surrey downlands.

Pleasure was a swirling, savage ocean, with surf-crested breakers which came crashing down upon them again and again. Amelia let out a long, low sigh as the tide carried her away, wild, untamable.

Together they lay on the battered straw palliasse, their breathing harmonizing as it grew slower, easier, deeper.

"Oh, Dorothea," sighed Amelia, all her fears momentarily forgotten.

"Hush, child." Dorothea put her finger to Amelia's lips. Amelia gave a delicious groan as she breathed in her own scent. The scent of purest sex.

Together they curled up on the straw mattress and

drifted off to sleep, their dreams filled with images of freedom and desire.

Shakhira looked on with silent satisfaction as the two young Englishwomen were brought before Bheli. She licked her lips, already anticipating the taste of their humiliation.

It had been she who had watched and waited through the long night hours, spying on the two captives through a tiny hole in the partition wall. They, the poor fools, had of course thought that they were safe from prying eyes, believing that their only guards were the two warrior priestesses slumbering outside the door.

How wrong they had been, thought Shakhira, exulting in her own special sense of victory. And how angry Bheli had been when she had gone to the senior slave with her tales of treachery and forbidden self-pleasure. Or had that anger been feigned? Shakhira was under no illusions about the sources of Bheli's sexual pleasure. She knew how Bheli loved to watch her errant slaves being punished…

The two English girls, naked and restrained by chains attached to their heavy leather collars, were forced to kneel before Bheli, her imperious dark eyes looking down on them with a stern, inquisitorial intensity.

“I am told that you have been behaving wickedly,” she began, pausing as though waiting for the two young women to perjure themselves. Amelia was not long in obliging her.

’lease, Ma'am, we have done nothing wrong,” she ’ed, her eyes brimming with moisture.

at so?” Bheli walked slowly up and down the ’le floor, her long white robe swishing about her impeccably manicured feet and revealing the scarlet-painted buttons of her toenails. "But my most trusted servants tell me that you have—both of you—indulged in forbidden pleasure." She flashed a quick glance at Shakhira, whose dark eyes were modestly lowered.

"No, Ma'am. Truly, we have done nothing…"

Bheli wheeled around, confronting her with a glittering stare.

"You dare to tell me that my servants have lied to me?"

Amelia opened her mouth to reply, but no sound came out. She knew instinctively when she was beaten.

"I put it to you, little English slut, that it is you who have been lying, not my faithful servant Shakhira."

Shakhira! So it was she who had spied on them and betrayed them. Amelia bit her lower lip, angry and ashamed and wishing fervently that she had been better able to resist Dorothea's insistent caresses. She hung her head in silence, too ashamed of her lie to speak.

Bheli turned her attention to the other English captive, the older girl they called Dorothea. This dark, steely-eyed woman with the cropped hair and the fiery temperament posed an even more interesting challenge than pretty little Amelia. It was plain to see that she considered herself far superior to her captors. Perhaps, after a little time in the temple harem, Dorothea Strong would begin to see things a little differently.

"What of you, my handsome bitch? What have you to say for yourself?"

Dorothea glared at her with utter venom, pursed her lips and spat at Bheli.

"That is all I care for your filthy rules! I am a free Englishwoman, not some little native slut."

The thick white gobbet of saliva struck the floor at Bheli's feet, but she stepped coolly over it, her eyes never leaving Dorothea's face.

"Is that so, Dorothea? Then why are you within these harem walls and not back in your home in England? Miss Strong, you may think you are special, but here in the citadel you are as nothing. You are less than a grain of sand, a guttering candle flame. Should I choose, I could snuff you out as easily as this." She dipped her hand over the smoky flame of the lamp, apparently feeling not the slightest discomfort, and the flame sputtered and went out. "Nothing, Dorothea. Do you understand that?"

"Let me go," growled Dorothea. "Let me go immediately." She wriggled and tried to claw at the collar about her neck, but the slave holding her simply jerked it back hard, forcing her head up, forcing her to look up into Bheli's dark, enigmatic eyes.

"No, Dorothea, I shall not let you go. You may consider yourself very fortunate indeed that I do not have you killed immediately. That is the usual fate of those who stray within the precincts of the citadel. But I have spoken of you to the high priestess Ishtar, and she has a fancy to train you..."

"Train me!" Dorothea let out a gasp of horror. "I will not permit this!"

"You will permit anything I choose, Dorothea," replied Bheli serenely. She was enjoying herself immensely. It was always diverting to be given charge of a postulant with a truculent, headstrong nature, for this made the breaking of the girl's spirit all the more exciting. Yes, Dorothea Strong would pose quite a challenge.

Dorothea struggled again to free herself from the slave's clutches but, just as before, she was restrained by the tight collar around her neck. Worse, Shakhira lifted the tawse and brought it down hard upon her breasts, making her grit her teeth in discomfort and leaving behind a rather pretty pattern of plum red marks.

"Please, Dorothea—do as she says," Amelia appealed to her, her eyes reflecting Dorothea's pain.

"Why should I pay her any attention?" snapped Dorothea, still clawing at her collar.

"You had better listen very carefully to me, Dorothea," continued Bheli, "because you are going to be here for the rest of your miserable life. On the night of the horned moon, you and Amelia will both be initiated as slaves in the Temple of the Rosebud Sutra."

Chapter 10

On some auspicious day, an assembly of women shall be convened in the temple, and they shall test one another in their knowledge of the sensual arts. The slaves who may be the most beautiful and who may have the power to attract the lusts of others shall here be done homage to. —The Rosebud Sutra

Amelia gazed through the window and into the courtyard beyond. Through the ornate tracery of brasswork which formed a pretty but impenetrable cage, she watched the priestesses making their preparations for the coming ceremonies.

She had been in the citadel for how long—a month? Two? It was hard to be certain. Time seemed dislocated and almost meaningless in this place, where there were few points of reference to mark its passing. Back at the academy in Jainapur, life had been infinitely structured—by the prompt awakening at five-thirty every morning, by the endless round of chapel services and lessons, and of course by the regular and often inexplicable chastisements meted out by Miss Catherstone.

The memories of Miss Catherstone's beatings were perhaps the last remaining link with that once familiar past. For it was Bheli's "training sessions" which now gave structure to Amelia's days. To Amelia's and also to Dorothea's, for the older woman had now also been assimilated into the harem's training routine, to be prepared for her initiation as a temple slave on the night of the horned moon.

Amelia drew her thin wrap around her and tried to remember her former life. It seemed barely more than a hazy blur, yet the ache of longing was still strong within her. More than anything she remembered Mary Bates, sweet, brave, irreverent Mary Bates with her insolent smile and her soft, knowing hands. How she wished they were together again and that Mary was teaching her the ways of love—not Bheli and Shakhira, with their whips and straps and chains.

Would she ever be free? In two nights' time the crescent moon would ride high in the night sky, a single star riding within its nether tip. And on that night, she and Dorothea would be initiated into their new life of servitude—initiated, that is, if they were successful in overcoming the trials that would be presented to them in the temple. And if not… The alternative hardly bore thinking about.

It seemed to Amelia that freedom was little more than an idle dream, yet Dorothea kept on and on about her plans and her determination to leave this place—not only free and alive, but carrying the *Rosebud Sutra* with her. Dorothea had tried on every possible occasion to persuade Amelia to accompany her in her escape, but a deep-seated fear held Amelia back. Illogical though it might seem, Amelia could not free her mind from the stories of terrible retribution that had been related to her. If she tried to leave the citadel with Dorothea, and Dorothea insisted on stealing away the *Rosebud Sutra*, then whatever fate might befall the archaeologist, Amelia would be certain to share it.

"Pay attention, do. It is time for your next training session."

Amelia looked up to see the eunuch standing barefoot beside the sunken pool. Its warm, pink waters moved in gentle ripples, stirred by the mountain breeze from the open window.

"Yes. I suppose it must be."

"You had better not be late this time," pointed out the boy, his crimson-painted lips forming a rather pretty moue of disapproval. "Mistress Bheli says you still have much to learn before your initiation, and you know how she abhors unpunctual slaves."

Suddenly, without the slightest provocation, tears flooded Amelia's bright blue eyes and she could hardly see.

"Oh, what am I to do?" she sobbed, not even bothering to dab the moisture from the corners of her eyes. Unchecked, the tears spilled over her lower eyelids and formed little rivulets that ran down her creamy pink cheeks. "Whatever am I to do?"

"Do?" The eunuch giggled nervously, quite astonished by this sudden outburst. It had never occurred to him that there might be any choice in the matter.

"Why—you must obey, like all the other slaves. What else could you do?"

"That's just it," sobbed Amelia. "I cannot…I simply cannot bear this any more. I want to learn, truly I do; I want to be obedient and do as I am bidden, but I am so afraid. I try to forget, but I still keep wishing I could go home—and then I remember that I don't have a home any more."

The eunuch looked pensive for a moment, wondering what it might be like to have a home beyond the citadel. He had been so young when he was brought here that he could remember nothing—nothing beyond the sensual desire to be like all the other slave girls, to share the immense pleasure that he was privileged to give them. This English girl's individuality both intrigued and irritated him.

"The temple harem is your home," he announced finally, his butterfly mind examining the conundrum, deciding it was nonsensical, and discarding it as it would discard any other toy it had grown bored with. His face broke into a faintly malicious smile. "Unless you fail the temple initiation, of course. You know what will happen to you then, don't you?" He drew an immaculately manicured nail across his bare throat.

Amelia wiped her eyes with the back of her hand, aware that she must look a complete fright. It was just as well she had not yet had her face painted this morning or the kohl and lip paint would be running all over the place. She didn't much like the eunuch, and certainly didn't trust him, but he seemed to be the only member of the temple harem who was prepared to talk to her at any length. The other slaves held themselves aloof, apparently loath to associate with a mere postulant—one whose fate hung so precariously in the balance, as had theirs, years or months before.

"What will happen—at the initiation?"

The eunuch sighed. "Such beautiful women." He half closed his eyelids, as though picturing the women in his mind, and his long silky lashes swept down onto his cheeks. "The priestesses and the slaves will assemble in the Temple of the Sutra for the ceremony of dedication, and they will all be dressed in the finest, most beautiful robes and jewelry. It will be so wonderful. If only I could be allowed to see it."

"And what about me? What will happen to me?"

"There will be a procession into the courtyard of the citadel, and then there will be trials for you to undergo. You and your troublesome friend will be set tasks of sexual endeavor. If you succeed in completing them, you will be honoured with the robes of a slave. If you fail..."

Amelia swallowed hard. She wasn't entirely sure she had wanted to talk about it, after all. It was as fantastical as some made-up adventure story in a child's book, yet it all felt uncomfortably close, uncomfortably real. It was really, truly, going to happen.

A figure appeared in the doorway, and she froze, catching her breath in dismay.

"You really are a disobedient little slut, aren't you?"

"I am sorry, Madam Shakhira. I..."

"I told her that Madam Bheli wished to see her, Madam Shakhira, but she would not come," butted in the eunuch hastily, his long lashes fluttering in feigned submission as he distanced himself from the offender.

"I am sure you did," replied Shakhira, an expression of malevolent enjoyment passing across her face. "After all, this little English slut is well-known as a source of disruption in the training house. When I tell Bheli of her repeated disobedience, there is sure to be some very special punishment in store for her. Come with me, slut. Madam Bheli will brook no further delay."

Her heart heavy, Amelia followed Shakhira silently out of the main chamber of the harem house, and along one of the many corridors which radiated out like the spokes of a wheel, at the hub of which were the quarters shared by Bheli and her most favoured senior slaves.

Amelia had never been in these rooms before, but she was not in the least surprised to find that they were more sumptuously decorated even than the marble-lined training room with the rosewater pool. Everywhere was cool white and mellow gold, the walls covered in exquisitely detailed paintings depicting women enjoying the fruits of each other's bodies. Amelia recognized some of the skills and positions of lovemaking which she had been taught by Bheli as a small introduction to the secrets of the *Rosebud Sutra*.

Bheli was waiting for her, reclining on a couch piled high with gold and silver cushions, but of Dorothea there was no sign.

"You are appallingly late, slave."

"I...am very sorry, Madam." She hung her head submissively, pressed her hands together and touched her bowed forehead with them, in the respectful manner she had been taught.

"You may raise your head."

Amelia did so and looked about her, suddenly very insecure, still hoping to see Dorothea waiting for her as she usually did, because she desperately needed this one ally to make her inevitable punishment more bearable.

Seeing Amelia's confusion, Bheli gave a long-suffering sigh.

"You have permission to speak, slave."

"Please, Madam, where is Dorothea?"

Bheli exchanged knowing glances with Shakhira, who smirked.

"I fear your fellow Englishwoman has transgressed once too often," replied Bheli rather enigmatically. "Her latest episode of defiance has tried my patience almost to the breaking point. She has been taken to the Chamber of Correction, where I trust I shall be able to teach her to practice better manners in the presence of her mistresses."

"Madam, the slave Amelia has also shown unforgivable disobedience," broke in Shakhira.

"Indeed? Tell me of this disobedience."

"She refused to obey the command when she was bidden to come to you," replied Shakhira. "And see—she has not even prepared herself for your glorious presence. Her lips have not been painted, there is no kohl outlining her eyes, and if I am not much mistaken, the little slut has even been weeping."

Amelia knew that the punishment must and would be a severe one. Weeping openly betrayed a lack of self-control, and was therefore one of the most heinous crimes a postulant slave could commit.

"Such a pity." Bheli rolled onto her belly and her shimmering white robes slid over the curves of her body, emphasizing the plump bounty of her delicious backside. "And I felt we had made a little progress with the slut over these past weeks. She almost appeared to be accepting her role as a submissive with dignity and grace, but the arrival of the other English slut seems to have halted her progress."

"Might I suggest some fitting punishment, Madam? Perhaps a severe beating? I have but lately obtained a wonderfully supple lash with leather thongs—it bites like a serpent's kiss. I would be honoured to take charge of the slut's chastisement."

Bheli shook her head loftily. "No, not a beating, Shakhira. Something a little more ingenious and more lasting, I think. Something that will bring her to a more complete recognition of her status. The ultimate mark of her servitude."

Bheli sat up and swung her long limbs over the side of the couch. The robe fell open around her thighs, showing Amelia a glimpse of the adorably plump shaven pussy beneath.

"In two nights' time, you know that you must face the ordeals of initiation," continued Bheli, making no attempt to cover herself. She was thoroughly enjoying Amelia's hungry gaze, the sweep of those yearning eyes begging for a sweetmeat from her mistress's table. "Do you seriously believe that you are ready to acquit yourself with honour?"

"I do not know, Madam. But I will try my best."

"I do not doubt it, my pretty slut, but have you the strength of body and spirit to withstand the pain, to take it and enjoy it, to turn it into a thing of the most exquisite pleasure?" Bheli did not wait for a reply, but slid her legs a little further apart so that her cunt-lips were more perfectly exposed. "I think that is something we ought to discover now, don't you?"

She watched with approving excitement as Amelia's tongue tip passed nervously over her pink lips. Although she would never let Amelia know, not for an instant, Bheli had been much pleased with her brace of English bitches: the one haughty and high-spirited; the other a pretty, tremulous, highly strung creature who was clearly terrified by her own immense capacity for wicked, sensual pleasure.

"Strip her, Shakhira. She is not much use to me clad in that ridiculous robe."

Shakhira stepped forward, silently excited, wondering what new and delightful punishment Bheli had dreamed up for the English girl. Shakhira knew that, even as the slut Amelia cried out in the pain of her chastisement, she also would feel it, welcoming its bite and burn as though it had come to her from the hand of Madam Bheli herself.

Stripped of her robe, Amelia felt almost more comfortable than semi-clothed. In this place, this citadel of women devoted to sensuality and sexual servitude, all clothing seemed an irrelevance, a lie concealing the truth of the passion beneath the filmy fabric.

Her long blonde braid swung gently from side to side as she stood waiting for Bheli to decide her fate. Its feathery tip, interwoven with a blue silk tassel, swished silently over the little hollow at the small of her back, the tassel dipping deliciously into the once forbidden crease at the very top of her buttocks.

"Tie her to the bench. Securely. I do not want any accidents."

Bheli indicated a very old, scrubbed wooden table, rather similar to the one Amelia had seen in the Chamber of Correction. Leather thongs hung down at its head and foot; thongs that might be tied so tightly that a captive would be incapable of any movement... Amelia felt an instant thrill of fear, and just as instantly felt a surge of guilt, unable to shake off the shame she still felt whenever she realized that fear or pain was exciting her.

But it was no use denying her arousal. It was already an oozing, trickling brooklet which seemed to begin at her nipples and slowly wind its way down through the pit of her stomach to the ache of her womb and the burning bud of her clitoris, whose dry heat could only be assuaged by more and yet more of the honeysweet nectar.

Amelia allowed herself to be led over to the punishment table, the bracelets of bells about her ankles jingling as she walked.

"Lie down," Shakhira instructed her.

Amelia got up onto the bench and stretched out on her back, in the submissive pose she had been taught by Bheli: eyes closed, thighs pressed chastely together, arms crossed over the breast as though she were some exquisitely decorated corpse. For, as Shakhira was always so ready to tell her, Amelia had no life except as the plaything and possession of her mistresses. It was for her mistresses to breathe life into her and direct all her actions and emotions, all her punishments—and pleasures.

"You must keep your eyes closed for now," Bheli continued. "Put your arms above your head and spread your legs."

Amelia did so, but to her surprise she was rewarded with a deft, stinging slap across the left breast. She dared not open her eyes, and screwed them tightly shut, refusing to let the tears come. For they were tears not of pain, but of humiliation. Once again, it seemed, she had failed to please her mistresses.

"Not like that!" snapped Shakhira. "Arms above your head, like that, but not with the hands together." Amelia moved them further apart, hardly daring to hope that she had done the right thing. "That is better.

Now open your legs. Wide apart, girl, and completely straight. Put your knees down, do you understand me?"

Shakhira's rapid-fire commands reminded Amelia of Miss Catherstone, her tall, angular figure stiffening with indignation whenever one of her charges failed to perform a task adequately. Eyes closed and her mind momentarily distracted by the thought, she was transported back to the schoolroom where, one sultry afternoon just before the July rains, she had been punished for her inadequacy in declining a Latin noun.

"Courtnay!"

Amelia had stumbled hurriedly to her feet, so flustered that she had dropped her pen and almost upset the full inkwell, its contents lapping dangerously at the rim.

"Miss Catherstone?"

"Pay attention, girl! I will not have my girls daydreaming in class. Tell me what we have just been discussing."

Amelia cast her mind back, suddenly so frantic that she could hardly remember who she was, let alone what the lesson was about. As a rule she paid very careful attention to what the headmistress was saying, but it was an oppressively hot day, her friends were waiting for her outside, and Latin was so dull...

"Please, Ma'am. You were teaching us about Latin nouns, Ma'am."

Miss Catherstone's thin lips pursed a fraction more tightly.

"Pray be more specific, Courtnay."

"I...I am not sure, Miss Catherstone." Amelia hung her head in utter shame, her cheeks crimson with embarrassment. Behind her, two of the class swots were sniggering. She wished the earth would open up and swallow her.

"Silence in class," snapped Miss Catherstone, her bright eyes scanning the classroom and commanding obedience. Silence fell, as thick and suffocating as a woolen blanket, and she turned her eyes back to Amelia, who by now was quaking with fear. She rapped out the command: "Give me the Latin word for war."

Relief swept over Amelia. This, at least, she knew.

"*Bellum*, Miss Catherstone."

"Good. Now decline it for me."

"All of it, Miss Catherstone?"

"All of its parts, Courtnay. In full."

Amelia swallowed very hard. Perhaps it would be all right. Perhaps she would be able to remember...

"*Bellum, bellum, bellum. Belli...*"

"Continue."

"Er...*belli, bello, bello. Bella...*"

"Yes, Courtnay?"

"I...I'm sorry."

"What was that? Speak up, child, so that all of us can hear."

"I'm sorry, Miss Catherstone. I can't remember the rest."

"*Bella, bella. Bellorum, bellis, bellis.* Is that it?"

"Yes, Miss Catherstone. I did know it, really I did. I'd just forgotten for the moment."

"Quite so."

Those two words, chilling and quiet, were enough to freeze Amelia's blood. She had no need to let her imagination run riot. She knew exactly what was coming next.

"Come and stand at the front of the class. Instantly!"

Amelia walked slowly and reluctantly toward the front of the class, her long school dress swishing against the desks as she passed. The afternoon heat was stifling, the air so thick and heavy that it was almost unbreathable, as though it formed a palpable cage about her far more effectively than the imprisoning gates of the Jainapur Academy for the Daughters of Gentlewomen. She could feel sweat trickling down her neck and back, down the smooth slope from throat to breast, and into the sleek furrow between her budding breasts.

"Bend over my desk," Miss Catherstone instructed her, with a studied coolness that belied the excitement within her own breast. Pretty little Amelia Courtnay was irritatingly submissive and generally so well behaved that she rarely had such a heaven-sent opportunity to discipline her. This would be a rare treat indeed. "At once, now."

Miss Catherstone's desk stood at the front of the classroom, and was raised on a small dais, as was common in English schools of the time. This allowed the teacher an unrivalled view of her pupils, and lent to Miss Catherstone's already imposing figure an authority which simply could not be denied. The desk itself was a heavy structure of dark wood with a sloping lid across which Amelia now draped her quivering form.

Half-standing, half-lying across the desk, Amelia closed her eyes so that she could not see the faces of her classmates, some white with shock, others contorted into suppressed grins and grimaces. And there would undoubtedly be many who envied Amelia her position now, as the sole focus of Miss Catherstone's formidable attentions.

Miss Catherstone signalled to a prefect to pull up Amelia's skirts and petticoats, and took the opportunity to carry out a cursory examination of Amelia's undergarments. Amelia dreaded such impromptu inspections, which were often carried out in addition to the daily morning inspection in the dormitory. Even as Miss Catherstone's eyes roamed over the linen-covered swell of her buttocks, she could feel the sweat running down her back, soaking the fabric and forming a little pool at the base of her spine.

"And so, Courtnay, I perceive that you have been indulging in impure thoughts again," announced the headmistress, her voice stern yet purring with satisfaction.

"No, Miss Catherstone, I have not! I promise you..."

"Be silent, wicked girl. It is clear from your undergarments that you have allowed yourself to indulge your impurity, for they are soaked through with the juices of your sinful lust."

This time Amelia held her tongue, reining in her impulse to protest against this injustice. For was this not just one more in a long line of instances of Miss Catherstone's seemingly arbitrary unkindness? At that time, Amelia had been far too innocent to imagine the true reason for this apparent cruelty, but now—after weeks of training in the temple harem—she was beginning to understand that Miss Catherstone had derived extreme pleasure from the beatings. More pleasure, even, than she, Amelia, had derived from being beaten...

She recalled how Miss Catherstone had selected a long, supple birch rod from the bundle she kept perpetually beside her desk for just such an eventuality. There was a different rod for every occasion, a different instrument of discipline for each creamy white backside, each flawless back and rosy, slender-fingered hand.

She heard Miss Catherstone test the birch rod once,

twice, three times, swishing it through the air with a quick, cutting movement.

"It will suffice," the headmistress muttered. "It will suffice very well indeed."

As Amelia lay on the punishment table in Bheli's chamber, she could not help remembering that first swinging cut across her bare back, then the second, which took her breath away as it sliced into the exposed flesh of her backside. That day, she remembered, she had experienced for the very first time something of the extraordinary pleasure which could be derived from punishment.

It had been the merest inkling, no more, and when the punishment was done, there had been tears and a burning pain from the red welts across her backside. But she also remembered the unaccustomed warm feeling between her legs and how she had wanted to rub herself there, where she had been forbidden to touch herself, though in those innocent days she had not understood why.

"Pay attention, slut. Madam Bheli is addressing you."

Shakhira's hand slapped down upon her bare thigh, and Amelia started, her body jerking at the sudden chastisement. Her ankles pulled instinctively inward, but they were impeded by the leather thongs Shakhira had bound securely around them. In a daze, Amelia realized that she was helpless—bound hand and foot to the table.

"Tie her more securely," said Bheli in a matter-of-fact voice. "It annoys me to see her squirming about like that."

"With pleasure, Madam," replied Shakhira. Amelia's blue eyes flashed open as she felt Shakhira's hands on her hair, tugging the long blonde plait so hard that she had to bite her lip to prevent herself from squealing with discomfort.

"You have not been given permission to open your eyes," remarked Bheli. "However, there is no reason why you should not have the pleasure of seeing what is to be done to you. The act will, I feel, have greater power if you are aware of each stage of it."

As Bheli was speaking, Shakhira was pulling Amelia's plait toward her, forcing the English girl to lie very still and look directly upward. At this stage, all she could see was the ceiling of the chamber: an octagonal dome, each segment decorated with an erotic mosaic in painted glass, through which the sun shone with a lascivious eagerness. Its multi-coloured rays cast shifting, flickering patterns on Amelia's spread-eagled body.

"It is done, Madam," announced Shakhira, making fast the leather thongs which tied Amelia to the punishment table by her hair. "What would you have me do next?"

"Bring me my box of sweet oils and my...instruments," replied Bheli.

Amelia listened in silence as Shakhira's soft footsteps moved across the tiled floor. She could hear the sound of a drawer opening, of something heavy being taken out.

"This is a punishment but it is also a great privilege, Amelia," Bheli told her.

"Yes, Madam," replied Amelia, though she still did not understand what was to be done to her.

"A punishment and a privilege," repeated Bheli, bending over the table so that her face was quite close to Amelia's. For a moment, Amelia had the strangest, the most delicious fantasy—the faint hope that Bheli would kiss her, pressing her ruby-painted lips against hers, forcing her young and tender body to express the depth of its desire. "The initial discomfort will in itself be a delight to you, I am certain of that, and in any case will be vastly outweighed by the self-discipline which the exercise will promote in you."

"Madam?" Amelia looked up questioningly into Bheli's eyes. "I do not understand."

"Then I shall explain." Bheli took something from Shakhira's hands and laid it gently on the low table beside the punishment bench. It made a soft scraping noise as she put it down, and then Amelia thought she heard the faint sound of a tiny key turning in a lock.

"I am going to pierce your body, Amelia. You have seen some of the women of the harem wearing jewels in their navels, in their breasts?"

"Yes, Madam." Amelia shivered, not sure if she feared or yearned for this doubtful honour. Perhaps both in equal measure...

"Others, my sweet English slut, wear their jewels in more discreet, more secret places." Bheli's skillful fingers traced a winding path down Amelia's belly, circling the neat little depression of her navel then walking a little further down, onto the plump flesh of her sex-mound, now denuded of its luxuriant blonde curls.

Amelia's breath escaped in an almost inaudible sigh. Could it be true that Bheli was going to honour her with one of those beautiful jewelled rings piercing the flesh of her cunt-lips? She thought of the pain and humiliation of the piercing, but it suddenly seemed trivial by comparison with the honor of bearing her mistress's mark.

"Oh, Madam..."

Then Bheli's finger slipped from her mount of Venus and continued its journey, exerting a light pressure which forced apart Amelia's sex-lips and opened up the coral pink wetness of the flesh within.

Amelia's whole body stiffened as Bheli's sharp-nailed fingertip explored the soft heart of her womanhood. All of a sudden, the game seemed much more serious. Disturbing yet arousing thoughts were tumbling over each other in her head. Thoughts of things she was almost too scared to picture. Thoughts of the slave Premila...

"What a fat little rosebud you have, my sweet," observed Bheli, taking Amelia's clitoris between her finger and thumb and giving it a hard squeeze.

Amelia almost fainted with the pain, but somehow she managed to stop herself from making any sound save a little drawing-in of breath. No, no, it couldn't be that. They couldn't do that to her...

"Yes, Amelia, I am going to pierce your clitoris. You may consider it a discipline and a great honor—the first of the trials you must undergo in order to become a temple slave."

Amelia gazed up at the glittering painted glass of the domed ceiling. The colours shifted as the sun rode slowly across the sky, picking out different areas of the mosaics as it did so. As though magnifying her own fears, the sun's rays blazed suddenly through the bright pink folds of a dancing girl's cunt, her head thrown back and her legs spread wide as she waited to receive the honor of her mistress's curled-up fist.

"Give her some of this to drink." Bheli handed Shakhira a small glass vial, half-filled with a dark orange liquid. "It will increase her desire and intensify all sensation."

Amelia did not want to drink the bitter-tasting concoction, but Shakhira forced it between her lips, and little by little it trickled down her throat. It tasted strong and acidic, and burned as she swallowed it; it had the strength of a powerful alcohol, mixed with bitter herbs whose taste the addition of a sugary syrup had done little to diminish.

Within moments she began to feel dizzy and light-headed. The octagon of images above her seemed to be spinning slowly like a roulette wheel, the sun's fiery disc, the white ball that fell, time and time again, on the coral pink of the dancing girl's parted sex-lips…

Her whole body seemed to be on fire. The merest breath of a breeze across her flesh felt like a lover's caress. She could feel each individual hair on her skin erecting in pleasure, yearning for more and greater sensations.

But not this. No, please, not this.

Amelia tried to close her eyes but she had not the will. Bheli was showing her the piercing instrument—a long, sharp-pointed spike like a fat darning needle. It glinted in the fierce sunlight blazing down from the ceiling, and seemed to burn right into Amelia's soul.

Shakhira's fingers were pinching her nipples now. Normally the sensation would have been pleasant, but now—because of the strong elixir she had been given to drink—every sensation was magnified ten, maybe a hundred times. Every touch was unbearably vivid, every caress so intense in its symphony of sensations that Amelia could have wept. She tried to twist and turn, but the leather straps held her fast, and she could not even look away because of the thongs holding her blonde plait to the punishment bench.

When Bheli touched her clitoris, she opened her mouth and howled like a wild beast, the pleasure so blindingly bright that she could not endure it even for a moment.

"Gag her," said Bheli. "She may scream her pleasure, but no one will hear her."

Pleasure? Could this be pleasure? Amelia's brain whirled in confusion as the thick rubber gag pushed its way between her teeth, so suddenly that it half choked her. All she wanted was for this to stop, now, this minute. Or was it truer to admit that she wanted it to go on forever and ever and never stop? This hellish mixture of pleasure and pain was like nothing she had ever imagined.

Surprisingly enough, the tip of the piercing instrument entered the flesh of Amelia's clitoris with little pain. It was so razor-sharp that it passed through the swollen head with little more than a sudden sharp sensation.

It was not until a few moments later, when the silver ring had been slipped into place, and the heaviness of the ruby was pulling and stretching and distending the swollen stalk, that the full flood of sensations washed over Amelia.

Throbbing, burning, pulsing with a strange inner energy, her clitoris seemed to have taken on a life of its own, and Amelia trembled in her bonds, pulling them this way and that in her frantic, fruitless attempt to escape from the terrible, tormenting pleasure that pursued her at every moment.

Bheli gazed down at the English girl with a dispassionate approval as she watched her body stiffen and jerk. As she had anticipated, the pain of the piercing was transforming rapidly into ecstasy, and even as Bheli looked on, Amelia entered the silent agony of this new and terrifying type of orgasm. The girl was becoming the woman. At last, Amelia Courtnay would have to admit to the strength of her desires.

Bheli turned to Shakhira and gave her a half-smile of satisfaction.

"The girl is almost ready for initiation," she announced. "You have done well. And as a reward you may spend this night with her and teach her to perfect her control of this new pleasure."

Shakhira felt the warmth of sudden pleasure wash over her, and in an impulse of gratitude, she fell to her knees before Bheli, bending low to plant kisses on her sandalled feet.

"Mistress," she breathed, and she shuddered with ecstasy as she felt Bheli's hand smoothing the dark cascade of her hair.

In the Chamber of Correction, nameless, faceless women served the high priestess Ishtar with unquestioning and silent obedience.

Dorothea did not struggle. To do so would prove futile now, for the iron manacles held her fast and she had come to understand that the only way to survive this ordeal was to feign submissive obedience.

At first she had fought like a she-cat, spitting and straining at the end of her slave chain, scratching and biting whenever anyone tried to fasten her wrists into the manacles. But each outburst of defiance had met with increasingly ferocious revenge beatings with paddle and cat and bullwhip, which left her flesh reddened and flecked with blood.

Little by little, she had realized that overt resistance was self-defeating. She must learn to be more cunning. Thinking back over the moments of danger she had faced in other expeditions, she decided to deceive and disarm her captors with a display of abject submission.

So now she hung, unmoving, from the manacles. Between her shackled wrists a chain was stretched, and this had been threaded through a large iron meat hook which was embedded in the ceiling of the punishment chamber.

She had lost track of how long she had been like this, and her arms ached from being pulled half out of their sockets. But the tongues of the naked slave girls felt cool and soothing on her wounded flesh as they lapped up the slow trickles of her blood.

At last, Ishtar clapped her hands, and to Dorothea's disappointment the slave-girls moved away.

"She is sufficiently cleansed now," announced Ishtar. "We may proceed with the second stage of the bitch's discipline. Open your mouth, slave."

Dorothea obeyed without a second thought. If this was the game she must play, then she would play it faultlessly. She was thinking of the initiation ceremony in two nights' time, when the *Rosebud Sutra*, the magnificently gilded book on its intricately wrought gold stand, would be brought out of the temple into the main courtyard. Then would be her chance of freedom, of glory.

Amelia might think that Dorothea had abandoned her plans to steal the *Rosebud Sutra*, but that was because Amelia was a silly child. The stupid girl had refused all Dorothea's pleas to join her in her escape, and in the end Dorothea had given up trying to persuade her. There were plenty more girls like Amelia Courtnay to be had, and once she had taken the *Rosebud Sutra* safely back to London, she would be so fabulously rich and famous that every pretty girl in England would be throwing herself at her feet.

The high priestess ran a wad of goat's wool over Dorothea's tongue. It was soaked in some sort of sweet, spicy oil which Dorothea found quite pleasant, rather soothing, like oil of cloves. Willingly she extended her tongue a little further, not for one second suspecting what was going to happen next.

When the piercing needle entered her tongue tip, she almost forgot her newfound submissiveness and screamed in pain, but she was so shocked that she just gave a long, noisy gasp. For a few seconds the pain was intense, a blinding, searing lightning bolt that left her breathless and incapable of the slightest movement.

And then the little golden stud was pushed into place and the sharpness of pain was gone, leaving only a dull, throbbing ache that might even be the precursor of pleasure.

The next thing Dorothea knew, the manacles had been unlocked from her wrists and she had fallen to her knees upon the uneven stone floor. And now the high priestess Ishtar was standing before her, her robes kilted to the waist and pushed through her intricate chain-mail belt.

The high priestess's pubis was plump and smooth. Dorothea breathed in its strong, spicy scent and felt her shock become excitement, her excitement becoming arousal…

"You have borne your punishment well," commented the high priestess, parting her tattooed love-lips with well-manicured, scarlet-tipped fingers. "And now, my little English slave, I shall teach you how to lick me out."

Chapter 11

She who is ingenious and wise, and who knows the intentions of others, may gain over even a woman who is very hard to be obtained. —The Rosebud Sutra

A single star glittered brightly within the curve of the crescent moon; now green, now red, now white; a token of what was to come.

All the stars were very bright tonight, thought Amelia as she gazed out through the bars of the harem window. But the deep blackness of the night sky reminded her how very far she was from what she had once thought of as civilization.

Had she been stupid to think of Jainapur as home and the European ways as far superior to the Indian?

Here in the citadel, she had been taught secrets she had never even dreamed existed. She had learned the dark truths about her desires and the greatest secret of all: that there could be exquisite pleasure even in pain and submission. Perhaps *especially*...

She barely thought about what she was doing as she accepted a soft towel from one of the slave girls and ran it over her body, dripping wet from the rosewater bath. Since that night when she had submitted to Dorothea's seductive caresses, she and the English archaeologist had seldom been permitted to see each other, let alone establish any sort of more intimate contact.

Dorothea, she had been told by Bheli, was considered to be a thoroughly bad influence upon her, and she had been taken away to undergo training which would cure her of her arrogant defiance, once and for all.

Whilst she did not trust Dorothea and certainly did not approve of her ridiculous and foolhardy plan to steal away the *Rosebud Sutra*, Amelia had very much missed having the company of another Englishwoman. Life in the harem alternated between the frightening and the dull, and few of the slaves would even talk to her. What's more, as life in Jainapur receded into the fuzzy memory pictures of a dream, she felt she needed Dorothea to tell her that it had been real: that she was Amelia Courtnay the English soldier's daughter, and not Amelia that little English slut, who was about to embark upon a life of unending sexual servitude in the Temple of the Rosebud Sutra.

As the eunuch held out a brass-rimmed mirror and she painted her lips in a scarlet bow, Amelia wondered to herself if Dorothea might perhaps have been right after all. Tonight would be her last chance to escape.

Through the barred window came the sounds of preparation, the priestesses raising their voices in a mystical chant to a statue of the goddess Akhtar as they prepared to proceed into the temple and emerge bearing the sacred *Rosebud Sutra.*

Her last chance ever... Ought she to take it? Find Dorothea somehow and tell her that she would go with her, even if it meant colluding in the theft of the ancient book?

The slave girl and the eunuch stood back, admiring her as though she were some fragile and delicate painting, some work of art crafted uniquely for the pleasure of the high priestess. Which, in a way, she was, Amelia mused to herself. She must get used to the idea that she had no existence any more, except as the high priestess's plaything and possession.

"She is pretty enough, I suppose," sniffed the eunuch. "But her breasts are very small." He managed to squeeze a whole universe of disdain into those few words, noted Amelia.

"She will suffice."

Amelia turned away and caught an unexpected sight of herself in the full-length mirror that stood beside one of the curtained alcoves. Her robe was made from the finest gold thread, woven into a semi-diaphanous tissue which clung to her body like a lover's embrace, at once veiling and revealing. Her feet were decorated with stencilled patterns and shod in jewelled sandals that sparkled in the smoky lamplight. It seemed to Amelia that she was now not so much a creature of living flesh and blood, as a moving statue, a chimerical creation of shadow and starlight.

"Come." The slave girl nodded to the eunuch. "We have done as we were bidden. Now the bitch must fend for herself." She turned sly eyes on Amelia. "You must wait here until the moon is at its zenith, and the star at the very centre of its crescent. Then, when the temple ceremonies are done, they will come for you." Her eyes raked up and down Amelia's form, critically appraising the youthful nakedness beneath the filmy robe. "If the Goddess wills it, you may perhaps survive the ordeal."

The boy sniggered as he followed the slave out of the chamber, half-turning to throw Amelia a last prurient look before the heavy wooden doors closed behind him. She was alone with her thoughts.

"Nasty little...," Amelia's breath escaped in an inarticulate hiss. She was afraid and she was angry. She didn't know whether to cry or to scream and shout her rage.

"Don't take any notice of him, Miss Amelia. I'm here now."

The familiar voice froze Amelia in her tracks. She was hallucinating, she must be. That was the only possible explanation. Slowly, very, very slowly, she turned around to face the source of the voice.

A shimmering, primrose-yellow curtain swished back and a tall, veiled figure stepped out of the alcove behind it. It was an anonymous figure, clad from head to toe in the dark red robes of a domestic servant, but there could be no mistaking those soft brown eyes, twinkling with a mischievous warmth above the draped red fabric which hid the lower part of her face. Even before the veil had fallen away, Amelia was mouthing the name that had haunted her ever since her abduction.

"Mary? Is it really you? How can it be...?"

The woman pushed back the red silk wrap which

covered her head, and shook her chocolate brown hair free. Her smile was as warm and fresh as a spring day in Jainapur.

"Couldn't let them do that to you, now could I, Miss Amelia? Just giving up and pretending it had never happened? Scandalous, that's what it was. Specially after I heard that old bitch Catherstone talking to Dorothea Strong. Seems they had a little financial arrangement between them—Strong's hard cash for your body."

"What!" All along, Amelia had sensed that Dorothea Strong was not to be trusted, and yet she had allowed her own girlish desires to overrule her common sense.

"But look here, Amelia. I didn't come here to talk about Dorothea Strong, now did I? I came to rescue you from this hellhole."

Mary's hands encircled her waist, firmly but with infinite gentleness. Their lips met, and a huge shudder of warm, soft pleasure ran right through Amelia's body.

"How could...how on earth did you manage to get in?"

"I was brought up in the East End, remember. Long before my old Dad brought us to India, I was running around Cheapside with the beggars and the petty thieves." She tapped the side of her nose. "You learn a lot on the streets—housebreaking, thieving, you name it.

"Mind you, once I set off after you into the mountains, I went and got myself well and truly lost. Wandered around in circles for days until I was half-dead from cold and hunger. Luckily, I happened on a tribe of nomads, and the women took me in and looked after me. A few of them spoke a dialect I could understand—same as the Indian servants at the academy—and after a little persuasion, they told me about the citadel. I was sure that must be where they'd taken you, especially when they told me a blonde-haired English girl had been seen with a party of outlaw women.

"It was a long journey, but I found the citadel two days ago. Two days and nights I've been waiting for my chance, just watching and waiting and planning. And now here I am."

"How...?"

Mary grinned.

"Got in over the wall, didn't I? Just like I used to do at nights, back at the academy. Remember?"

Amelia rested her head on Mary's shoulder, suddenly feeling very weary and more than a little tearful.

"Oh, Mary... It's so good to see you, but how can you possibly save me from this? They will be coming to take me to the ceremony soon. If they find you here, they will kill you. You must go, you must save yourself before it's too late...."

Mary's arms tightened about Amelia's waist, her right hand roaming down over the smooth, creamy globe of her buttocks, so imperfectly veiled by the flimsy robe.

"It's taken me weeks to find you, Amelia," she said firmly. "And if you think I'm leaving you now, you've got another think coming. Tonight, Amelia, I'm taking you away from this place, and you're never coming back."

From the journal of Dorothea Strong, 1885

I have now been incarcerated in the citadel for more than two weeks and have suffered the most indescribable indignities at the hands of my captors.

It is their intention to initiate me into the ranks of their temple slaves, for tonight is their annual festival, which they call the Night of the Horned Moon. On this night many young women and girls will be brought to the central courtyard of the citadel from the training houses of the harem in which they have been held in preparation for this night. Among these women will be Amelia Courtnay—and myself.

At least, that is the plan which has been outlined to me by my instructress, a slave known as Bheli, and by the high priestess Ishtar, who has made of me a special favorite because of my apparently miraculous conversion to docile submission. My submission is, of course, entirely feigned, since I have no intention of becoming yet another of Ishtar's hapless playthings.

Tonight, I shall leave the citadel—and if all goes according to plan, I shall leave with the *Rosebud Sutra* in my possession.

As I sit beside the window of the cell in which I have been incarcerated, I can observe the preparations for tonight's ceremonies. From a purely anthropological perspective, these are entirely fascinating. In the central courtyard a dais has been built, on which stands a golden couch and a whipping post with manacles and anklets of purest gold. This, I have been told, is where the trials of initiation will take place.

At the commencement of the ceremony, the priestesses will proceed out of the temple, carrying a litter bearing the high priestess Ishtar who, according to their primitive system of belief, is said to be the incarnation of their Goddess.

They will be followed by six naked slaves harnessed to a gilded cart. On this cart will be the *Rosebud Sutra* on its golden stand, and to bear it is considered the greatest honor that a slave may be accorded. All year the slaves vie with each other for their mistresses' favor, for only those who greatly please the high priestess and her senior priestesses may aspire to take part in the ceremony. Behind them will follow the postulants who are to be presented for initiation.

I have little interest in the ceremony itself, for my intentions are entirely focused upon my acquisition of the *Sutra*. Once it is installed in the courtyard, the priestesses and slaves will kneel to honour it, pressing their foreheads upon the earth, and it is at this moment that I shall make my move.

They have not shackled me, as they did in the Chamber of Correction. Nor have they made any attempt to search my person, for each postulant slave must prepare herself as she sees fit for the ceremony. As soon as they left me alone in my cell, it was a simple matter to retrieve my trusty pistol from its hiding place beneath a loosened floor tile.

The pistol is now concealed beneath my cloak. I reach beneath the folds of fabric to touch its cold metal hilt and it feels reassuring, solid and dependable. It will protect me from any attempts on my life by the slaves, for all must go unarmed on this sacred night, and I give no credence to the ludicrous tales of terrible vengeance which the priestesses tell in order to protect their precious sacred book from theft. The *Sutra* is now as close within reach as the golden African statuette which I so nearly won. This time I shall not fail.

I have reluctantly reached the conclusion that Amelia Courtnay is an ignorant, silly, immature girl who is unworthy of my attentions. Perhaps in this life of ignominious submission she has found her true vocation. But I refuse utterly to submit myself to such degradation.

I hear footsteps and voices in the outer chamber. I know that I am soon to be summoned to the place of initiation, but I am more than ready for them all.

Tonight I leave the citadel—with the *Rosebud Sutra* as my prize.

Mary and Amelia talked in hushed whispers. As far as they knew, there was no one else inside the harem house, but they could not be certain. A moment's incaution and they would be certain to lose everything.

"Poor Amelia," murmured Mary, tracing the faded scars of Amelia's last punishment through the golden tissue of her gown. "You shouldn't have let them do this to you, you know."

"What choice did I have?"

"Everybody has a choice," retorted Mary, pushing Amelia back onto the softness of the couch and rucking up her robe with gently insistent fingers. "I chose to come and find you, didn't I? And now I'm choosing... I'm choosing to make love to you."

"We can't!" exclaimed Amelia in an agonized whisper, though her body was crying yes, yes, yes. "If someone comes in and finds us..."

"They won't. You said yourself you would be left alone until the ceremony was about to begin. Come on, Amelia, let me love you."

"But there isn't time. If we're to get away..."

"There is plenty of time. We can't leave the harem

house until the priestesses have all gone into the temple for the first preparation ritual. Once they go in there and they start drinking and dancing, they won't notice what's going on in front of their own eyes. We should have plenty of time to slip away before they come to fetch you and realize that you've gone—if they even notice, once they're half out of their minds on that sacred wine of theirs." She kissed Amelia, very tenderly but very firmly, almost as a man kisses a woman whose body he has just bought for a handful of silver coins. "The boy will wait outside the walls of the citadel with the horses. I've paid him well—he won't let us down."

Amelia's body was taking over from her mind, forcing her to relax as only a day before Bheli had forced her to submit. How could she admit to Mary that she had felt a kind of pleasure in that submission, that even now she was taking delight in Mary's gentle insistence?

How she had changed since she had come to the citadel. Forced to confront the truth about herself, she had come to understand why Miss Catherstone's beatings had so excited as well as terrified her. Even then, there had been a part of her that craved the security of the strictest discipline. How the punishments had pained her, but how wonderful it had felt, afterwards, to feel the warm glow of forgiveness and the coolness of healing salve spreading over her smarting flesh...

"What about Dorothea?" gasped Amelia, trying hard to be altruistic even though she knew now that Dorothea's motives had never been anything other than self-seeking. "We can't just abandon her here, can we?"

"Is she still determined to steal the *Rosebud Sutra?*"

Amelia nodded. "I tried to persuade her, but..."

"Then I don't see how we can help her. She's a

greedy fool. If she wants to get herself killed, that's her affair—but we can't let her destroy us, can we?"

Amelia fell silent, feeling guilty but knowing that Mary was talking good sense. More than that, she recognized the authority in Mary's voice and responded to it instinctively, as she had been so efficiently instructed over these past weeks.

"Can we, Amelia?" Mary repeated, pinching Amelia's nipple to gain her attention.

Amelia gave a little gasp of delicious pain and blurted out her instinctive response, the response which she had been trained to give at the initiation ceremony: "No, Mistress."

Mary drew back, her eyes wide with surprise.

"What did you say?"

Amelia reddened, but it was too late to cover up her faux pas. She lowered her eyes, hardly daring to look Mary in the face. But Mary took hold of her chin and gently raised it so that their eyes met.

"You called me 'Mistress,' didn't you? Now why would you do a thing like that?"

"I..." Where could she begin? How on earth could she explain in a way that Mary would understand?

"Tell me."

"It's...it's something they taught me to say...at the initiation ceremony tonight. As a temple slave, I would have to serve my mistress, do whatever she tells me. I don't know why I called you Mistress just then...I suppose it must be second nature to me now. That's what they've done to me, Mary, I can hardly recognize myself." She lowered her eyes and her voice became a hushed whisper. "You see, being told what to do, it sort of, I don't know...it sort of excites me. Does that make sense to you?"

"You'd have to promise to do anything your mistress told you?"

Amelia looked into Mary's curious brown eyes and gave a shiver of excitement. She surprised herself as she answered: "Yes. Anything."

Mary got up from the couch and turned away, hiding her confusion from Amelia. This was a very new and unexpected development. She was experienced in the ways of love, but she had never thought of playing this intriguing game before. Slowly, her heart thumping with excitement, she stooped and picked up an ivory-handled cat-o'-nine-tails from one of the low tables, running the deceptively soft and supple thongs over the palm of her hand.

She turned to face Amelia again, and this time her face was filled with the most miraculous, joyous excitement.

"If you wanted me to, Amelia, I could be your mistress."

It was surprisingly easy for Mary and Amelia to slip away into the shadows as the priestesses congregated in the temple to drink their sacred wine and sing hymns to the goddess Akhtar.

"What happens when they realize we are gone?" whispered Amelia nervously as they pressed themselves into a pool of darkness and eased themselves along the base of one of the high walls.

"You have seen how distracted they are—distracted with wine and aphrodisiacs. We shall be far away before they even notice. Feel for the rope and climb it. It cannot be far ahead."

"You should go first. And what about Dorothea?" Even at this late hour, Amelia was thinking of the woman who had never brought her anything but misfortune.

"For goodness' sake find the rope and climb it!" Mary was taking surprisingly easily to the role of dominatrix, and she rewarded her charge's dilatory response with a deft but affectionate slap across the rump.

Galvanized into action, Amelia fumbled along the rough wall and succeeded in catching the end of the rope—a long, dangling string of knotted cloths that felt as though it were far too frail to take even her slight weight. But Mary hoisted her up a few feet and she seized hold of it, bracing her bare feet against the stones and feeling for footholds as she hauled herself upward with aching arms.

When she was only halfway up the shadowed wall, the sounds of music from the temple began to sound noticeably nearer.

"Mary!" she gasped in horror. "What do I do now…?"

"Keep climbing. Quickly! The procession is coming out into the courtyard." Mary urged Amelia upward, and she scrambled a few yards higher up the wall, skinning elbows and chipping her painted toenails on the rough slabs.

Almost at the top of the wall now, Amelia lunged with all her strength for the last of the stones and heaved herself up, her frail arms almost giving way as she pulled herself, puffing and panting, onto the broad, flat top of the high wall. A moment later she felt the rope jerk suddenly, and knew that Mary was climbing up to join her.

Twenty feet below, she could see saffron-robed figures with shaven heads bearing the high priestess into the courtyard on a gilded litter. Ishtar looked very beautiful and very menacing, her tattooed head crowned with a headdress of many-headed silver serpents, and an enormous silver phallus clasped between the scarlet-tipped talons of her long and slender fingers.

Behind the litter came a wheeled cart, pulled by six naked slave girls. Their nipples were pierced and linked by silver chains so heavy that their fleshy globes were stretched and distended into pendulous udders as they bent to pull the cart.

Amelia looked down and saw Mary's face, white and tense in the moonlight.

"The *Sutra,*" she gasped as she pulled herself toward Amelia. "Look—can you see it?"

Amelia gazed at it in wonderment as two priestesses lifted it with difficulty out of the cart and set it down on the stone flags of the courtyard. On a stand of gilded wood, about four feet high, lay the most wonderful book Amelia had ever seen. She had only glimpsed it briefly before, for she had been banished from the temple after her first meeting with Ishtar. No postulant could be permitted to read the secrets of the *Sutra* until after her initiation. Now she saw it in its full beauty, its intricately gilded cover complemented by the most exquisite golden figurines of demons, their bodies twisted, their faces those of gargoyles, half woman, half mythical beast. In the light from the blazing torches, their ruby eyes seemed to glitter with a fierce inner intelligence.

Mary joined her at the top of the wall just as the most extraordinary and terrifying events began to take shape. As the *Sutra* was placed in its position of honour in the middle of the courtyard, all the priestesses and slaves sank to their knees on the bare stone floor, bowing so low that their foreheads touched the ground as they began a long, low chant of homage.

At that moment, a figure broke ranks. It was one of the postulant slaves—a figure clad in flowing red and black, with cropped hair and white, smooth skin.

"Dorothea? No, it can't be!" exclaimed Mary. "The bloody fool..."

Amelia watched in silent, open-mouthed terror as Dorothea rushed through the crowd of worshippers, a gleaming pistol held rock-steady in her right hand, and approached the *Rosebud Sutra*.

Dorothea must have known that she only had seconds in which to accomplish the deed, for she snatched at the holy book as eagerly as a child stealing sweets, tearing it from its stand with such ferocity that the fine gold chain holding it there snapped instantly in two.

A terrible high scream filled the air, the screaming of a hundred voices raised in a thin, ethereal keening. Yet the worshippers were still praying devoutly, their faces pressed to the ground as though they were frozen there, paralyzed or too afraid to raise their heads. Where was that terrible, blood-curdling sound coming from? It seemed to fill the whole air, so shrill and high that Amelia had to put her hands over her ears. And still it got louder and more insistent.

When Amelia looked again at Dorothea, she too screamed in terror. For—impossible as it might seem—the golden statuettes of the demon women were coming to menacing life, their bodies swelling and uncoiling, their eyes flashing, their bony hands reaching out with clawlike fingers. Dorothea was standing stock-still and ashen-faced, the *Rosebud Sutra* clutched to her breast with one arm whilst the other fired four, five, six futile gunshots into the invulnerable bodies of her assailants.

And now they were her pursuers, their arms entwining about her body with a subtle, inexorable insistence as she tried to run away, their bodies coiling about her, their fingers tearing at her clothes, exposing the hard-crested hummocks of her bare breasts.

As the terrible, inhuman pleasure overtook her, the *Rosebud Sutra* fell from her hand and another scream was joined to the high, ethereal keening.

"Come on." Mary spoke to Amelia a third time, and at last she heard. "We must go. We have to get away. Now."

"But Mary—Dorothea..."

Mary took a last, long look down into the courtyard, filled now with the golden, seething shapes of the many-headed demons that had dragged Dorothea to her doom, completely obscuring her body in their teeming lust of vengeful desire. She gave Amelia's hand a squeeze.

"We can't help her now. Throw the rope over the other side of the wall and slide down it."

"But Mary..."

"Do it!"

As they slid down the rope and jumped down onto the stony ground outside the citadel, Amelia heard the terrible wailing sound rise to a discordant crescendo, and then, suddenly...

Silence. Not a sound but the distant howling of a mountain wind across the barren mountainside.

Chapter 12

All young maids must study the Rosebud Sutra *and the arts and sciences thereto, alone or with a confidential friend. For a maid must learn to pleasure her mistress.*

—The Rosebud Sutra

It was a fine Sunday afternoon in Jainapur, and girls in crisp white dresses with starched collars were taking the air, their eyes modestly lowered but their well-tutored cunnies and bumcheeks burning with newly discovered agonies of pleasure, ably taught to them by their generous mistresses at the academy.

All was as it should be. The annual rains had come and gone and the sun was shining down beatifically out of a cloudless blue sky. To the outward eye at least, little had changed in the hill station of Jainapur over the last year, despite Miss Catherstone's sudden dismissal from her post as headmistress at the academy. As it later transpired, the trustees had discovered certain irregularities in her administration, and she had been instantly removed from her duties.

Shortly afterwards, the academy had acquired a new assistant mistress. The appointment had been a natural choice, for who could combine the laudable qualities of fortitude, self-reliance, and feminine modesty more perfectly than Miss Amelia Courtnay, the beautiful heroine of Jainapur since her escape with Mary Bates from the citadel? Under her stern but kindly guidance, the young girls of the academy would surely blossom into accomplished ladies, more than able to find their way in the world.

On this perfect afternoon, Mary stood at the window of the senior dormitory where she had once paid illicit visits to Amelia, and smiled to herself, thinking over what had happened. She had now been promoted to matron of the academy, a role which required her to exert the firmest authority over the pupils. It was a role which, she was rapidly discovering, suited her rather well.

It was unfortunate about Dorothea, of course, but truthfully the woman had only herself to blame. No one could be quite sure what had happened to her, but it was perhaps best not dwelt upon. The odd thing was that one volume of Dorothea's diary had arrived at the academy only days ago, wrapped in a small oilskin packet and addressed to Amelia. Mary had persuaded her to keep this new development secret, along with the full story of what had happened to them in the mountaintop fortress. Who could tell what dangers might ensue if the outside world knew too much about the secret Temple of the Rosebud Sutra?

A small sound behind her made Mary turn around, her long skirts swishing and her high-heeled, patent-leather boots tapping on the parquet floor. She smiled.

"Good morning, Amelia."

"Good morning, Mistress."

Amelia knelt respectfully at Mary's feet, raising her head to plant a kiss on Mary's folded hands. Mary contemplated the intricate, glossy coils of Amelia's bright blonde hair.

"Your hair is a little askew today."

Amelia's hands instantly shot up to her hair, her fingers trying hurriedly to put it right.

"You may rectify it later," continued Mary with generous good humour. She was enjoying the game every bit as much as Amelia was. At last they had both discovered their true vocations in life, the relative stations which best suited their temperaments. "But mind that it does not happen again—this is the second time in a week."

"No, Mistress. I am sorry, Mistress."

"Overall, I have been quite pleased with your efforts this week."

Amelia beamed with pride.

"As your reward, you may share my bed tonight. But first..."

"Mistress?"

"It has been too long since you had refreshment. If you are thirsty you may lick out my cunny."

As she raised her skirts and felt Amelia's fingers fluttering over the bare lips of her shaven cunt, Mary dreamed up new and delicious games that she and Amelia could play together.

It would not be too difficult, she mused. After all, even in the few moments that she had spent hiding in the temple, she had made a more than cursory examination of the *Rosebud Sutra*. And if she could not understand much of the text, what did it matter?

The exquisite illustrations had proved most instructive...

LINDSAY WELSH
Bad Habits
$4.95 (CANADA $5.95) ROSEBUD

JEAN STINE

SEASON OF THE WITCH

"A future in which it is technically possible to transfer the total mind (personality, character, memory, intelligence) of a rapist killer into the brain dead but physically living body of his female victim.

"Remarkable for intense psychological technique. There is eroticism but it is necessary to mark the differences between the sexes and the subtle altering of a man into a woman." —*The Science Fiction Critic* **268-X**

JOHN WARREN

THE LOVING DOMINANT

Everything you need to know about an infamous sexual variation—and an unspoken type of love. Mentor—a longtime player in the dominance/submission scene—guides readers through this rarely seen world, and offers clear-eyed advice guaranteed to enlighten the most jaded erotic explorers. Mentor reveals the too-often hidden basis of the D/S relationship: the care, trust and love between partners. **218-3**

GRANT ANTREWS

SUBMISSIONS

Another stunning, sensitive tale from the author of ***My Darling Dominatrix***. Once again, Antrews portrays the very special elements of the dominant/submissive relationship with restraint—this time with the story of a lonely man, a winning lottery ticket, and a demanding dominatrix. Grant Antrews is one of erotica's most discerning writers; never leering, he explores his lovers' exotic world and the remarkable bonds it engenders. **207-8**

MY DARLING DOMINATRIX

A remarkable and uncompromising debut novel from major talent. When a man and a woman fall in love it's supposed to be simple, uncomplicated, easy—unless that woman happens to be a dominatrix. Curiosity gives way to unblushing desire in this story of one man's awakening to the joys to be experienced as the willing slave of a powerful woman. This unpretentious love story captures the richness and depth of this very special kind of love. **3055-5**

SARA ADAMSON

THE SLAVE

The second volume in the astonishing "Marketplace" trilogy. ***The Slave*** covers the experience of one exceptionally talented submissive who longs to join the ranks of those who have proven themselves worthy of entry into the Marketplace. But the price, while delicious, is staggeringly high.... Adamson's plot thickens, as her trilogy moves to a mindblowing conclusion in the forthcoming ***The Trainer***. **173-X**

THE MARKETPLACE

"Merchandise does not come easily to the Marketplace.... They haunt the clubs and the organizations, their need so real and desperate that they exude sensual tension when they glide through the crowds. Some of them are so ripe that they intimidate the poseurs, the weekend sadists and the furtive dilettantes who are so endemic to that world. And they never stop asking where we may be found...." A compelling tale of the ultimate training academy, where only the finest are accepted and trained for service beyond their wildest dreams **3096-2**

RHINOCEROS BOOKS $6.95

THE CATALYST

After viewing a controversial, explicitly kinky film full of images of bondage and submission, several audience members find themselves deeply moved by the erotic suggestions they've seen on the screen. Each inspired coupling explores their every imagined extreme, as long-denied urges explode! **3015-6/$4.95**

DAVID AARON CLARK

SISTER RADIANCE

From the author of the acclaimed ***The Wet Forever***, comes a chronicle of obsession, rife with Clark's trademark vivisections of contemporary desires, sacred and profane. The vicissitudes of lust and romance are examined against a backdrop of urban decay and shallow fashionability in this testament to the allure—and inevitability—of the forbidden. **215-9**

THE WET FOREVER

The story of Janus and Madchen, a small-time hood and a beautiful sex worker, ***The Wet Forever*** examines themes of loyalty, sacrifice, redemption and obsession amidst Manhattan's sex parlors and underground S/M clubs. Its combination of sex and suspense makes ***The Wet Forever*** singular, uncompromising, and strangely arousing—and led Terence Sellers to proclaim it "evocative and poetic." **117-9**

ALICE JOANOU

TOURNIQUET

A heady collection of stories and effusions from the pen of one our most dazzling young writers. Strange tales abound, from the story of the mysterious and cruel Cybele, to an encounter with the sadistic entertainment of a bizarre after-hours cafe. By turns lush and austere, Joanou's intoxicating command of language and image makes ***Tourniquet*** a sumptuous feast for all the senses. Strong stuff from a writer at the beginning of her career. **3060-1**

CANNIBAL FLOWER

"She is waiting in her darkened bedroom, as she has waited throughout history, to seduce the men who are foolish enough to be blinded by her irresistible charms. She is Salome, Lucrezia Borgia, Delilah—endlessly alluring, the fulfillment of your every desire.... She is the goddess of sexuality, and ***Cannibal Flower*** is her haunting siren song."—Michael Perkins **$4.95/72-6**

MICHAEL PERKINS

EVIL COMPANIONS

A handsome edition of this cult classic that includes a new preface by Samuel R. Delany on the creation of this brutal novel. Set in New York City during the tumultuous waning years of the Sixties, ***Evil Companions*** has been hailed as "a frightening classic." A young couple explore the nether reaches of the erotic unconscious in a shocking confrontation with the extremes of passion. This acclaimed novel, out of print for years, returns with a special Afterword by the author. **3067-9**

AN ANTHOLOGY OF CLASSIC ANONYMOUS EROTIC WRITING

Michael Perkins, acclaimed authority on erotic literature, has collected the very best passages from the world's erotic writing—especially for Rhino*ceros* readers. "Anonymous" is one of the most infamous bylines in publishing history—and these steamy excerpts show why! Masterpieces of an underground genre. **140-3**

CARRIE'S STORY *Molly Weatherfield*

"I had been Jonathan's slave for about a year when he told me he wanted to sell me at an auction. I wasn't in any condition to respond when he told me this..." Desire and depravity run rampant in this story of uncompromising mastery and irrevocable submission. Mind-boggling excess makes *Carrie's Story* one of the hottest novels ever published. 228-0

CHARLY'S GAME *Bren Flemming*

Charly's a no-nonsense private detective facing the fight of her life. A rich woman's gullible daughter has run off with one of the toughest leather dykes in town—and Charly's hired to lure the girl back. One by one, wise and wicked women ensnare one another in their lusty nets—until the final explosive encounter! 221-3

ANDREA AT THE CENTER *J.P. Kansas*

"You're going to be part of a special community for a few months. You'll be treated well here at the center. It's going to be the most enlightening experience of your life. When it's over, you'll be returned to where you come from." Kidnapped! Lithe and lovely young Andrea is, without warning, whisked away to a distant retreat. Gradually, she is introduced to the ways of the Center, and soon becomes quite friendly with its other inhabitants—all of whom are learning to abandon all restraint in their pursuit of the deepest sexual satisfaction. 206-X

ASK ISADORA *Isadora Alman*

An essential volume, collecting six years' worth of Isadora Alman's syndicated columns on sex and relationships. Alman's been called a "hip Dr. Ruth," and a "sexy Dear Abby," based upon the wit and pertinence of her advice. Today's world is more perplexing than ever—and Isadora Alman is just the expert to help untangle the most personal of knots. 61-0

LESSONS AND LOVERS *Elaine Platero*

"Hettie felt like a kind of sex-doll for the other two, a living breathing female body to demonstrate the responses and vulnerabilities of womankind to a young man who was hungry for knowledge...." When a repressed widow, her all-too-willing manservant, a voluptuous doctor and an anxious neophyte take a country weekend together, crucial lessons are learned by all! 196-9

THE SLAVES OF SHOANNA *Mercedes Kelly*

Shoanna, the cruel and magnificent, takes four maidens under her wing—and teaches them the ins and outs of pleasure and discipline. The four are trained in every imaginable way: from simple fleshly joys to techniques for the handling of unimaginable instruments. Slutty students! 164-0

MASTER OF TIMBERLAND *Sara H. French*

Luscious slaves serve randy tourists in this ultimate vacation paradise. Only the most willing and voluptuous are admitted, and trained to accommodate every whim of the horny vacationers—all of whom choose their slaves with discretion, and rule with an iron fist. 3059-8

STASI SLUT *Anthony Bobarzynski*

Adina lives in East Germany, far from the sexually liberated, uninhibited debauchery of the West. She meets a group of ruthless and corrupt STASI agents who use her as a pawn in their political chess game as well as for their own perverse gratification—until she uses her talents and attractions in a final bid for total freedom in the revolutionary climax of this *Red*-hot Cold War thriller! 3052-0

BLUE TANGO *Hilary Manning*

Ripe and tempting Julie is haunted by the sounds of extraordinary passion beyond her bedroom wall. Alone, she fantasizes about taking part in the amorous dramas of her hosts, Claire and Edward. When she finds a way to watch the nightly debauch, her curiosity turns to full-blown lust! 3037-7

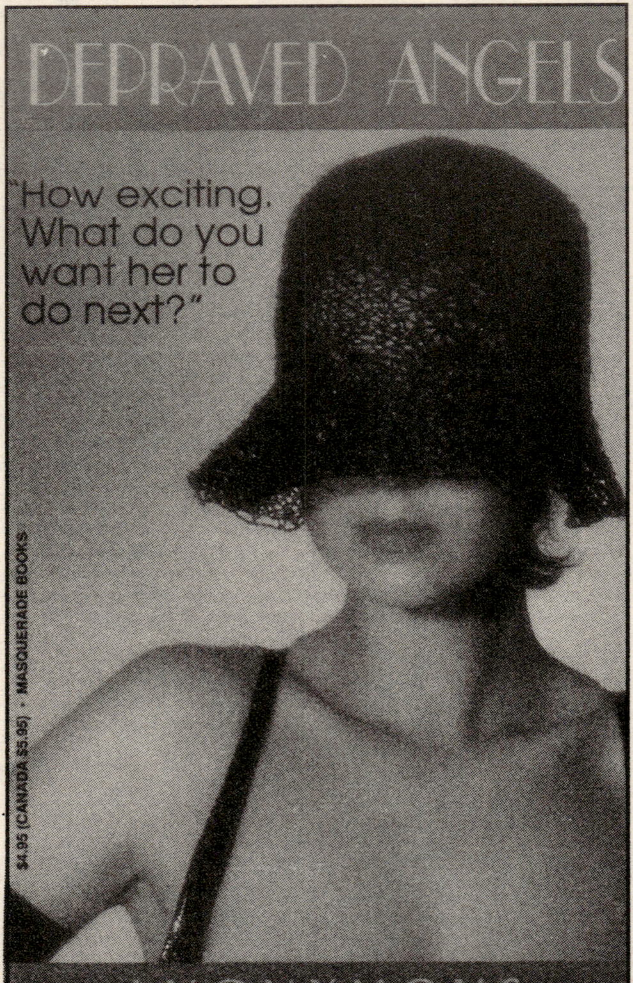
DEPRAVED ANGELS
"How exciting. What do you want her to do next?"
$4.95 (CANADA $5.95) • MASQUERADE BOOKS
ANONYMOUS

LOUISE BELHAVEL

FRAGRANT ABUSES

The saga of Clara and Iris continues as the now-experienced girls enjoy themselves with a new circle of worldly friends whose imaginations match their own. Polymorphous perversity follows the lusty ladies around the globe! 88-2

DEPRAVED ANGELS

The final installment in the incredible adventures of Clara and Iris. Together with their friends, lovers, and worldly acquaintances, Clara and Iris explore the frontiers of depravity at home and abroad. 92-0

TITIAN BERESFORD

JUDITH BOSTON

Young Edward would have been lucky to get the stodgy old companion he thought his parents had hired for him. Instead, an exquisite woman arrives at his door, and Edward finds his compulsively lewd behavior never goes unpunished by the unflinchingly severe Judith Boston! 87-4

NINA FOXTON

An aristocrat finds herself bored by amusements for "ladies of good breeding." Instead of taking tea with proper gentlemen, Nina invents a contraption to "milk" them of their most private essences. No man ever says "No" to Nina! 145-4

A TITIAN BERESFORD READER

A captivating collection! Beresford's fanciful settings and outrageous fetishism have established his reputation as one of modern erotica's most imaginative and spirited writers. Wild dominatrixes, deliciously perverse masochists, and mesmerizing detail are the hallmarks of the Beresford tale. 114-4

CINDERELLA

Beresford triumphs again with castle dungeons and tightly corseted ladies-in-waiting, naughty viscounts and impossibly cruel masturbatrixes—nearly every conceivable method of erotic torture is explored and described in lush, vivid detail. 3024-5

CHINA BLUE

KUNG FU NUNS

"When I could stand the pleasure no longer, she lifted me out of the chair and sat me down on top of the table. She then lifted her skirt. The sight of her perfect legs clad in white stockings and a petite garter belt further mesmerized me. I lean particularly towards white garter belts." The infamous China Blue returns! 3031-8

SECRETS OF THE CITY

China Blue, the infamous Madame of Saigon, a black belt enchantress in the martial arts of love, is out for revenge. Her search brings her to Manhattan, where she intends to call upon her secret sexual arts to kill her enemies at the height of ecstasy. 03-3

HARRIET DAIMLER

DARLING • INNOCENCE

In *Darling*, a virgin is raped by a mugger. Driven by her urge for revenge, she searches New York for him in a furious sexual hunt that leads to rape and murder. In *Innocence*, a young invalid determines to experience sex through her voluptuous nurse. Two critically acclaimed novels in one volume! 3047-4

THE PLEASURE THIEVES

They are the Pleasure Thieves, two lusty and larcenous men whose sexually preoccupied targets are set up by luscious Carol Stoddard. She forms an ultra-hot sexual threesome with them, trying every combination from two-on-ones to daisy chains—but always on the sly, because pleasures are even sweeter when they're stolen! 036-X

erotic
PLAYGIRL
romance
SPANISH
HOLIDAY
$4.95 • EROTIC PLAYGIRL ROMANCE
LIZBETH DUSSEAU

THREE WOMEN
They could never get enough...
$4.95 (CANADA $5.95) • MASQUERADE BOOKS
ANONYMOUS

THE WILD HEART

A luxury hotel is the setting for this artful web of sex, desire, and love. A newlywed sees sex as a duty, while her hungry husband tries to awaken her to its tender joys. A Parisian entertains wealthy guests for the love of money. Each episode provides a new variation in this lusty Grand Hotel! **3007-5**

DEMON HEAT

An ancient vampire stalks the unsuspecting in the form of a beautiful and utterly irresistible woman. But this fiend doesn't drink blood; she craves a different kind of potion. When her insatiable appetite has drained every last drop of juice from her victims, they hunger for more—even if it means being sucked to death! **79-3**

HAREM SONG

Young, sensuous Amber flees her cruel uncle and provincial village in search of a better life, but finds she is no match for the glittering light of London. Soon Amber becomes a call girl and is sold into a lusty Sultan's harem—a vocation for which she possesses more than average talent! **73-4**

JADE EAST

Laura, passive and passionate, follows her husband Emilio to Hong Kong. He gives her to Wu Li, a connoisseur of sexual perversions, who passes her on to Madeleine, a flamboyant lesbian. Madeleine's friends make Laura the centerpiece in Hong Kong's underground orgies. Soon Laura becomes one of Emilio's steamy slaves for sale! **60-2**

RAWHIDE LUST

Diana Beaumont, the young wife of a U.S. marshal, is kidnapped as an act of vengeance against her husband. Jack Beaumont sets out on a long journey to get his wife back, but finally catches up with her trail only to learn that she's been sold into white slavery in Mexico. **55-6**

THE JAZZ AGE

The time: the Roaring Twenties. A young attorney becomes suspicious of his mistress while his wife has an fling with a lesbian lover. ***The Jazz Age*** is a romp of erotic realism from the heyday of the flapper and the speakeasy. **48-3**

AMARANTHA KNIGHT

THE DARKER PASSIONS: *DR. JEKYLL AND MR. HYDE*

It is an old story, one of incredible, frightening transformations achieved through mysterious experiments. Now, Amarantha Knight explores the steamy possibilities of a tale where no one is quite who—or what—they seem. Victorian bedrooms explode with hidden demons. **227-2**

THE DARKER PASSIONS: *DRACULA*

From the realm of legend comes the grand beast of eros, the famed and dreaded defiler of innocence. His name is Dracula, and no virgin is protected from his unspeakable ravishments. One by one he brings his victims to the ecstasy that will make them his—forever. A classic fiend recast as the ultimate voluptuary. **147-0**

ALIZARIN LAKE

THE EROTIC ADVENTURES OF HARRY TEMPLE

Temple's memoirs chronicle his amorous adventures from his initiation at the hands of insatiable sirens, through his stay at a house of hot repute, to his encounters with a chastity belted nympho—and other twisted partners. **127-6**

EROTOMANIA

The bible of female sexual perversion! It's all here, everything you ever wanted to know about kinky women past and present. From simple nymphomania to the most outrageous fetishism, all secrets are revealed in this look into the forbidden rooms of feminine desire. **128-4**

TEARS OF THE INQUISITION

Best–selling author Paul Little delivers a staggering account of pleasure and punishment. "There was a tickling inside her as her nervous system reminded her she was ready for sex. But before her was...the Inquisitor!" Wild and pleasurable penalties abound in this story set during one of histories most notorious periods. **146-2**

DOUBLE NOVEL

Two of Paul Little's bestselling novels in one spellbinding volume! ***The Metamorphosis of Lisette Joyaux*** tells the story of an innocent young woman initiated into a new world of lesbian lusts. ***The Story of Monique*** reveals the clandestine sexual rituals that beckon to the ripe and willing Monique. **86-6**

CHINESE JUSTICE AND OTHER STORIES

The notorious Paul Little indulges his penchant for punishment in these wild tales. ***Chinese Justice*** is already a classic—the story of the excruciating pleasures and delicious punishments inflicted on foreigners under the tyrannical leaders of the Boxer Rebellion. One by one, each foreign woman is brought before the authorities and grilled. Scandalous tortures are inflicted upon the helpless females by their relentless, merciless captors. **153-5**

SLAVES OF CAMEROON

This sordid tale is about the women who were used by German officers for salacious profit. These women were forced to become whores for the German army in this African colony. The most perverse forms of erotic gratification are depicted in this unsavory tale of women exploited in every way possible.. No limits are acknowledged in this volume dedicated to the unleashed lusts for flesh and power! One of the infamous Paul Little's most ferocious volumes of punishing passion. **3026-1**

THE PRISONER

Judge Black has built a secret room below a women's penitentiary, where he sentences the prisoners to hours of exhibition and torment while his friends watch from their luxurious box seats. An endless array of errant beauties is brought down and sentenced in Judge Black's House of Corrections—a demonic and inescapable dungeon equipped with one purpose in mind: to administer his own brand of rough justice—and sizzling punishments—to the tenderest skin of his helpless captives! **3011-3**

ALL THE WAY

Two excruciating novels from Paul Little in one hot volume! ***Going All the Way*** features an unhappy man who tries to purge himself of the memory of his lover with a series of quirky and uninhibited women. ***Pushover*** tells the story of a serial spanker and his celebrated exploits in California. **3023-7**

THE AUTOBIOGRAPHY OF A FLEA III

That incorrigible voyeur, the Flea, returns! This time Flea visit Provence to spy on the younger generation, now coming into ripe maturity. With the same eye for lurid detail, the Flea's observations won't fail to titillate yet again! **94-7**

END OF INNOCENCE

The early days of Women's Emancipation are the setting for this story of some very independent ladies. These girls were willing to go to any lengths to fight for their sexual freedom, and willing to endure any punishment in their desire for total liberation. **77-7**

POOR DARLINGS

Here are the impressions and feelings, the excitement and lust, that young women feel when they submit to desire. Not just with male partners—but with women too. Desperate, gasping, scandalous sex turns these ladies into insatiable beasts of prey! **33-5**

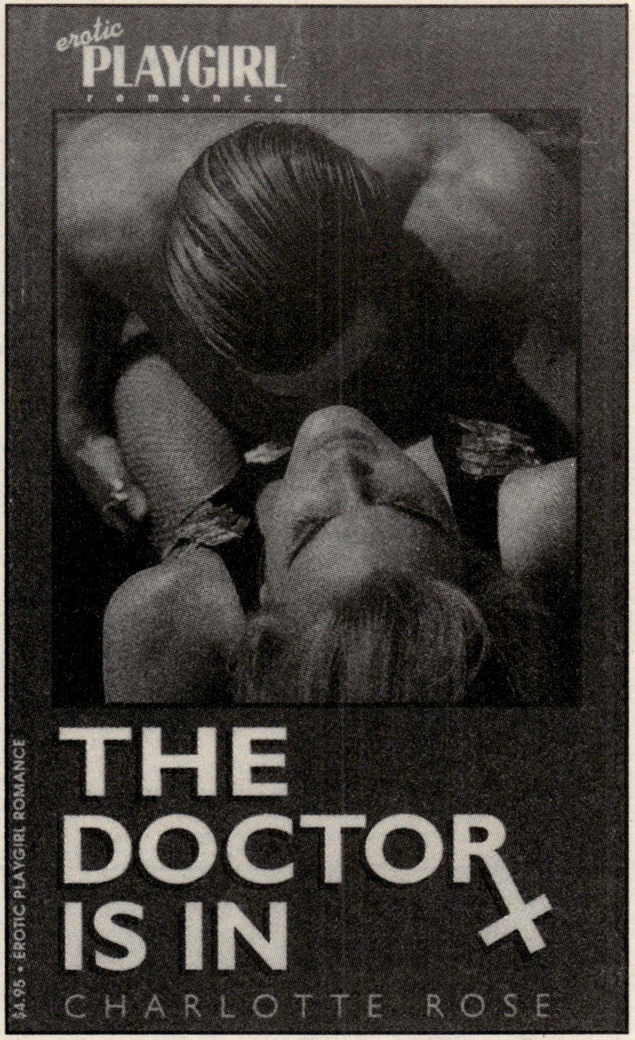
erotic
PLAYGIRL
romance
THE DOCTOR IS IN
CHARLOTTE ROSE
$4.95 • EROTIC PLAYGIRL ROMANCE

DANIEL VIAN
illusions

THE
HAVEN
VALENTINA CILESCU
$4.95 ROSEBUD

WAYWARD
She tossed aside her single garment and stood revealed in all her lusciousness...
$4.95 (CANADA $5.95) • MASQUERADE BOOKS
ANONYMOUS

MAUDE RIVERS

Under the tutelage of Charles, Maude learns to abandon the restraints of her strict upbringing and embrace the rewards of unbridled sexual indulgence. The lustful Charles leads his lovely charge on an erotic journey of breathtaking variety, and introduces her to a cast of insatiable accomplices. **3087-3**

KATE PERCIVAL

Kate, the "Belle of Delaware," divulges the secrets of her scandalous life, from her earliest sexual experiments to the deviations she learns to love. Nothing is secret, and no holes are barred in this titillating tell-all that reveals the hidden lives of turn-of-the-century lads and ladies. Sexual lunacy rules in this tale of an earlier America! **3072-5**

THE STORY OF MONIQUE

Between the lesbians who came to Sonia's parties, and the convent where nuns and monks fell upon each other in orgiastic madness, Monique soon discovered within herself an endless appetite for sex! Luckily, Monique would never find that appetite unsatisfied—thanks to an insatiable circle of acquaintances. **42-4**

THE FURTHER ADVENTURES OF MADELEINE

"What mortal pen can describe these driven orgasmic transports?" writes Madeleine as she explores Paris' sexual underground. She discovers that the finest clothes may cover the most twisted personalities of all! **04-1**

THE AMERICAN COLLECTION

LUST *Palmiro Vicarion*

A wealthy and powerful man of leisure recounts his rise up the corporate ladder and his corresponding descent into debauchery. Adventure and political intrigue provide a stimulating backdrop for this tale of a classic scoundrel with an uncurbed appetite for sexual power! **82-3**

WAYWARD *Peter Jason*

A mysterious countess hires a tour bus for an unusual vacation. Traveling through Europe's most notorious cities, she picks up friends, lovers, and acquaintances from every walk of life in pursuit of unbridled sensual pleasure. Countless orgies, outrageous acts, and endless deviation! **3004-0**

LOVE'S ILLUSION

Elizabeth Renard yearned for the body of Dan Harrington. Then she discovers Harrington's secret weakness: a need to be humiliated and punished. She makes him her slave, and together they commence a journey into depravity that leaves nothing to the imagination—*nothing!* **100-4**

THE RELUCTANT CAPTIVE

Sarah is kidnapped by ruthless outlaws who kill her husband and burn their prosperous ranch. Her journey takes her from the bordellos of the Wild West to the bedrooms of Boston, until she is bought at last by a mysterious stranger from her past. **3022-9**

LUSTY LESSONS

The privileged and attractive David Elston had everything except the ability to fulfill the unrelenting demands of his passion. His efforts end in failure until he meets a stranger who takes him to a forbidden land of pleasure. **31-9**

DANCE HALL GIRLS

The dance hall studio in Modesto was ruthless trap for men and women of all ages. They learned to dance under the tutelage of sexual professionals. So grateful were they for the attention, they opened their hearts and their wallets. Scandalous sexual slavery! **44-0**

GUILLERMO BOSCH

RAIN

An adult fairy tale, *Rain* takes place in a time when the mysteries of Eros are played out against a background of uncommon deprivation. The tale begins on the 1,537th day of drought—when one man comes to know the true depths of thirst. In a quest to sate his hunger for some knowledge of the wide world, he is taken through a series of extraordinary, unearthly encounters that promise to change not only his life, but the course of civilization around him. ***232-9***

MICHAEL LASSELL

THE HARD WAY

Virtually all of the material in this book was written and published between 1983 and 1993, although it covers all the years I can remember. The focus, of course, is on the post-Stonewall Liberation Years.... I am, like most writers, horrified to read work written as recently as ten days ago, much less ten years ago, but I have bitten the bullet and made few changes, except when some reference is so out of cultural currency as to obscure my own obscure point, or when I can't remember what the hell I meant by something. But what you see here, is pretty much the way it was the first time it appeared in black and white....

The first collection of renowned gay writer Michael Lassell's poetry, fiction and essays. Widely anthologized and a staple of gay literary and entertainment publications nationwide, Lassell is regarded as one of the most distinctive and accomplished talents of his generation. As much a chronicle of post-Stonewall gay life as a compendium of a remarkable writer's work, ***The Hard Way*** is sure to appeal to anyone interested in the state of contemporary writing. ***231-0***

SAMUEL R. DELANY

THE MAD MAN

For his thesis, graduate student John Marr researches the life and work of the brilliant Timothy Hasler: a philosopher whose career was cut tragically short over a decade earlier. Marr encounters numerous obstacles, as other researchers turn up evidence of Hasler's personal life that is deemed simply too unpleasant. On another front, Marr finds himself increasingly drawn toward more shocking, depraved sexual entanglements with the homeless men of his neighborhood, until it begins to seem that Hasler's death might hold some key to his own life as a gay man in the age of AIDS.

This new novel by Samuel R. Delany not only expands the parameters of what he has given us in the past, but fuses together two seemingly disparate genres of writing and comes up with something which is not comparable to any existing text of which I am aware.... What Delany has done here is take the ideas of Marquis de Sade one step further, by filtering extreme and obsessive sexual behavior through the sieve of post-modern experience.... *—Lambda Book Report*

The latest novel from Hugo- and Nebula-winning science fiction writer and critic Delany... reads like a pornographic reflection of Peter Ackroyd's Chatterton *or A.S. Byatt's* Possession.... *The pornographic element... becomes more than simple shock or titillation, though, as Delany develops an insightful dichotomy between [his protagonist]'s two worlds: the one of cerebral philosophy and dry academia, the other of heedless, 'impersonal' obsessive sexual extremism. When these worlds finally collide ... the novel achieves a surprisingly satisfying resolution....* *—Publishers Weekly*

hardcover 193-4/$23.95

RICHARD KASAK BOOKS $12.95

DAVID MELTZER

THE AGENCY TRILOGY

...'The Agency' is clearly Meltzer's paradigm of society; a mindless machine of which we are all 'agents' including those whom the machine supposedly serves.... —Norman Spinrad

With the Essex House edition of ***The Agency*** in 1968, the highly regarded poet David Meltzer took America on a trip into a hell of unbridled sexuality. The story of a supersecret, Orwellian sexual network, ***The Agency*** explored issues of erotic dominance and submission with an immediacy and frankness previously unheard of in American literature, as well as presented a vision of an America consumed and dehumanized by a lust for power. ***216-7***

CARO SOLES

MELTDOWN!

An Anthology of Erotic Science Fiction and Dark Fantasy for Gay Men

Editor Caro Soles has put together one of the most explosive, mind-bending collections of gay erotic writing ever published. ***Meltdown!*** contains the very best examples of this increasingly popular sub-genre: stories meant to shock and delight, to send a shiver down the spine and start a fire down below. An extraordinary volume, ***Meltdown!*** presents both new voices and provocative pieces by world-famous writers Edmund White and Samuel R. Delany. ***203-5***

BIZARRE SEX

BIZARRE SEX AND OTHER CRIMES OF PASSION

Edited by Stan Tal

Stan Tal, editor of *Bizarre Sex*, Canada's boldest fiction publication, has culled the very best stories that have crossed his desk—and now unleashes them on the reading public in ***Bizarre Sex and Other Crimes of Passion***. Over twenty small masterpieces of erotic shock make this one of the year's most unexpectedly alluring anthologies. Including such masters of erotic horror and fantasy as Edward Lee, Lucy Taylor, Nancy Kilpatrick and Caro Soles, ***Bizarre Sex and Other Crimes of Passion***, is a treasure-trove of arousing chills. ***213-2***

PAT CALIFIA

SENSUOUS MAGIC

Sensuous Magic *is clear, succinct and engaging even for the reader for whom S/M isn't the sexual behavior of choice.... Califia's prose is soothing, informative and non-judgmental—she both instructs her reader and explores the territory for them.... When she is writing about the dynamics of sex and the technical aspects of it, Califia is the Dr. Ruth of the alternative sexuality set....* *—Lambda Book Report*

Don't take a dangerous trip into the unknown—buy this book and know where you're going! *—SKIN TWO*

131-4

SKIN TWO

THE BEST OF *SKIN TWO* *Edited by Tim Woodward*

For over a decade, *Skin Two* has served as the bible of the international fetish community. A groundbreaking journal from the crossroads of sexuality, fashion, and art, *Skin Two* specializes in provocative, challenging essays by the finest writers working in the "radical sex" scene. Collected here, for the first time, are the articles and interviews that have established the magazine's singular reputation. Including interviews with cult figures Tim Burton, Clive Barker and Jean Paul Gaultier. ***130-6***

PAT
CALIFIA
SENSUOUS
MAGIC
A GUIDE FOR ADVENTUROUS COUPLES

GAUNTLET

THE BEST OF *GAUNTLET* *Edited by Barry Hoffman*

No material, no opinion is taboo enough to violate Gauntlet's *purpose of 'exploring the limits of free expression'—airing all views in the name of the First Amendment.*

—Associated Press

Dedicated to "exploring the limits of free expression," *Gauntlet* has, with its semi-annual issues, taken on such explosive topics as race, pornography, political correctness, and media manipulation—always publishing the widest possible range of opinions. Only in *Gauntlet* might one expect to encounter Phyllis Schlafley *and* Annie Sprinkle, Stephen King *and* Madonna—often within pages of one another. The very best, most provocative articles have been gathered by editor-in-chief Barry Hoffman, to make ***The Best of Gauntlet*** a most provocative exploration of American society's limits. ***202-7***

MICHAEL PERKINS

THE GOOD PARTS: An Uncensored Guide to Literary Sexuality

Michael Perkins, one of America's only serious critics to regularly scrutinize sexual literature, presents an overview of sex a seen in the pages of over 100 major volumes from the past twenty years.

I decided when I wrote my first column in 1968 that I would take the opportunity presented by Screw *to chronicle the inevitable and inexorable rise of an unfairly neglected genre of contemporary writing. I wondered if I would remain interested in the subject for very long, and if the field would not eventually diminish so there would be nothing to review.... Every week since then I have published a thousand-word review, and occasionally a longer essay, devoted to discovering and reporting on the manifestations of sexuality in all kinds of fiction, nonfiction, and poetry. In my columns I cast a wide net (a million words so far) over a subject no one else wanted to take a long look at. It has indeed held my interest.* ***186-1***

LARS EIGHNER

ELEMENTS OF AROUSAL

Critically acclaimed gay writer Lars Eighner—whose *Travels with Lizbeth* was chosen by the *New York Times Book Review* as one of the year's notable titles—develops a guideline for success with one of publishing's best kept secrets: the novice-friendly field of gay erotic writing.

In ***Elements of Arousal***, Eighner details his craft, providing the reader with sure advice. Eighner's overview of the gay erotic market paints a picture of a diverse array of outlets for a writer's work. Because, after all, writing is what ***Elements of Arousal*** is about: the application and honing of the writer's craft, which brought Lars Eighner fame with not only the steamy *Bayou Boy*, but the profoundly illuminating *Travels with Lizbeth.* ***230-2***

JOHN PRESTON

HUSTLING:
A GENTLEMAN'S GUIDE TO THE FINE ART OF HOMOSEXUAL PROSTITUTION

John Preston solicited the advice of "working boys" from across the country in his effort to produce the ultimate guide to the hustler's world. ***Hustling*** covers every practical aspect of the business, from clientele and payment options to "specialties," sidelines and drawbacks. No stone is left unturned in this guidebook to the ins and outs of this much-mythologized trade.

...fun and highly literary. What more could you expect from such an accomplished activist, author and editor?

—Drummer

137-3

MY LIFE AS A PORNOGRAPHER

And Other Indecent Acts

*...essential and enlightening...His sex-positive stand on safer-sex education as the only truly effective AIDS-prevention strategy will certainly not win him any conservative converts, but AIDS activists will be shouting their assent.... [**My Life as a Pornographer**] is a bridge from the sexually liberated 1970s to the more cautious 1990s, and Preston has walked much of that way as a standard-bearer to the cause for equal rights....* *—Library Journal*

*Preston's a model essayist; he writes pellucid prose in a voice that, like Samuel Johnson's, combines authority with entertainment.... **My Life as a Pornographer**...is not pornography, but rather reflections upon the writing and production of it. Preston ranges from really superb journalism of his interviews with denizens of the S/M demimond, particularly a superb portrait of a Colt model Preston calls "Joe" to a brilliant analysis of the "theater" of the New York sex club, The Mineshaft.... In a deeply sex-phobic world, Preston has never shied away from a vision of the redemptive potential of the erotic drive. Better than perhaps anyone in our community, Preston knows how physical joy can bridge differences and make us well.* *—Lambda Book Report*

135-7

MARCO VASSI

THE STONED APOCALYPSE

"...Marco Vassi is our champion sexual energist."—VLS

During his lifetime, Marco Vassi was hailed as America's premier erotic writer and most worthy successor to Henry Miller. His work was praised by writers as diverse as Gore Vidal and Norman Mailer, and his reputation was worldwide. ***The Stoned Apocalypse*** is Vassi's autobiography, financed by the other groundbreaking erotic writing that made him a cult sensation. Chronicling a cross-country trip on America's erotic byways, it offers a rare glimpse of a generation's sexual imagination. ***132-2***

A DRIVING PASSION

"Let me leave you with A Driving Passion. It is, in effect, an introduction and overview of all his other books, and my hope is that it will lead readers to explore the bold literary contribution of Marco Vassi." —Norman Mailer

While the late Marco Vassi was primarily known and respected as a novelist, he was also an effective and compelling speaker. ***A Driving Passion*** collects the wit and insight Vassi brought to his infamously revealing lectures, and distills the philosophy—including the concept of Metasex—that made him an underground sensation. An essential volume. ***134-9***

THE EROTIC COMEDIES

A collection of stories from America's premier erotic philosopher. Marco Vassi was a dedicated iconoclast, and ***The Erotic Comedies*** marked a high point in his literary career. Scathing and humorous, these stories reflect Vassi's belief in the power and primacy of Eros in American life, as well as his commitment to the elimination of personal repression through carnal indulgence. A wry collection for the sexually adventurous. ***136-5***

THE SALINE SOLUTION

During the Sexual Revolution, Marco Vassi established himself as an intrepid explorer of an uncharted sexual landscape. During this time he also distinguished himself as a novelist, producing ***The Saline Solution*** to great acclaim. With the story of one couple's brief affair and the events that lead them to desperately reassess their lives, Vassi examines the dangers of intimacy in an age of extraordinary freedom. A remarkably clear-eyed look at the growing pains of a generation. ***180-2***

THE MASQUERADE EROTIC LIBRARY

ADAM&EVE	93-9	$4.95
AFFINITIES	3113-6	$4.95
ALIZARIN LAKE READER, AN	3106-3	$4.95
ALL THE WAY	3023-7	$4.95
ALL-STUD	3104-7	$4.95
AMERICAN PRELUDE	170-5	$4.95
ANDREA AT THE CENTER	206-X	$4.95
ANGELA	76-9	$4.95
ANIMAL HANDLERS	264-7	$4.95
ANTHOLOGY OF CLASSIC ANONYMOUS EROTIC WRITING, AN	3140-3	$6.95
APPLICANT, THE	3038-5	$4.95
ARENA, THE	3083-0	$4.95
ASK ISADORA	61-0	$4.95
AUTOBIOGRAPHY OF A FLEA III	94-7	$4.95
B.M.O.C.	3077-6	$4.95
BAD HABITS	3068-7	$4.95
BADBOY EROTIC LIBRARY, VOL. 1, THE	190-X	$4.95
BADBOY FANTASIES	3049-0	$4.95
BAYOU BOY	3084-9	$4.95
BEAST OF BURDEN	3105-5	$6.95
BEST OF MARY LOVE, THE	3099-7	$4.95
BIG SHOTS	3112-8	$4.95
BIZARRE DREAMS	187-X	$4.95
BONE	177-2	$4.95
BOUDOIR, THE	85-8	$4.95
CANDY LIPS	182-9	$4.95
CANNIBAL FLOWER	72-6	$4.95
CAPTIVE MAIDENS	3014-8	$4.95
CARNAL DAYS OF HELEN SEFERIS, THE	3086-5	$4.95
CAROLINE'S CONTRACT	3122-5	$4.95
CAROUSEL	3051-2	$4.95
CATALYST, THE	3015-6	$4.95
CHAINS	3158-6	$4.95
CHARLY'S GAME	221-3	$4.95
CHINESE JUSTICE & OTHER STORIES	3154-3	$4.95
CINDERELLA	3024-5	$4.95
CITADEL, THE	198-5	$4.95
CLAIRE'S GIRLS	3108-X	$4.95
CLARA	80-7	$4.95
COMPLETE EROTIC READER , THE	3063-6	$4.95
COMPLETE PLAYGIRL FANTASIES, THE	3075-X	$4.95
CRUMBLING FAÇADE	3043-1	$4.95
DANCE HALL GIRLS	44-0	$4.95
DANGEROUS LESSONS	32-7	$4.95
DARLING • INNOCENCE	3047-4	$4.95
DEADLY LIES	3076-8	$4.95
DELICIOUS DAUGHTER, THE	3155-1	$4.95
DEMON HEAT	79-3	$4.95
DEPRAVED ANGELS	92-0	$4.95
DEVA-DASI	29-7	$4.95
DISCIPLINE OF ODETTE, THE	3033-4	$4.95
DISTANT LOVE	3056-3	$4.95
DOCTOR IS IN, THE	195-0	$4.95
DREAM CRUISE	3045-8	$4.95
DUKE COSIMO	3052-0	$4.95
ECSTASY ON FIRE	3080-6	$4.95
EIGHTH WONDER	200-0	$4.95
END OF INNOCENCE	77-7	$4.95
ENGLISH GOVERNESS, THE	43-2	$4.95
ENTER WITH TRUMPETS	197-7	$6.95
EQUINOX	3157-8	$6.95
EROTIC ADVENTURES OF HARRY TEMPLE, THE	3127-6	$4.95
EROTOMANIA	3128-4	$4.95
EVIL COMPANIONS	3067-9	$4.95
EXPOSED	3126-8	$4.95
FAUSTUS CONTRACT, THE	167-5	$4.95
FESTIVAL OF VENUS	37-8	$4.95
FIRST PERSON	179-9	$4.95
FLESH FABLES	243-4	$4.95
FOR A PIRATE'S KISS	3156-X	$4.95

THE MASQUERADE EROTIC LIBRARY

FOR SALE BY OWNER	3064-4	$4.95
FRAGRANT ABUSES	88-2	$4.95
FURTHER ADVENTURES OF MADELEINE, THE	04-1	$4.95
GARDEN OF DELIGHT	3058-X	$4.95
GAY ADVENTURES OF CAPTAIN GOOSE, THE	169-1	$4.95
GLORIA'S INDISCRETION	3094-6	$4.95
GOLDEN YEARS	3069-5	$4.95
HAREM SONG	73-4	$4.95
HAVEN, THE	165-9	$4.95
HEAT WAVE	3159-4	$4.95
HEIR • THE KING, THE	3048-2	$4.95
HELEN AND DESIRE	3093-8	$4.95
HELOISE	3073-3	$4.95
HIGHWAYWOMAN, THE	174-8	$4.95
HITTING HOME AND OTHER STORIES	222-1	$4.95
HUCK & BILLY	245-0	$4.95
ICE MAIDEN, THE	3001-6	$4.95
IF THE SHOE FITS	223-X	$4.95
ILLUSIONS	3074-1	$4.95
IMAGE OF THE BEAST, THE	166-7	$6.95
IMRE	3019-9	$4.95
INITIATION OF PB 500, THE	3141-1	$4.95
INITIATION RITES	3120-9	$4.95
INSTRUMENTS OF THE PASSION, THE	3010-5	$4.95
IN THE ALLEY	3144-6	$4.95
INTIMATE PLEASURES	38-6	$4.95
JADE EAST	60-2	$4.95
JAZZ AGE, THE	48-3	$4.95
JENNIFER	3107-1	$4.95
JENNIFER AGAIN	220-5	$4.95
JUDITH BOSTON	273-6	$4.95
KAMA HOURI	39-4	$4.95
KATE PERCIVAL	3072-5	$4.95
KATY'S AWAKENING	74-2	$4.95
KIDNAP	90-4	$4.95
KIM'S PASSION	162-4	$4.95
KISS OF LEATHER	3161-6	$4.95
KUNG FU NUNS	3031-8	$4.95
LADY F.	3102-0	$4.95
LAVENDER ROSE	208-6	$4.95
LEATHERWOMEN	3095-4	$4.95
LEATHERWOMEN II	229-9	$4.95
LESSONS AND LOVERS	196-9	$4.95
LETHAL SILENCE	3125-X	$4.95
LEWD CONDUCT	3091-1	$4.95
LONG LEATHER CORD, THE	201-9	$4.95
LOVE AND SURRENDER	3082-2	$4.95
LOVE IN WARTIME	3044-X	$4.95
LOVE'S ILLUSION	3100-4	$4.95
LOVING DOMINANT, THE	218-3	$6.95
LUST	82-3	$4.95
LUST OF THE COSSACKS	41-6	$4.95
LUSTFUL TURK, THE	163-2	$4.95
LUSTY LESSONS	31-9	$4.95
MAN SWORD	188-8	$4.95
MAN WITH A MAID	3065-2	$4.95
MAN WITH A MAID II	3071-7	$4.95
MAN WITH A MAID: THE CONCLUSION	3013-X	$4.95
MANEATER	3103-9	$6.95
MANSEX	3160-8	$4.95
MARKETPLACE, THE	3096-2	$6.95
MASQUERADE READER, A	84-X	$4.95
MASTER OF TIMBERLAND	3059-8	$4.95
MASTERING MARY SUE	3005-9	$4.95
MAUDE CAMERON	3087-3	$4.95
MEMBER OF THE CLUB	3079-2	$4.95
MEN AT WORK	3027-X	$4.95
MEN WHO LOVED ME	274-4	$6.95
MIKE AND ME	3035-0	$4.95
MILES DIAMOND	3116-7	$4.95
MISS HIGH HEELS	3066-0	$4.95

THE MASQUERADE EROTIC LIBRARY

MISTRESS MINE	3109-8	$4.95
MR. BENSON	3041-5	$4.95
MUSCLE BOUND	3028-8	$4.95
MY DARLING DOMINATRIX	3055-5	$4.95
MY LIFE AND LOVES (THE 'LOST' VOLUME)	52-1	$4.95
NAUGHTIER AT NIGHT	3030-X	$4.95
NUNNERY TALES, THE	20-3	$4.95
OBSESSIONS	3012-1	$4.95
ODD WOMEN	3123-3	$4.95
ORF	3110-1	$6.95
PASSAGE & OTHER STORIES	3057-1	$4.95
PASSION IN RIO	54-8	$4.95
PAULA	3036-9	$4.95
PAULINE	3129-2	$4.95
PERSUASIONS	183-7	$4.95
PLEASURE THIEVES, THE	36-X	$4.95
PLEASURES & FOLLIES	26-2	$4.95
PRISONER, THE	3011-3	$4.95
PRIVATE LESSONS	3116-0	$4.95
PROFESSIONAL CHARMER	3003-2	$4.95
PROTESTS, PLEASURES & RAPTURES	204-3	$4.95
PROVINCETOWN SUMMER	3040-7	$4.95
RAWHIDE LUST	55-6	$4.95
RED DOG SALOON	68-8	$4.95
RELUCTANT CAPTIVE, THE	3022-9	$4.95
REPENTANCE OF LORRAINE, THE	3124-1	$6.95
REUNION IN FLORENCE	3070-9	$4.95
RITUALS	168-3	$4.95
ROMANCES OF BLANCHE LE MARE, THE	3101-2	$4.95
ROPE ABOVE, THE BED BELOW, THE	269-8	$4.95
ROSEBUD SUTRA	242-6	$4.95
ROSEMARY LANE	3078-4	$4.95
RUN, LITTLE LEATHER BOY	3143-8	$4.95
SABINE	3046-6	$4.95
SACRED PASSIONS	21-1	$4.95
SCARLET PANSY, THE	189-6	$4.95
SCHOOL DAYS IN PARIS	205-1	$4.95
SCHOOL FOR SIN	89-0	$4.95
SCORPIUS EQUATION, THE	3119-5	$4.95
SCRAPBOOK	225-6	$4.95
SECRET DANGER	3111-X	$4.95
SEASON OF THE WITCH	268-X	$4.95
SECRET RECORD, THE	3039-3	$4.95
SECRETS OF THE CITY	03-3	$4.95
SENSATIONS	3081-4	$6.95
SEXPERT, THE	3034-2	$4.95
SEX SHOW	225-6	$4.95
SEXUAL ADVENTURES OF SHERLOCK HOLMES, THE	3097-0	$4.95
SHADOWMAN	178-0	$4.95
SILK AND STEEL	3032-6	$4.95
SINS OF THE CITIES OF THE PLAIN	3016-4	$4.95
SISTER RADIANCE	215-9	$6.95
SKIN DEEP	265-5	$4.95
SKIRTS	3115-2	$4.95
SLAVE, THE	173-X	$6.95
SLAVE ISLAND	3006-7	$4.95
SLAVE PRINCE, THE	199-3	$4.95
SLAVES OF CAMEROON	3026-1	$4.95
SLAVES OF SHOANNA	164-0	$4.95
SLAVES OF THE EMPIRE	3054-7	$4.95
SLOW BURN	3042-3	$4.95
SORRY I ASKED	3090-3	$4.95
SPANISH HOLIDAY	185-3	$4.95
STASI SLUT	3050-4	$4.95
STOLEN MOMENTS	3098-9	$4.95
STORY OF MONIQUE, THE	42-4	$4.95
STUDENTS OF PASSION	22-X	$4.95
SUBMISSIONS	207-8	$6.95
SUBMISSION HOLDS	266-3	$4.95
SWEET DREAMS	3062-8	$4.95
SWEETEST FRUIT, THE	95-5	$4.95